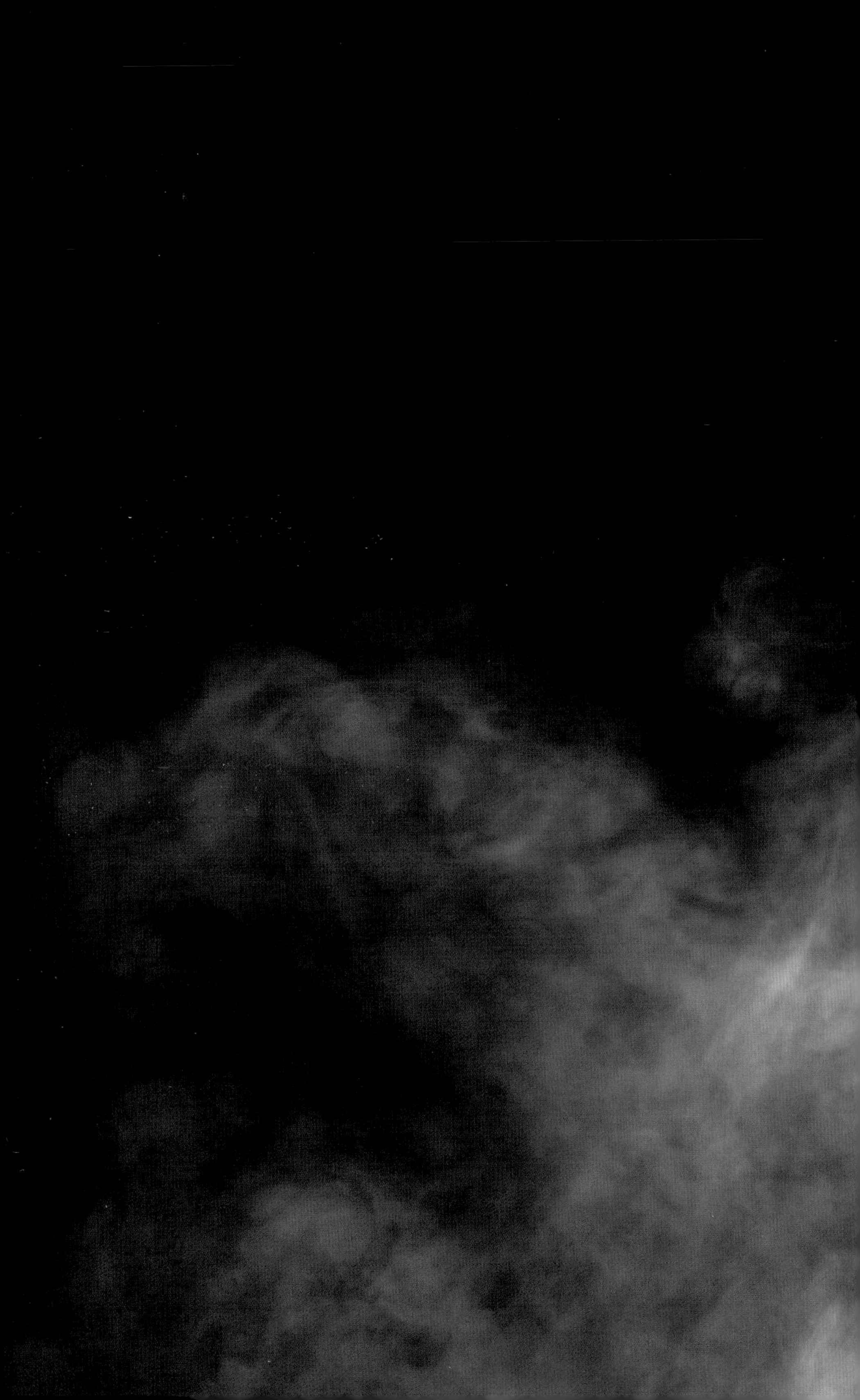

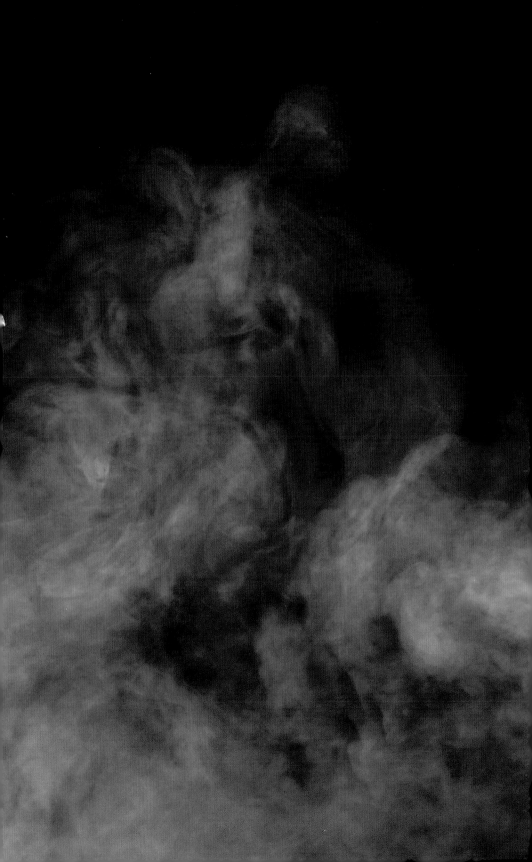

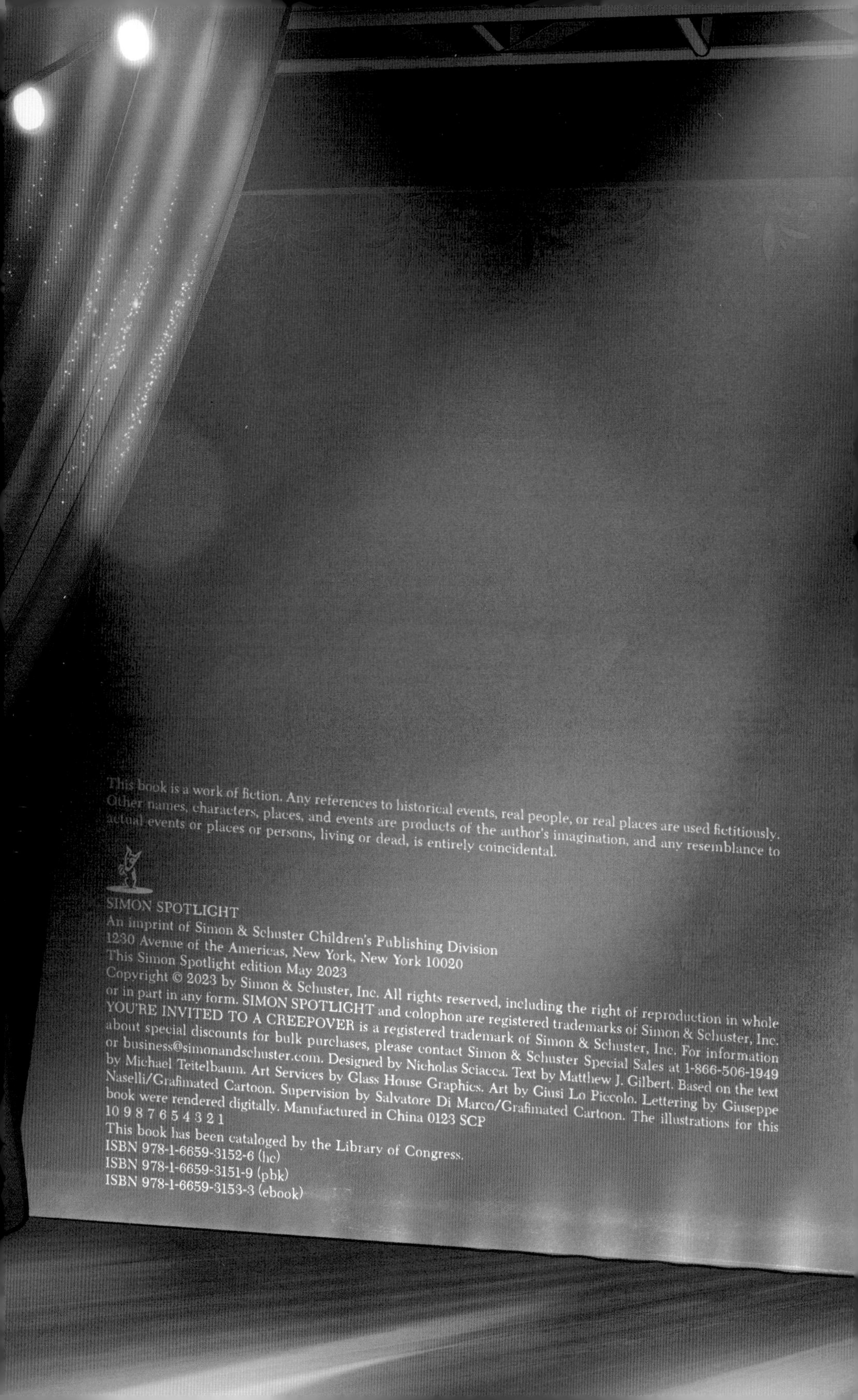

SIMON SPOTLIGHT

An imprint of Simon & Schuster Children's Publishing Division
1230 Avenue of the Americas, New York, New York 10020
This Simon Spotlight edition May 2023
Copyright © 2023 by Simon & Schuster, Inc. All rights reserved, including the right of reproduction in whole or in part in any form. SIMON SPOTLIGHT and colophon are registered trademarks of Simon & Schuster, Inc. YOU'RE INVITED TO A CREEPOVER is a registered trademark of Simon & Schuster, Inc. For information about special discounts for bulk purchases, please contact Simon & Schuster Special Sales at 1-866-506-1949 or business@simonandschuster.com. Designed by Nicholas Sciacca. Text by Matthew J. Gilbert. Based on the text by Michael Teitelbaum. Art Services by Glass House Graphics. Art by Giusi Lo Piccolo. Lettering by Giuseppe Naselli/Grafimated Cartoon. Supervision by Salvatore Di Marco/Grafimated Cartoon. The illustrations for this book were rendered digitally. Manufactured in China 0123 SCP
10 9 8 7 6 5 4 3 2 1
This book has been cataloged by the Library of Congress.
ISBN 978-1-6659-3152-6 (hc)
ISBN 978-1-6659-3151-9 (pbk)
ISBN 978-1-6659-3153-3 (ebook)

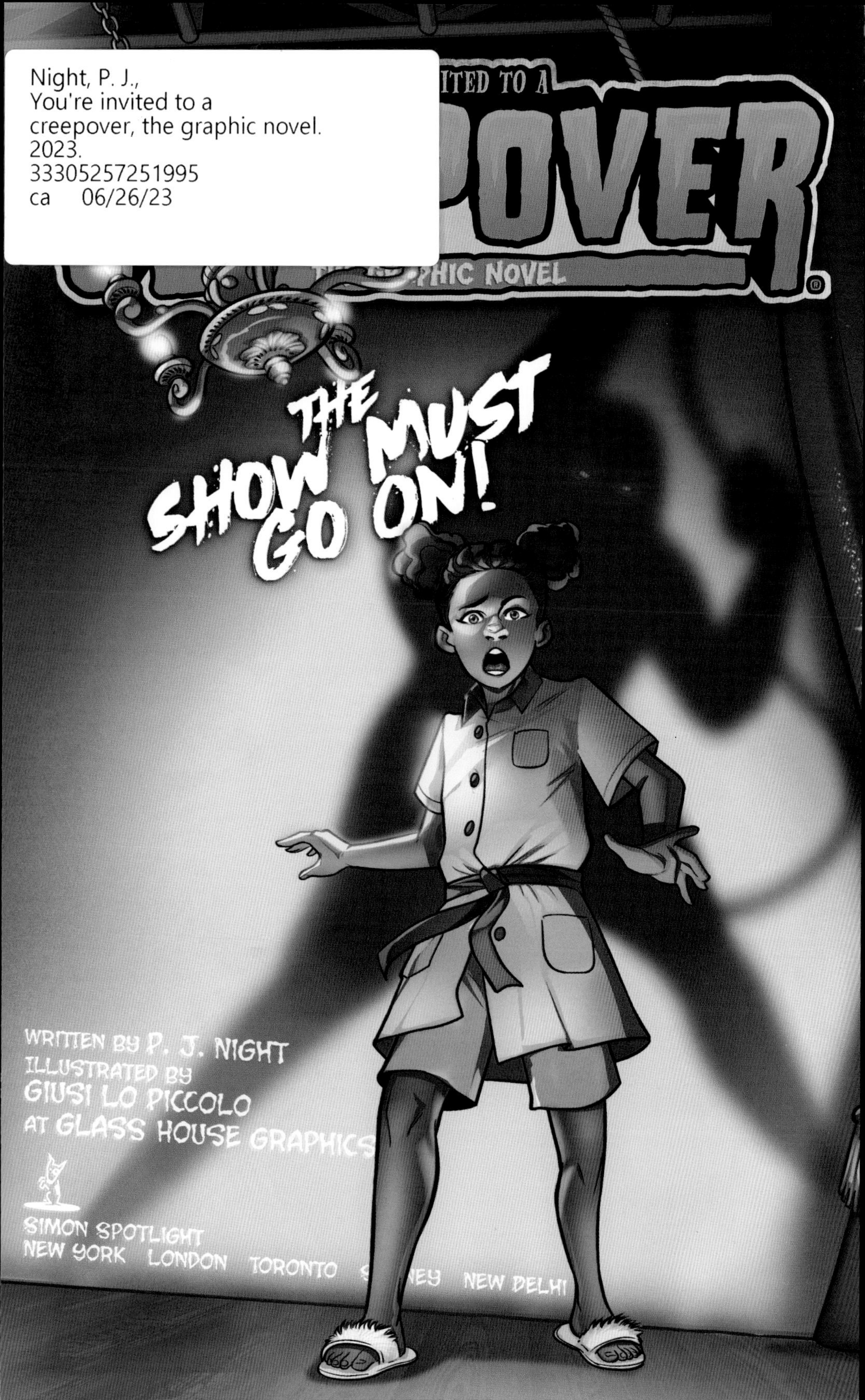
THE SHOW MUST GO ON!
WRITTEN BY P. J. NIGHT
ILLUSTRATED BY
GIUSI LO PICCOLO
AT GLASS HOUSE GRAPHICS
SIMON SPOTLIGHT
NEW YORK LONDON TORONTO NEW DELHI

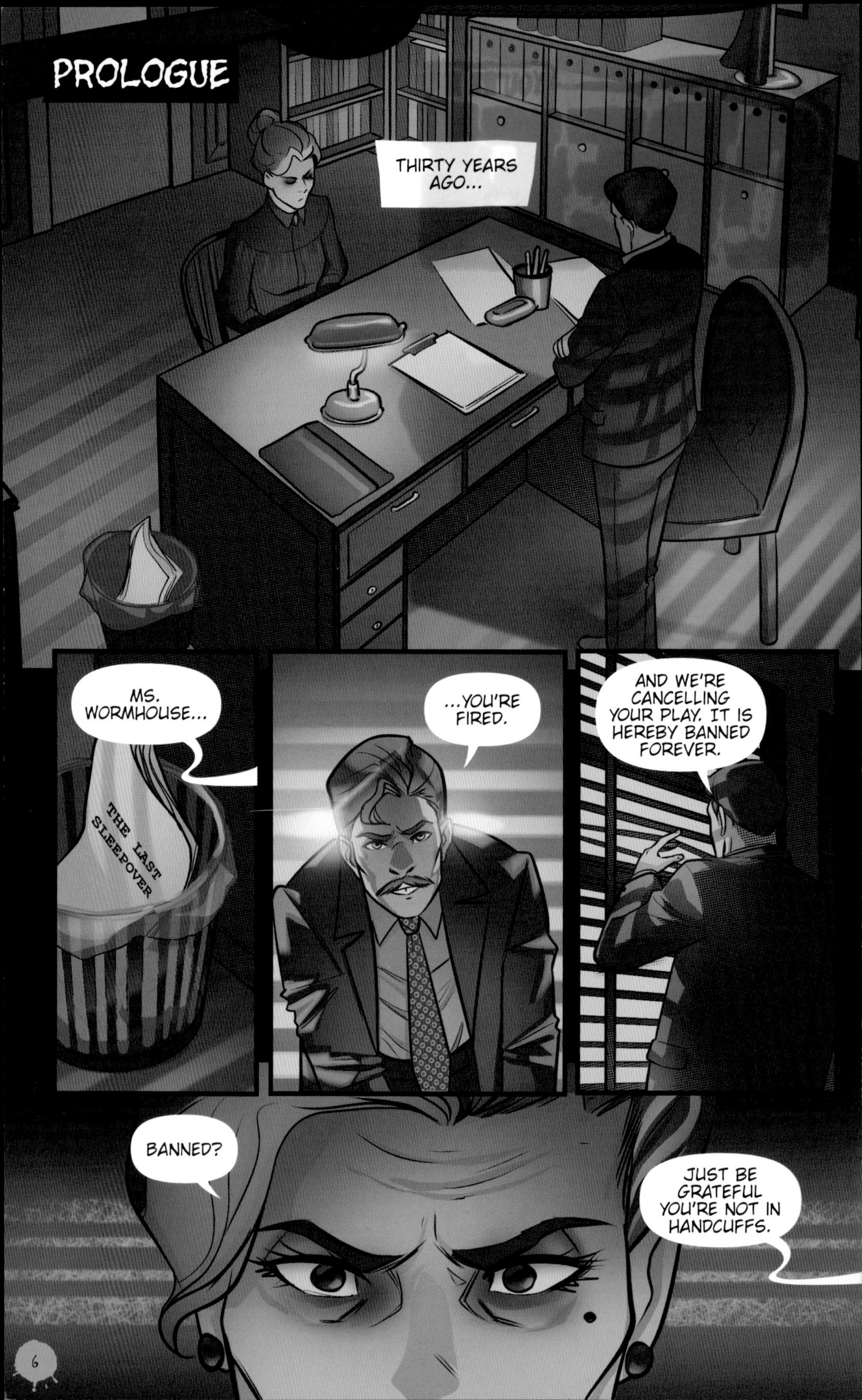
PROLOGUE
THIRTY YEARS AGO...
MS. WORMHOUSE...
THE LAST SLEEPOVER
...YOU'RE FIRED.
AND WE'RE CANCELLING YOUR PLAY. IT IS HEREBY BANNED FOREVER.
BANNED?
JUST BE GRATEFUL YOU'RE NOT IN HANDCUFFS.

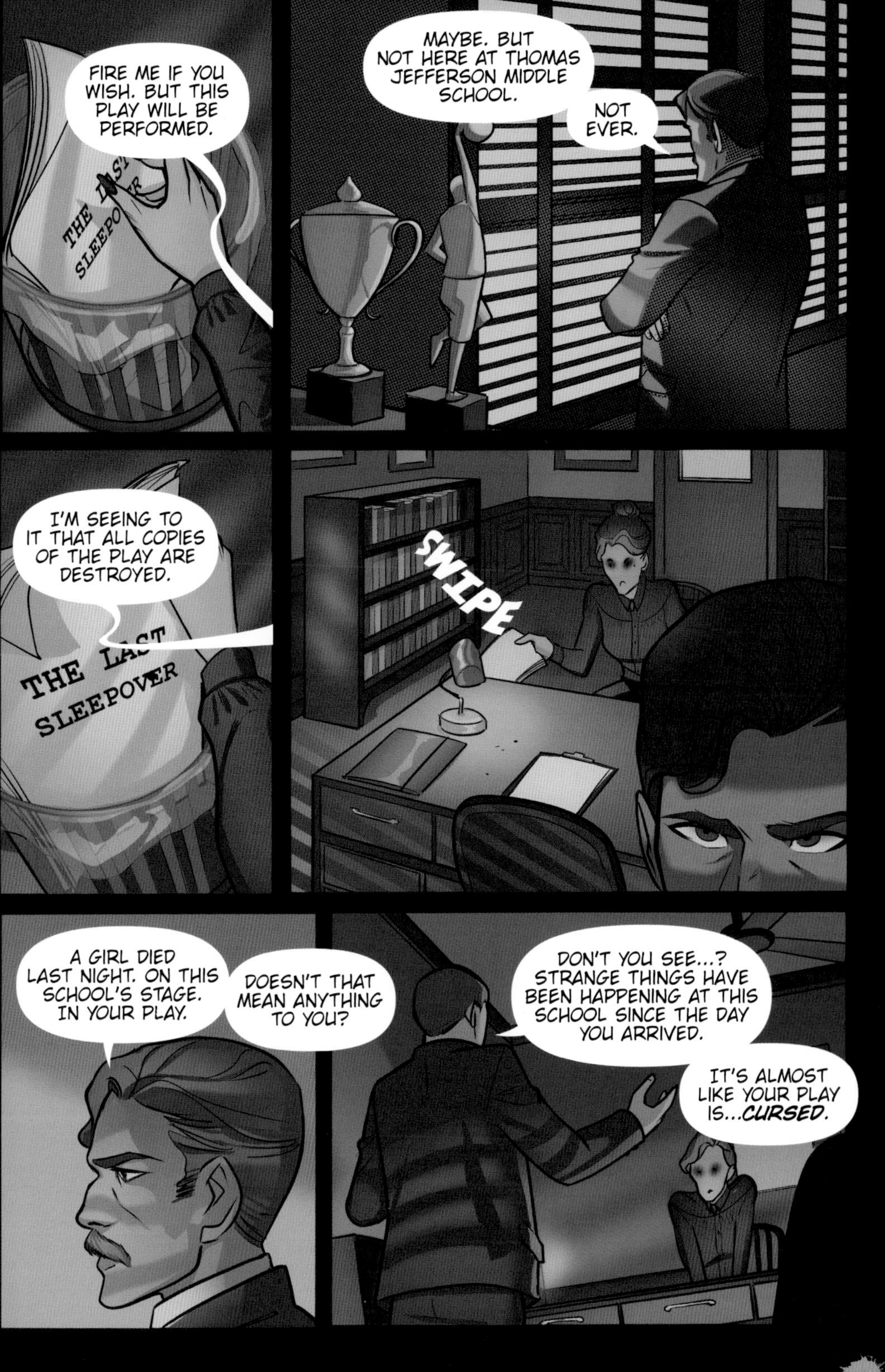
FIRE ME IF YOU WISH. BUT THIS PLAY WILL BE PERFORMED.
THE LAST SLEEPOVER
MAYBE. BUT NOT HERE AT THOMAS JEFFERSON MIDDLE SCHOOL.
NOT EVER.
I'M SEEING TO IT THAT ALL COPIES OF THE PLAY ARE DESTROYED.
THE LAST SLEEPOVER
SWIPE
A GIRL DIED LAST NIGHT. ON THIS SCHOOL'S STAGE. IN YOUR PLAY.
DOESN'T THAT MEAN ANYTHING TO YOU?
DON'T YOU SEE...? STRANGE THINGS HAVE BEEN HAPPENING AT THIS SCHOOL SINCE THE DAY YOU ARRIVED.
IT'S ALMOST LIKE YOUR PLAY IS...*CURSED*.

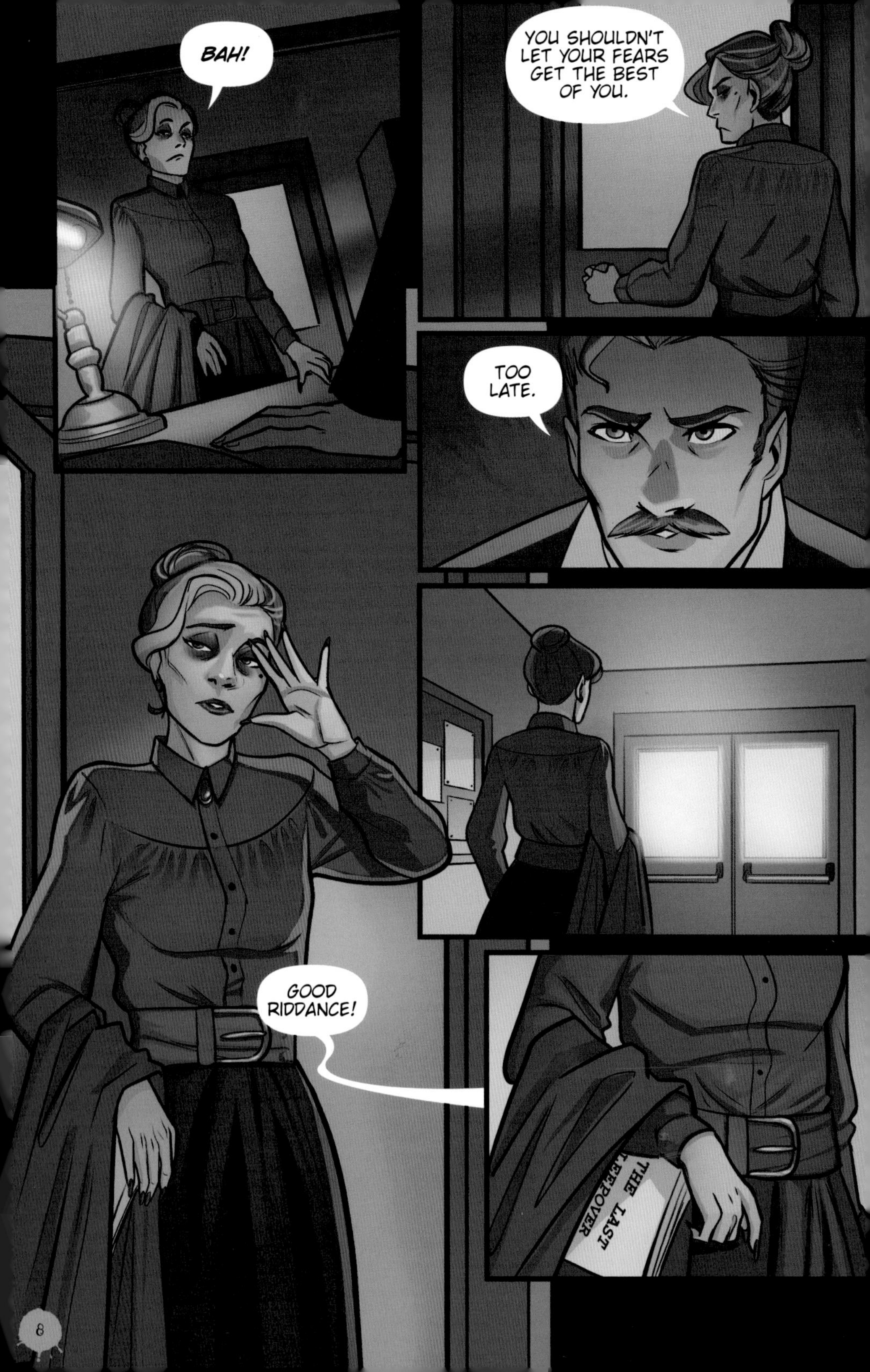
BAH!
YOU SHOULDN'T LET YOUR FEARS GET THE BEST OF YOU.
TOO LATE.
GOOD RIDDANCE!
THE LAST
LEEPOVER

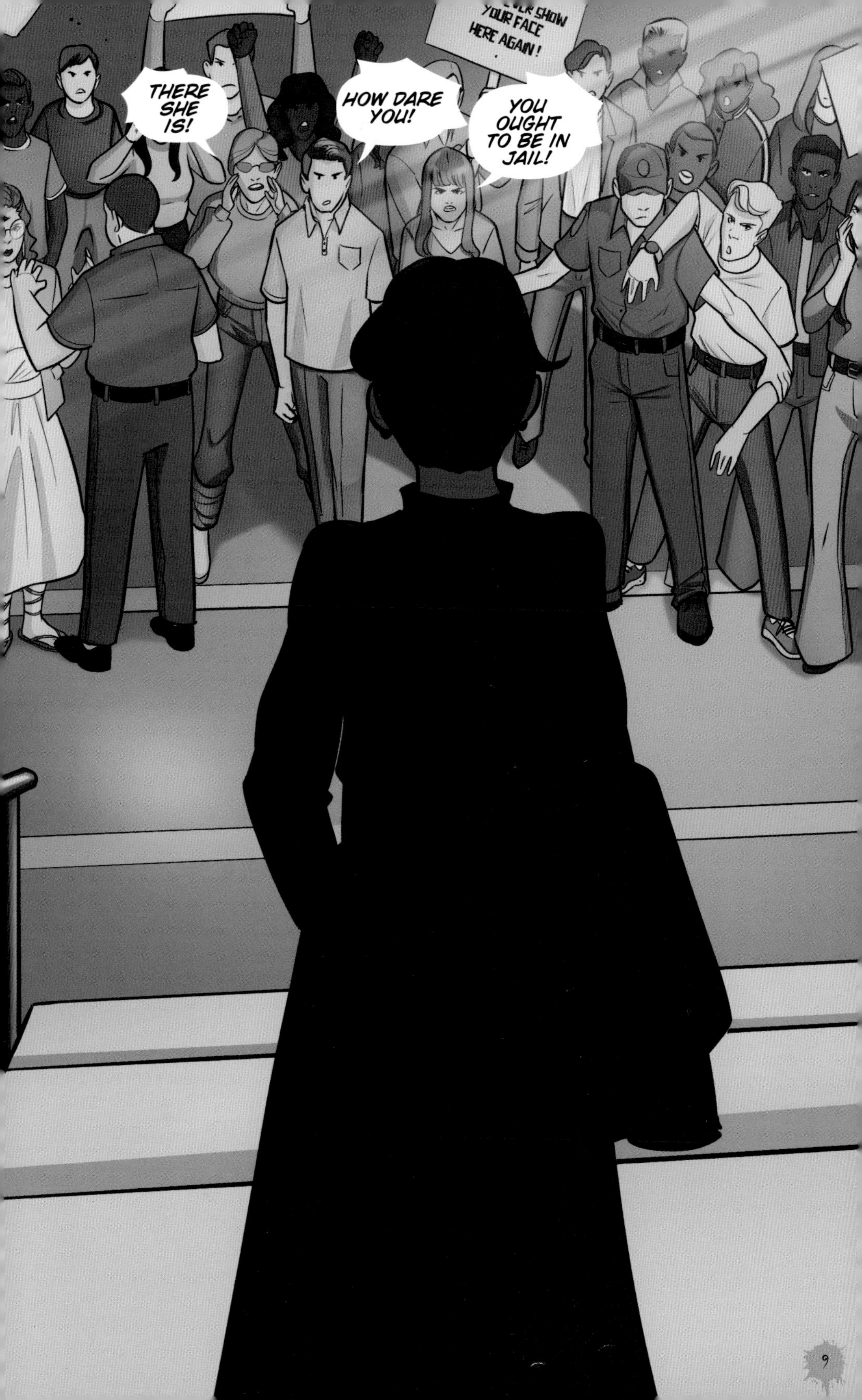
YOUR FACE
HERE AGAIN!
THERE SHE IS!
HOW DARE YOU!
YOU OUGHT TO BE IN JAIL!

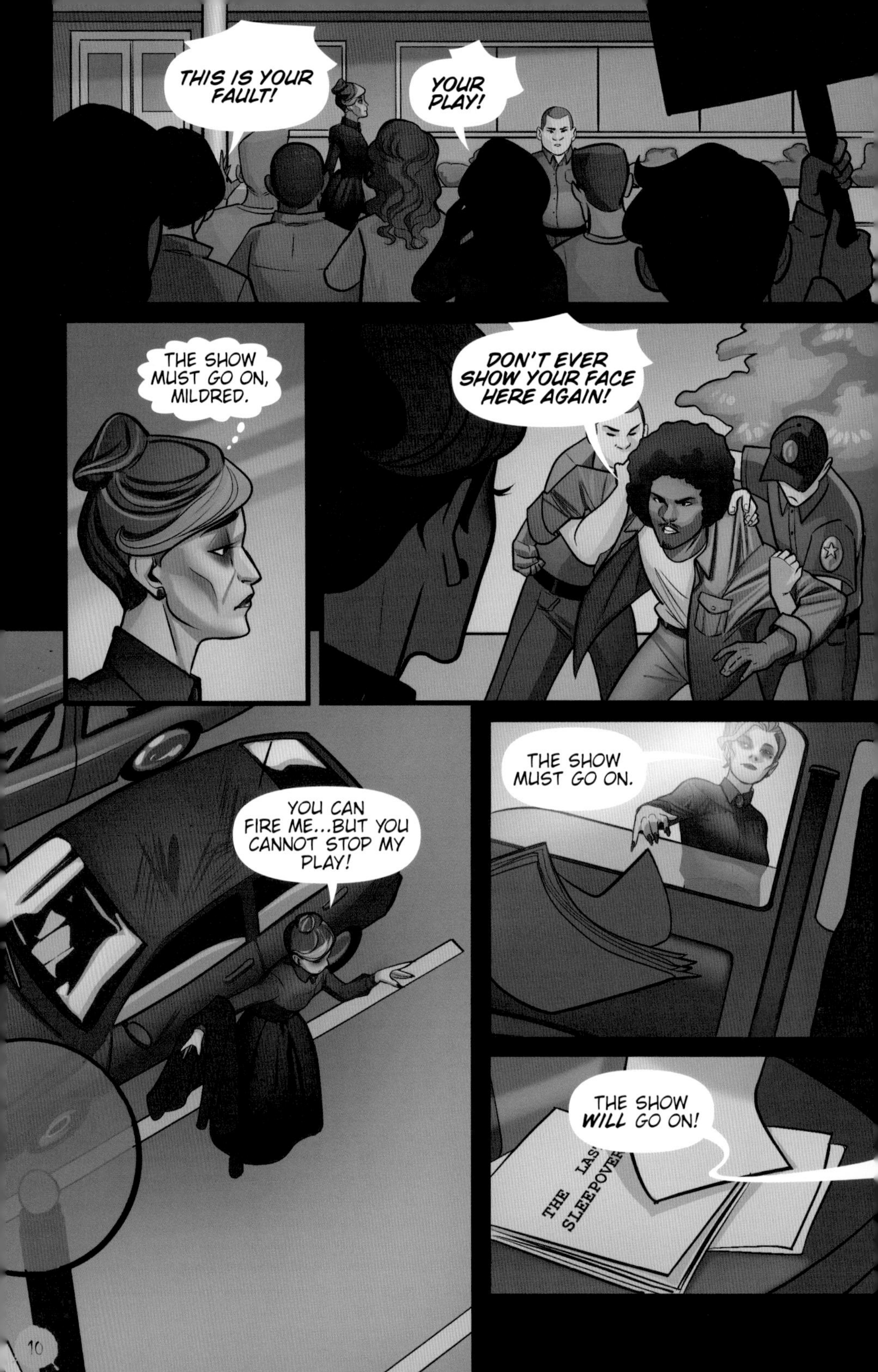
THIS IS YOUR FAULT!
YOUR PLAY!
THE SHOW MUST GO ON, MILDRED.
DON'T EVER SHOW YOUR FACE HERE AGAIN!
YOU CAN FIRE ME...BUT YOU CANNOT STOP MY PLAY!
THE SHOW MUST GO ON.
THE SHOW WILL GO ON!
THE LAS SLEEPOVER

CHAPTER 1

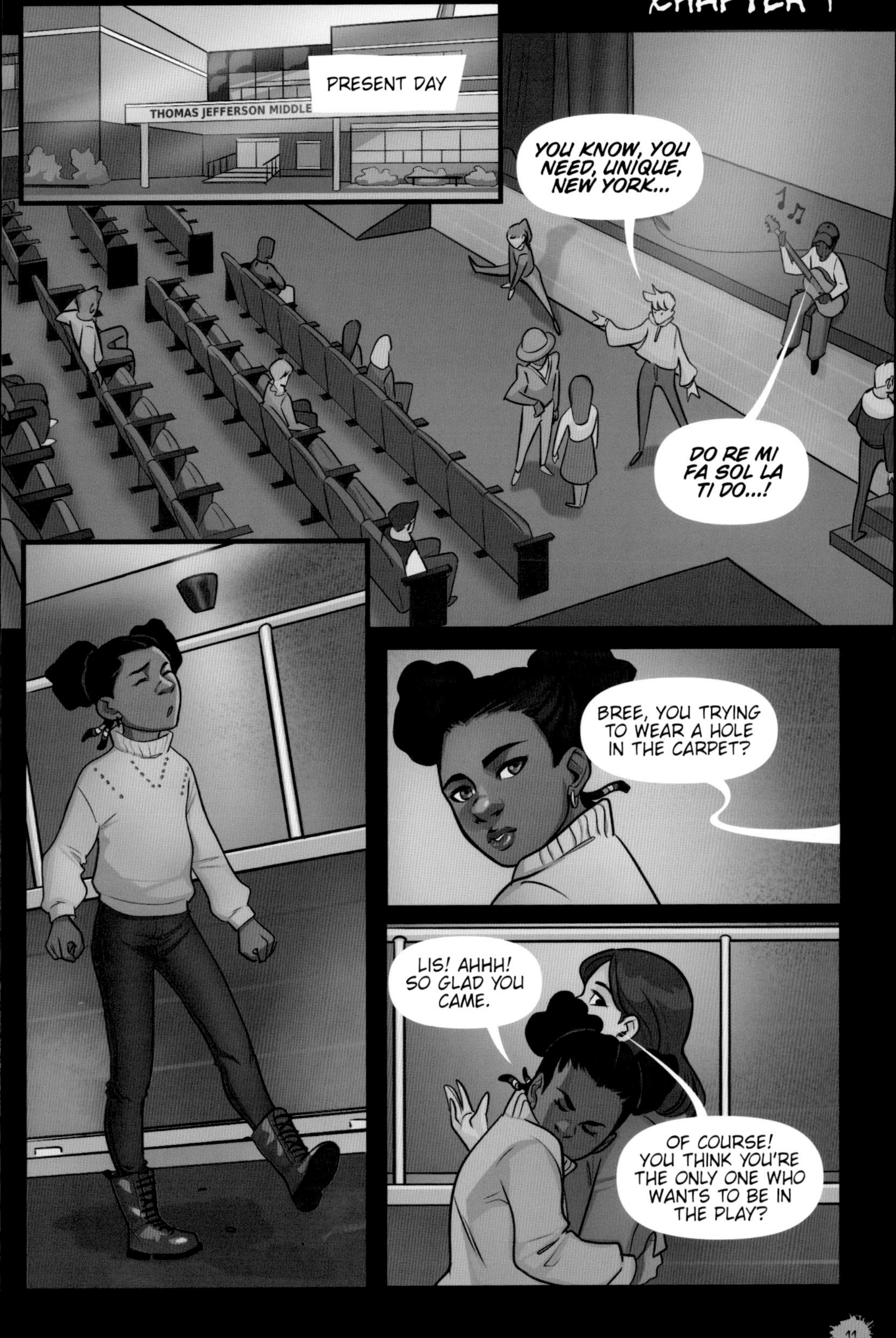
PRESENT DAY
THOMAS JEFFERSON MIDDLE
YOU KNOW, YOU NEED, UNIQUE, NEW YORK...
DO RE MI FA SOL LA TI DO...!
BREE, YOU TRYING TO WEAR A HOLE IN THE CARPET?
LIS! AHHH! SO GLAD YOU CAME.
OF COURSE! YOU THINK YOU'RE THE ONLY ONE WHO WANTS TO BE IN THE PLAY?

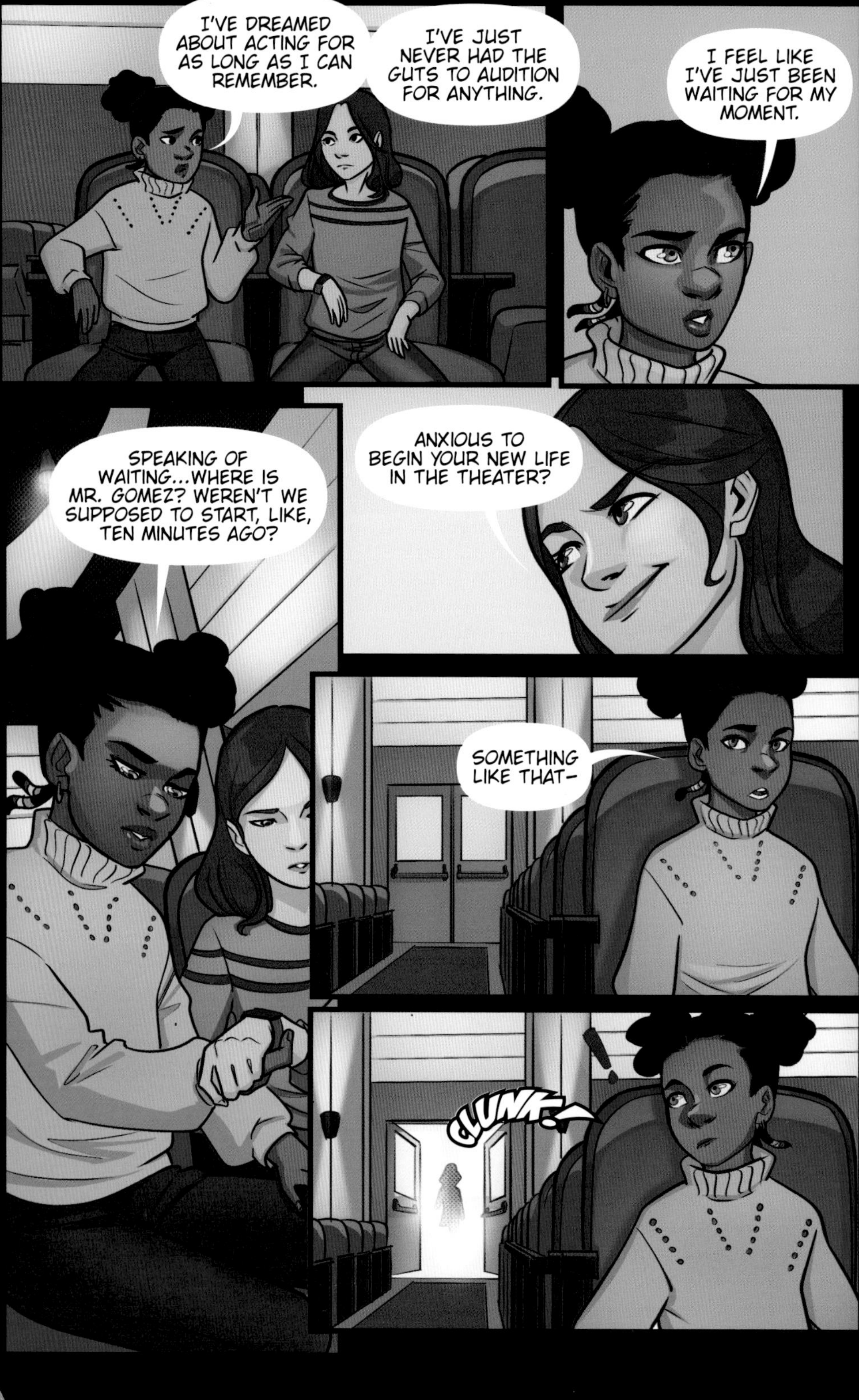
I'VE DREAMED ABOUT ACTING FOR AS LONG AS I CAN REMEMBER.
I'VE JUST NEVER HAD THE GUTS TO AUDITION FOR ANYTHING.
I FEEL LIKE I'VE JUST BEEN WAITING FOR MY MOMENT.
ANXIOUS TO BEGIN YOUR NEW LIFE IN THE THEATER?
SPEAKING OF WAITING...WHERE IS MR. GOMEZ? WEREN'T WE SUPPOSED TO START, LIKE, TEN MINUTES AGO?
SOMETHING LIKE THAT—
CLUNK!
!

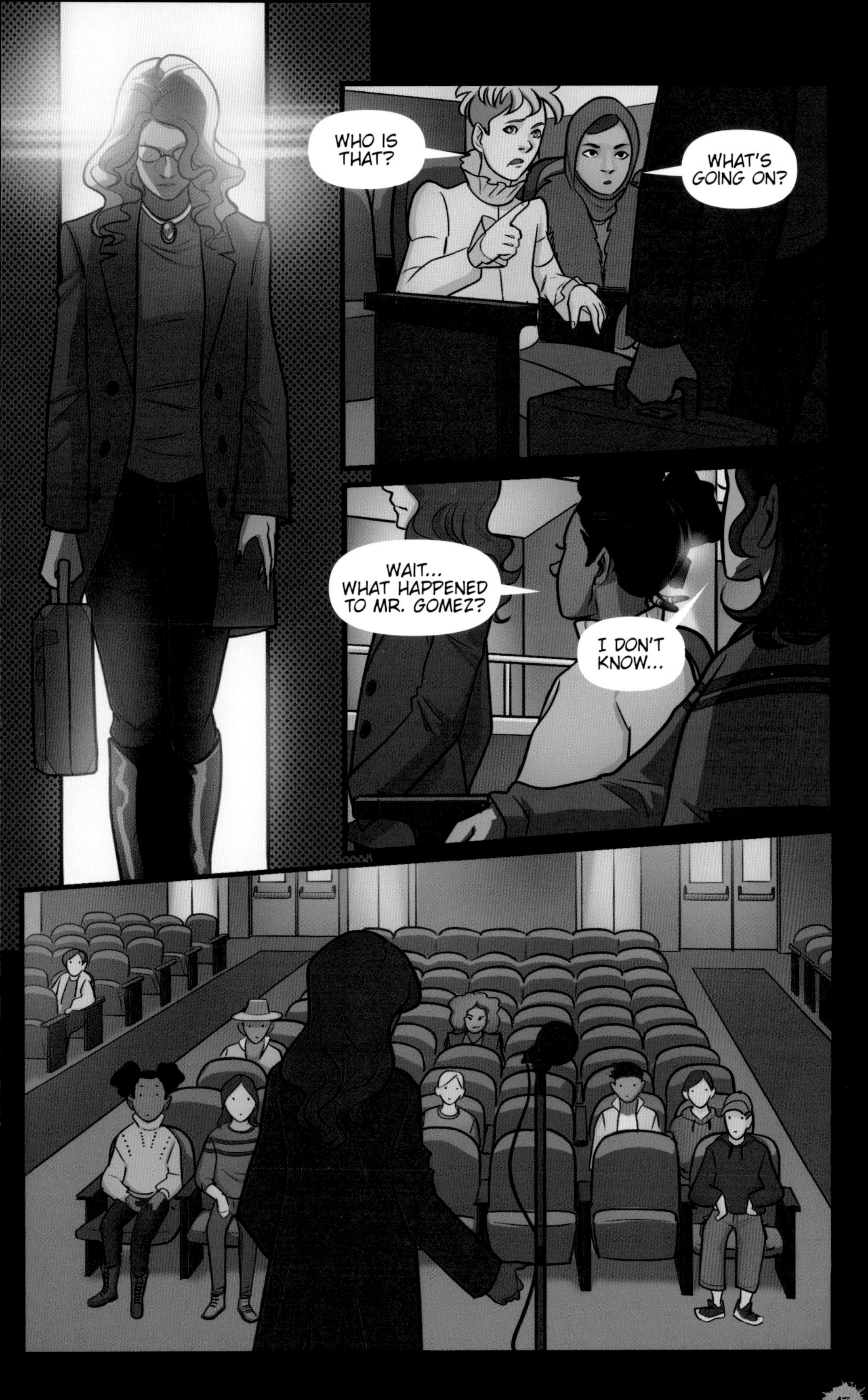
WHO IS THAT?
WHAT'S GOING ON?
WAIT... WHAT HAPPENED TO MR. GOMEZ?
I DON'T KNOW...

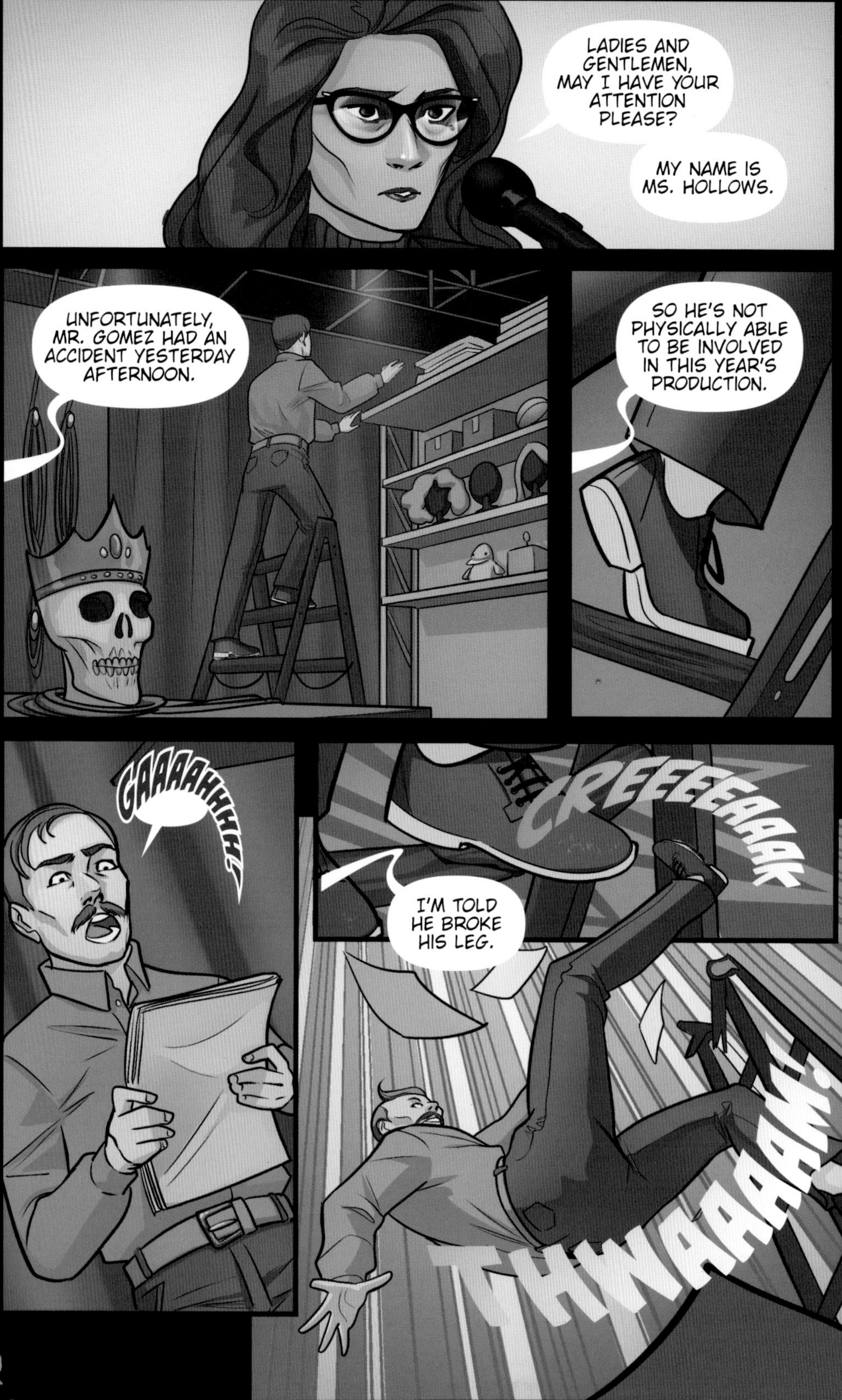
LADIES AND GENTLEMEN, MAY I HAVE YOUR ATTENTION PLEASE?
MY NAME IS MS. HOLLOWS.
UNFORTUNATELY, MR. GOMEZ HAD AN ACCIDENT YESTERDAY AFTERNOON.
SO HE'S NOT PHYSICALLY ABLE TO BE INVOLVED IN THIS YEAR'S PRODUCTION.
GAAAAHHHH!
CREEEEAAAK
I'M TOLD HE BROKE HIS LEG.
THWAAAAM!

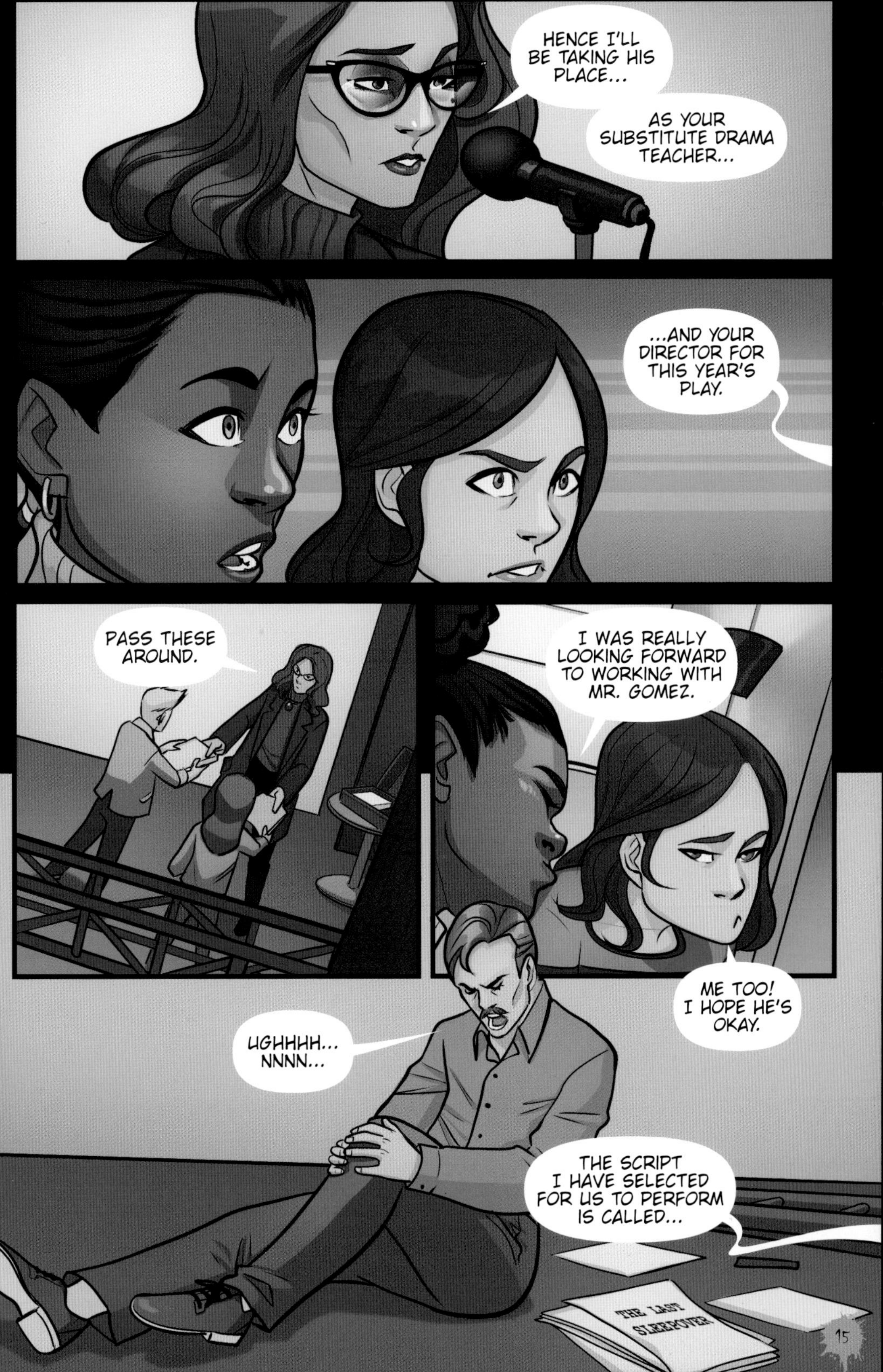

HENCE I'LL BE TAKING HIS PLACE...
AS YOUR SUBSTITUTE DRAMA TEACHER...
...AND YOUR DIRECTOR FOR THIS YEAR'S PLAY.
PASS THESE AROUND.
I WAS REALLY LOOKING FORWARD TO WORKING WITH MR. GOMEZ.
ME TOO! I HOPE HE'S OKAY.
UGHHHH... NNNN...
THE SCRIPT I HAVE SELECTED FOR US TO PERFORM IS CALLED...
THE LAST SLEEPOVER

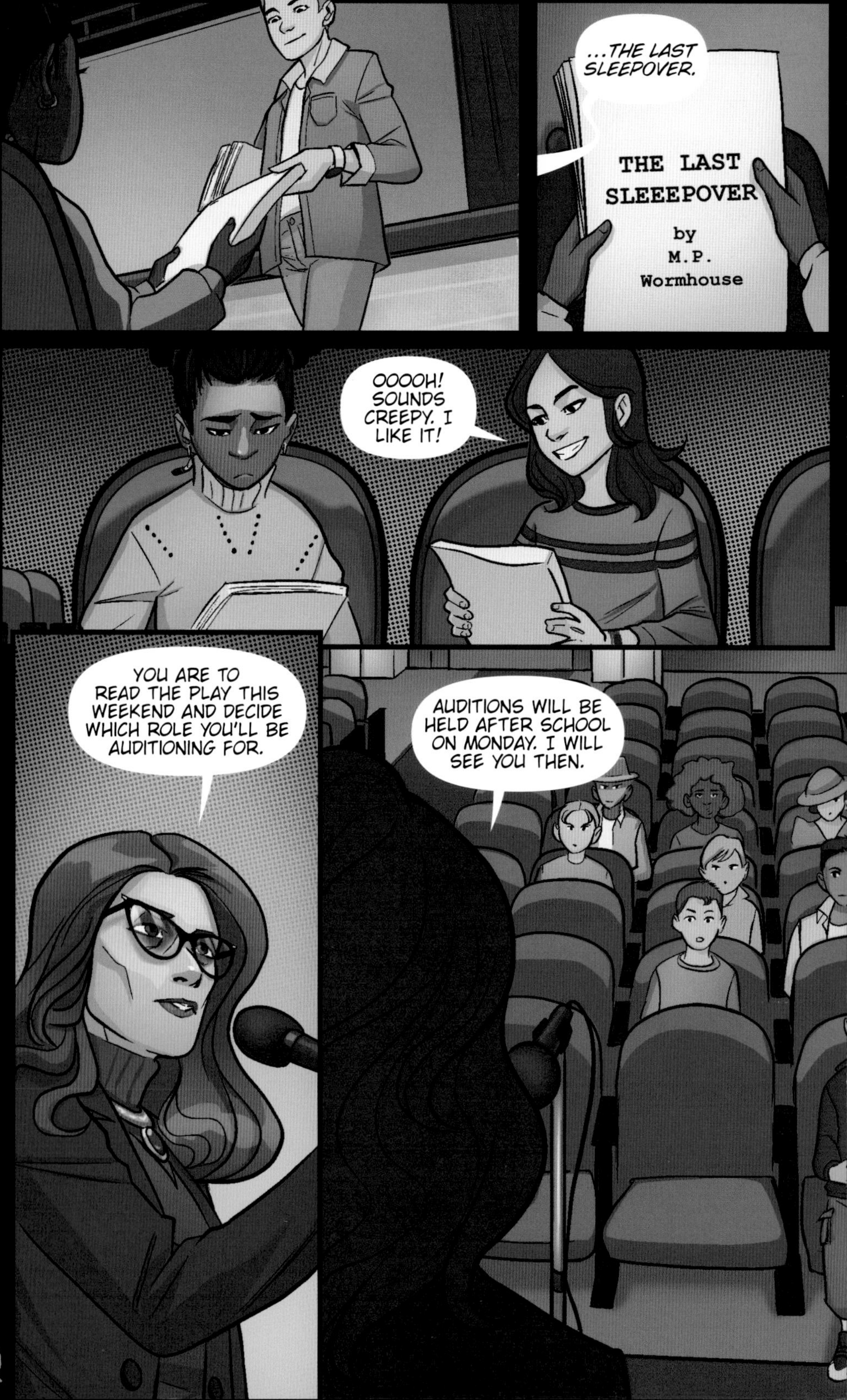
...THE LAST SLEEPOVER.
THE LAST SLEEEPOVER
by
M.P.
Wormhouse
OOOOH! SOUNDS CREEPY. I LIKE IT!
YOU ARE TO READ THE PLAY THIS WEEKEND AND DECIDE WHICH ROLE YOU'LL BE AUDITIONING FOR.
AUDITIONS WILL BE HELD AFTER SCHOOL ON MONDAY. I WILL SEE YOU THEN.

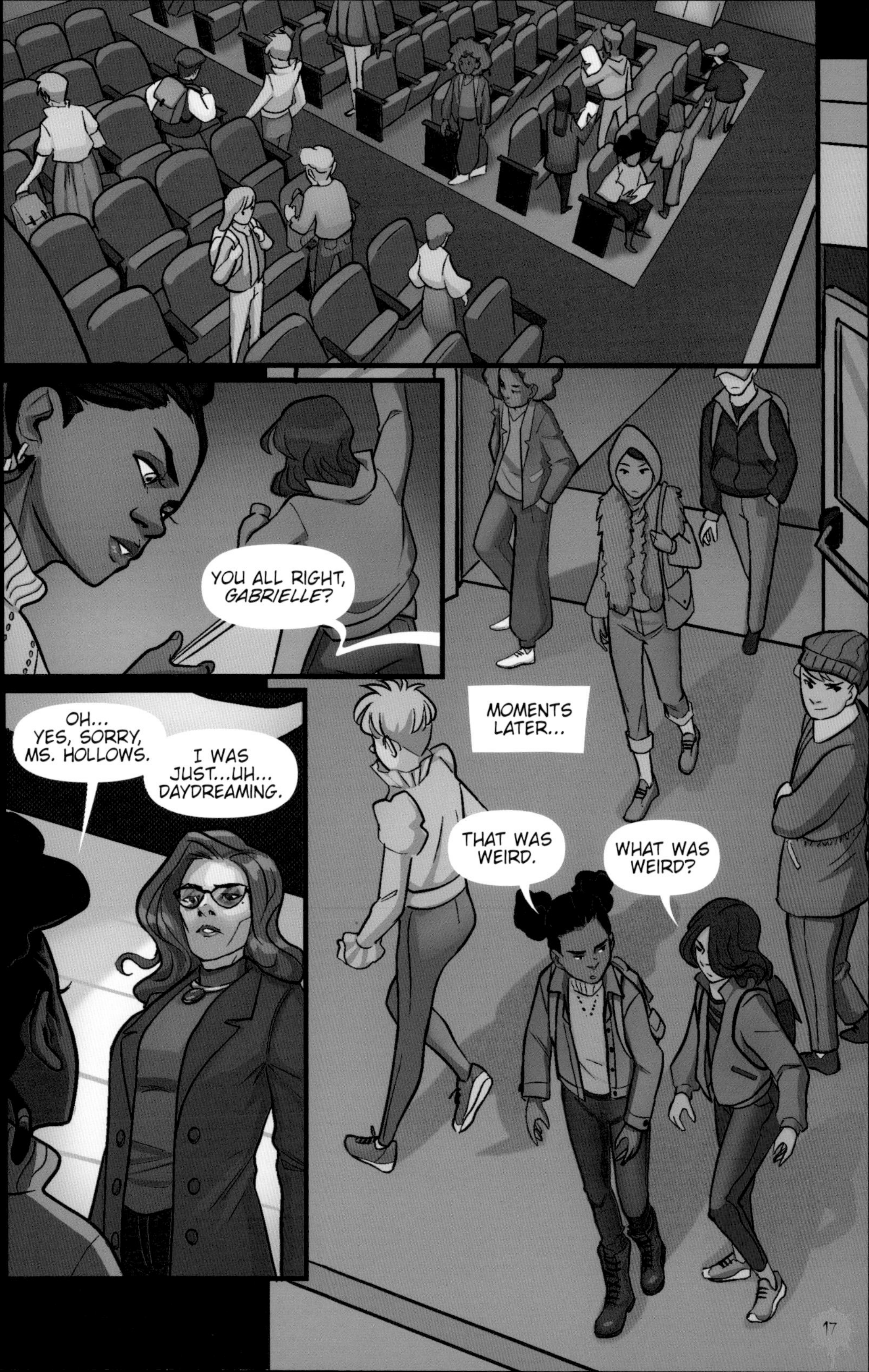
YOU ALL RIGHT, GABRIELLE?
OH... YES, SORRY, MS. HOLLOWS.
I WAS JUST...UH... DAYDREAMING.
MOMENTS LATER...
THAT WAS WEIRD.
WHAT WAS WEIRD?

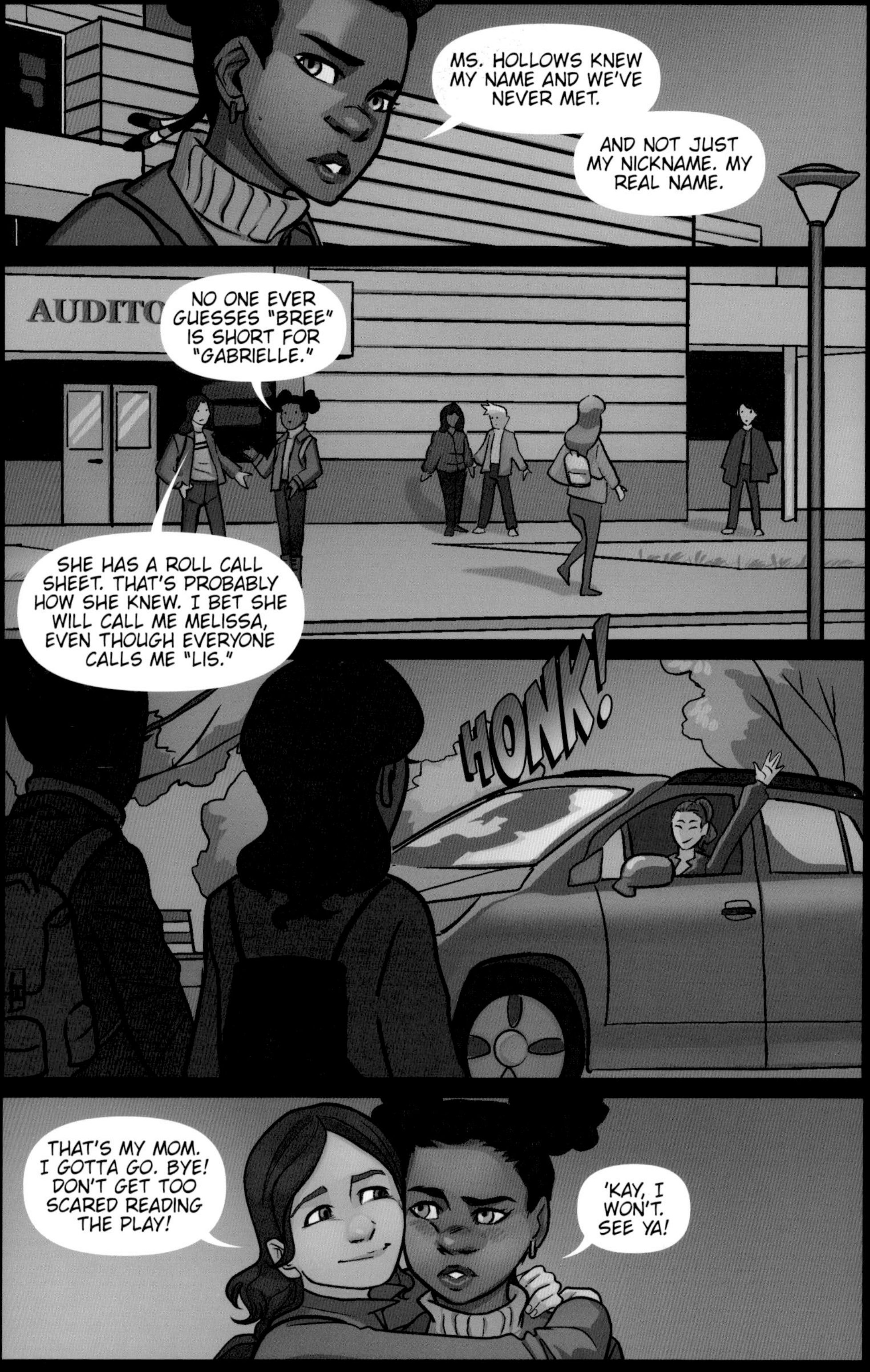
MS. HOLLOWS KNEW MY NAME AND WE'VE NEVER MET.
AND NOT JUST MY NICKNAME. MY REAL NAME.
AUDITO
NO ONE EVER GUESSES "BREE" IS SHORT FOR "GABRIELLE."
SHE HAS A ROLL CALL SHEET. THAT'S PROBABLY HOW SHE KNEW. I BET SHE WILL CALL ME MELISSA, EVEN THOUGH EVERYONE CALLS ME "LIS."
HONK!
THAT'S MY MOM. I GOTTA GO. BYE! DON'T GET TOO SCARED READING THE PLAY!
'KAY, I WON'T. SEE YA!

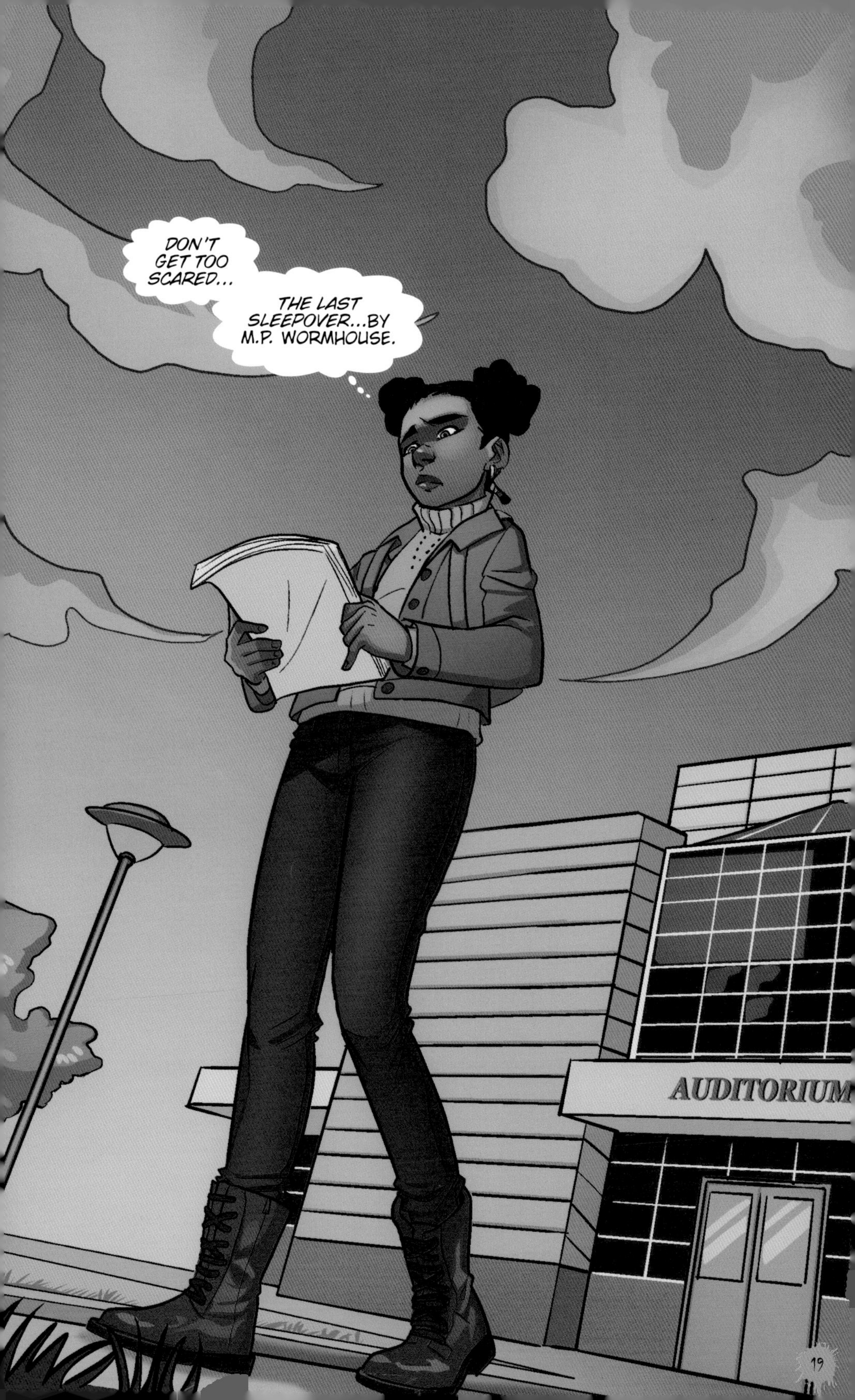
DON'T GET TOO SCARED...
THE LAST SLEEPOVER...BY M.P. WORMHOUSE.
AUDITORIUM

CHAPTER 2

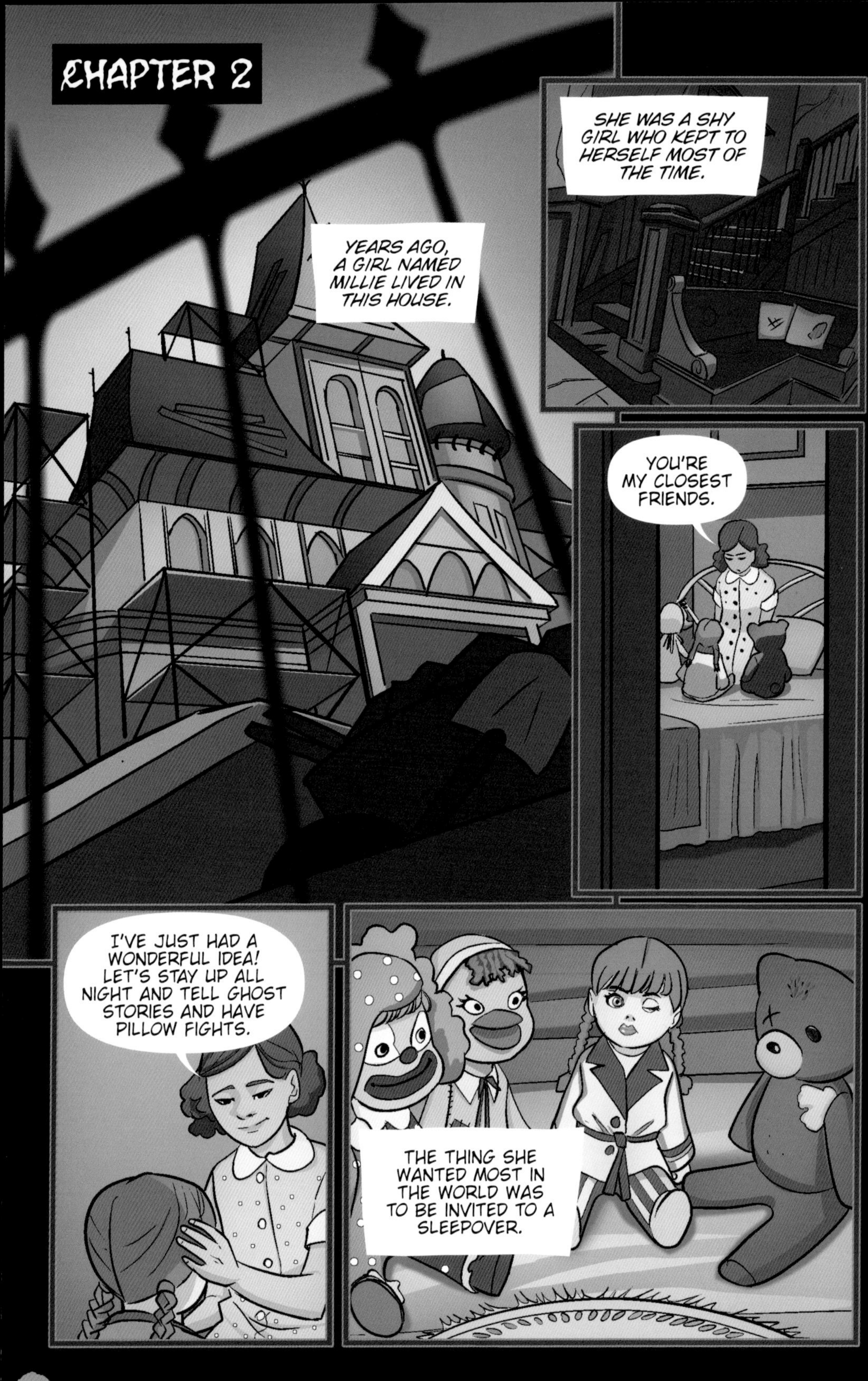
YEARS AGO, A GIRL NAMED MILLIE LIVED IN THIS HOUSE.
SHE WAS A SHY GIRL WHO KEPT TO HERSELF MOST OF THE TIME.
YOU'RE MY CLOSEST FRIENDS.
I'VE JUST HAD A WONDERFUL IDEA! LET'S STAY UP ALL NIGHT AND TELL GHOST STORIES AND HAVE PILLOW FIGHTS.
THE THING SHE WANTED MOST IN THE WORLD WAS TO BE INVITED TO A SLEEPOVER.

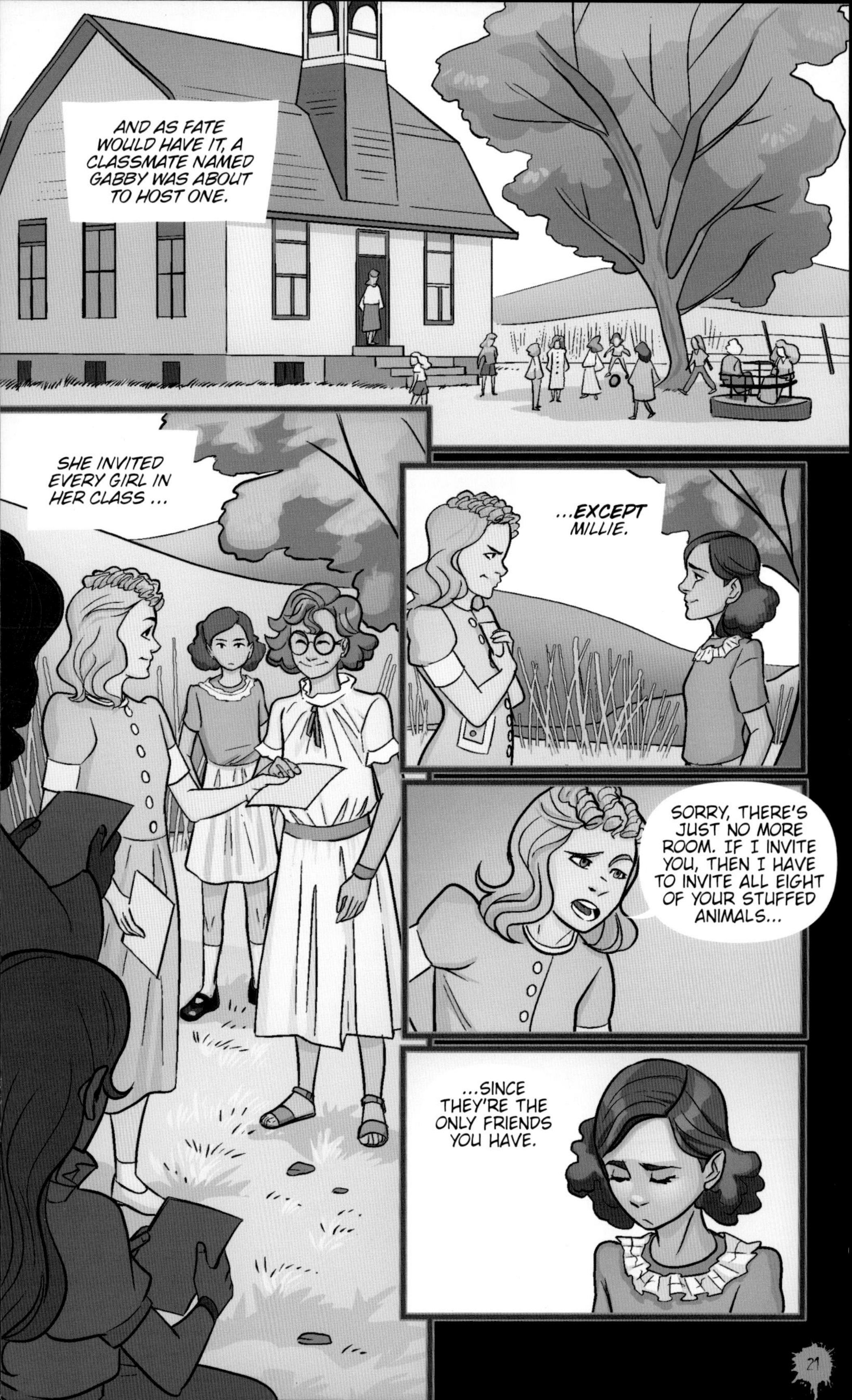
AND AS FATE WOULD HAVE IT, A CLASSMATE NAMED GABBY WAS ABOUT TO HOST ONE.
SHE INVITED EVERY GIRL IN HER CLASS ...
...EXCEPT MILLIE.
SORRY, THERE'S JUST NO MORE ROOM. IF I INVITE YOU, THEN I HAVE TO INVITE ALL EIGHT OF YOUR STUFFED ANIMALS...
...SINCE THEY'RE THE ONLY FRIENDS YOU HAVE.

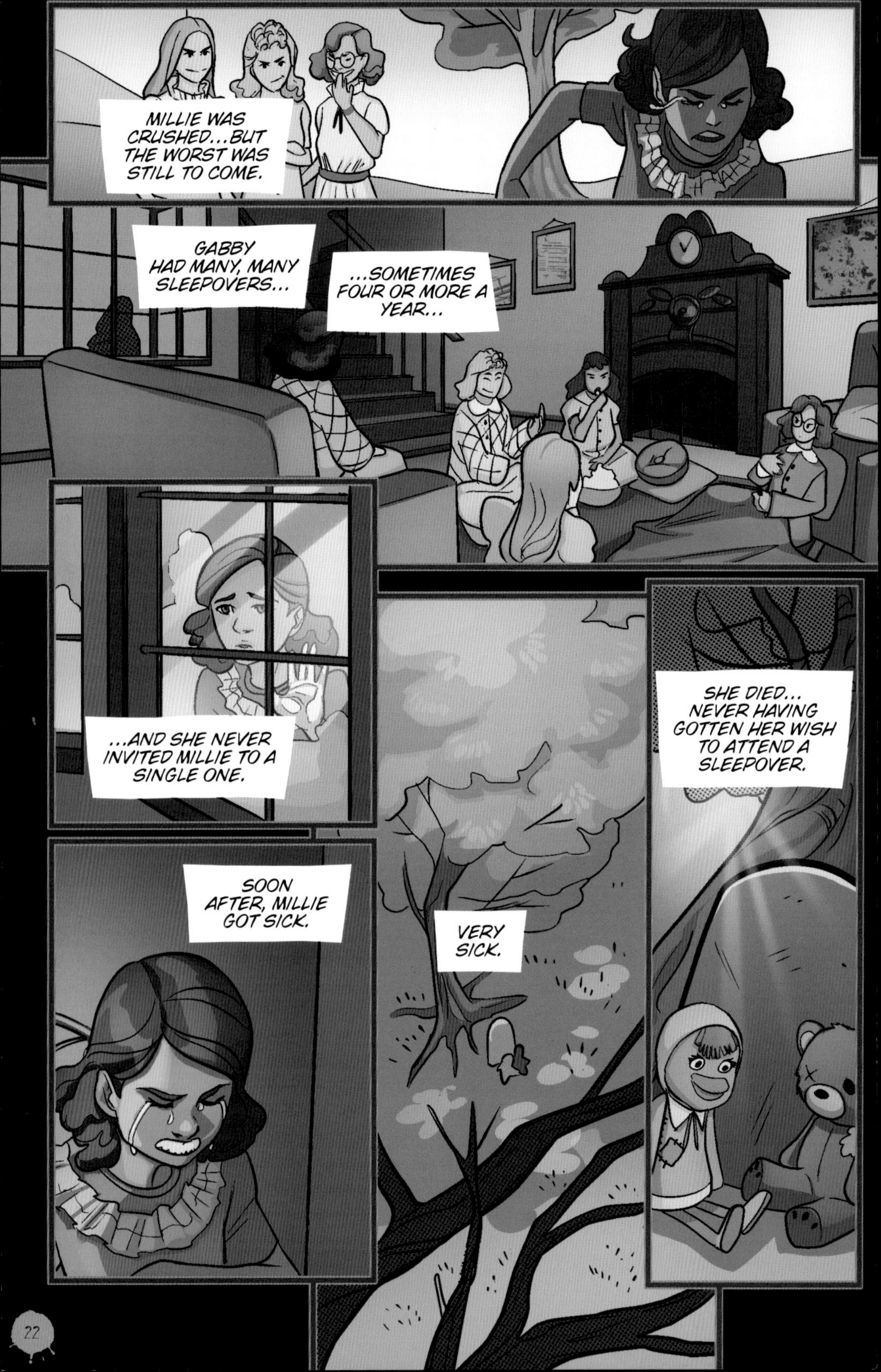
MILLIE WAS CRUSHED…BUT THE WORST WAS STILL TO COME.
GABBY HAD MANY, MANY SLEEPOVERS…
…SOMETIMES FOUR OR MORE A YEAR…
…AND SHE NEVER INVITED MILLIE TO A SINGLE ONE.
SOON AFTER, MILLIE GOT SICK.
VERY SICK.
SHE DIED… NEVER HAVING GOTTEN HER WISH TO ATTEND A SLEEPOVER.

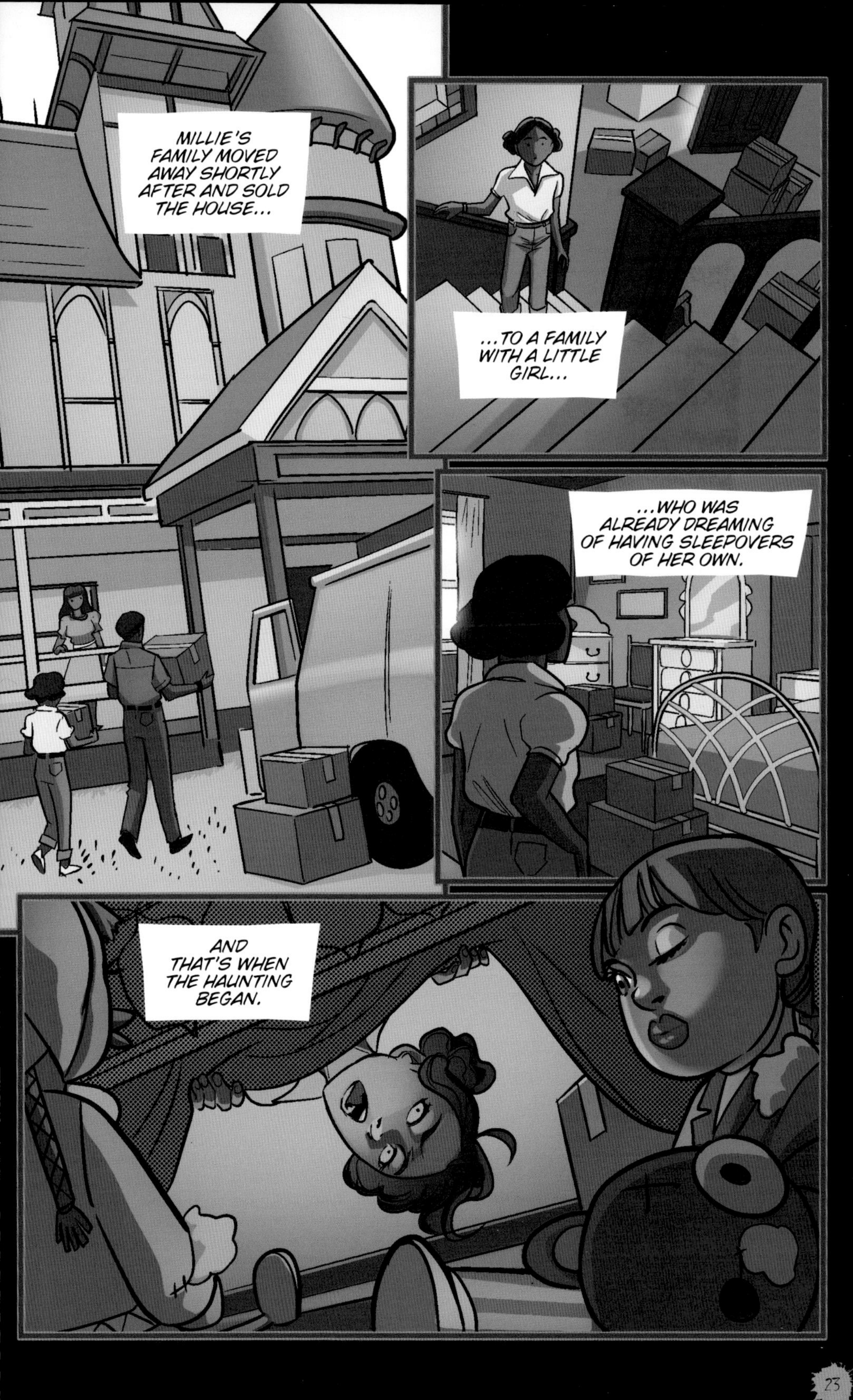
MILLIE'S FAMILY MOVED AWAY SHORTLY AFTER AND SOLD THE HOUSE...
...TO A FAMILY WITH A LITTLE GIRL...
...WHO WAS ALREADY DREAMING OF HAVING SLEEPOVERS OF HER OWN.
AND THAT'S WHEN THE HAUNTING BEGAN.

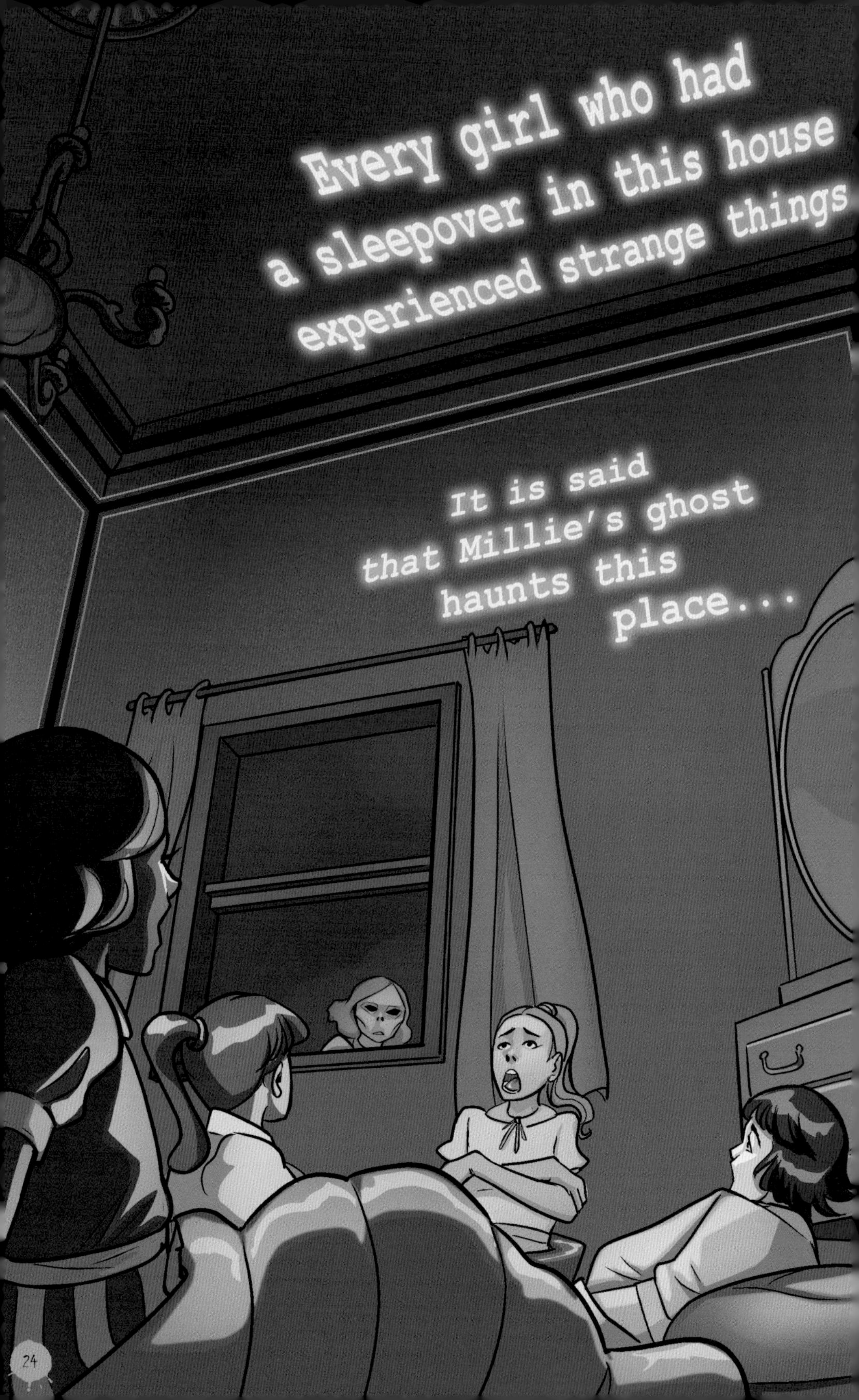
Every girl who had a sleepover in this house experienced strange things
It is said that Millie's ghost haunts this place...

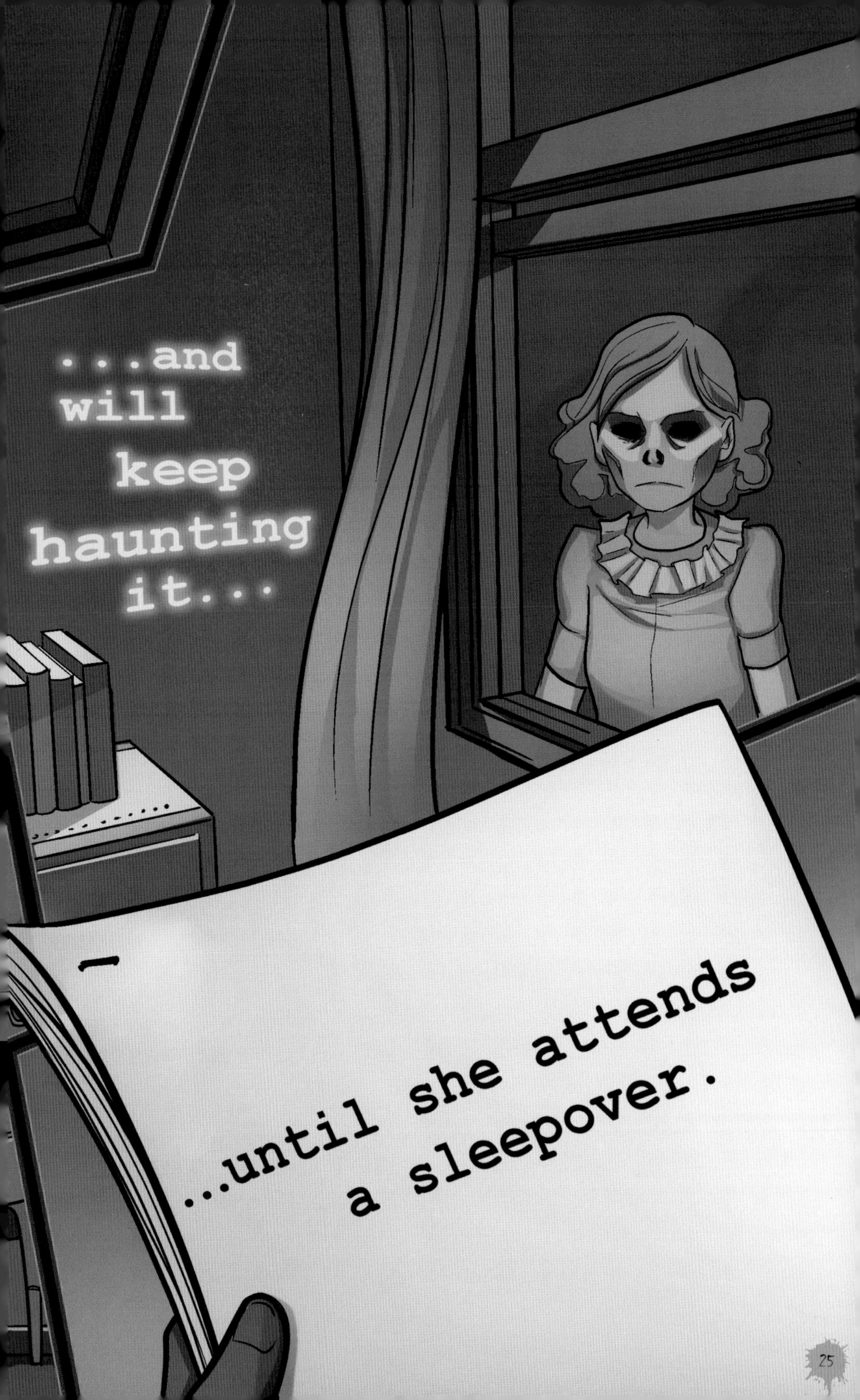
...and will keep haunting it...
...until she attends a sleepover.

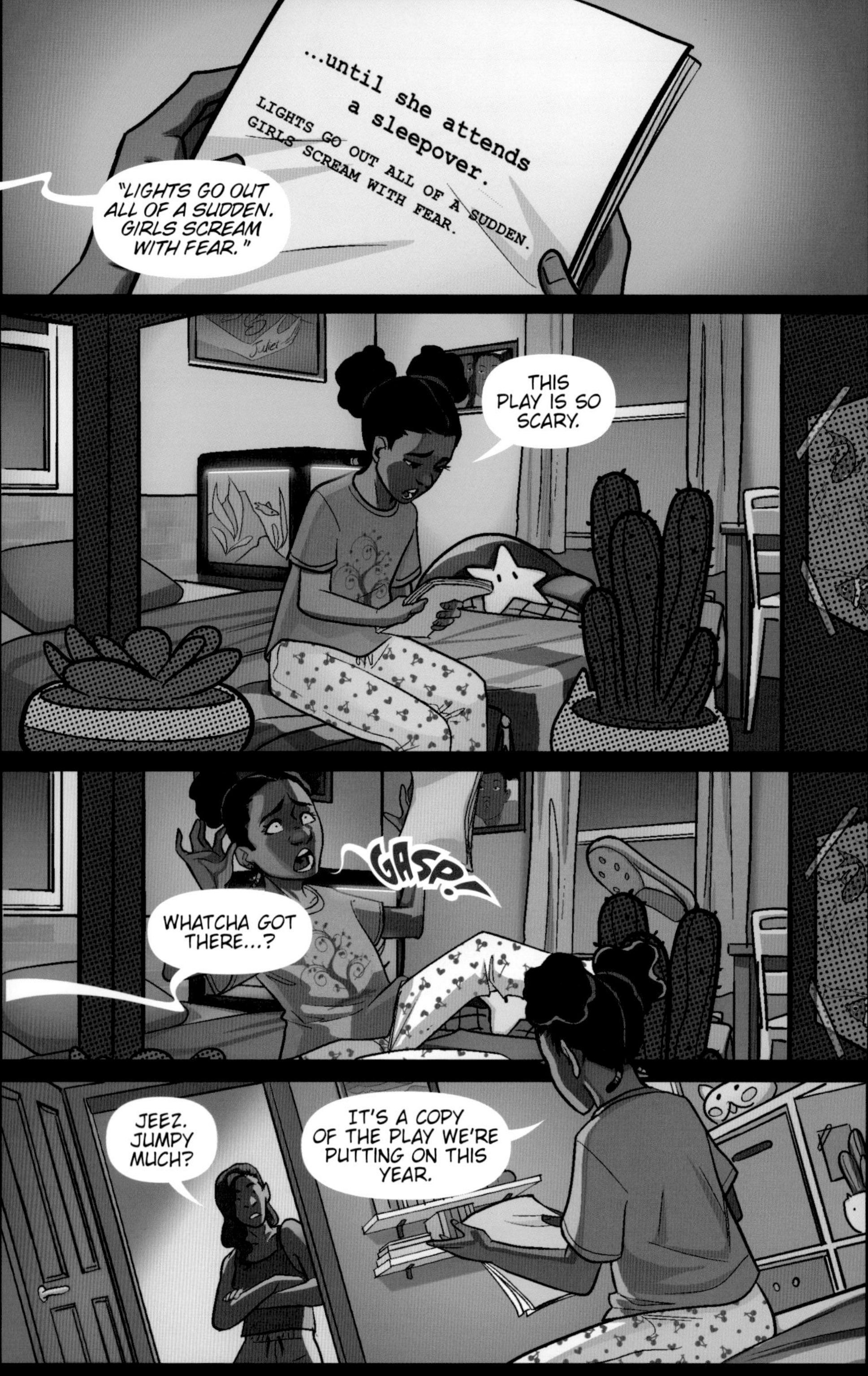
...until she attends a sleepover.
LIGHTS GO OUT ALL OF A SUDDEN.
GIRLS SCREAM WITH FEAR.
"LIGHTS GO OUT ALL OF A SUDDEN. GIRLS SCREAM WITH FEAR."
THIS PLAY IS SO SCARY.
GASP!
WHATCHA GOT THERE...?
JEEZ. JUMPY MUCH?
IT'S A COPY OF THE PLAY WE'RE PUTTING ON THIS YEAR.

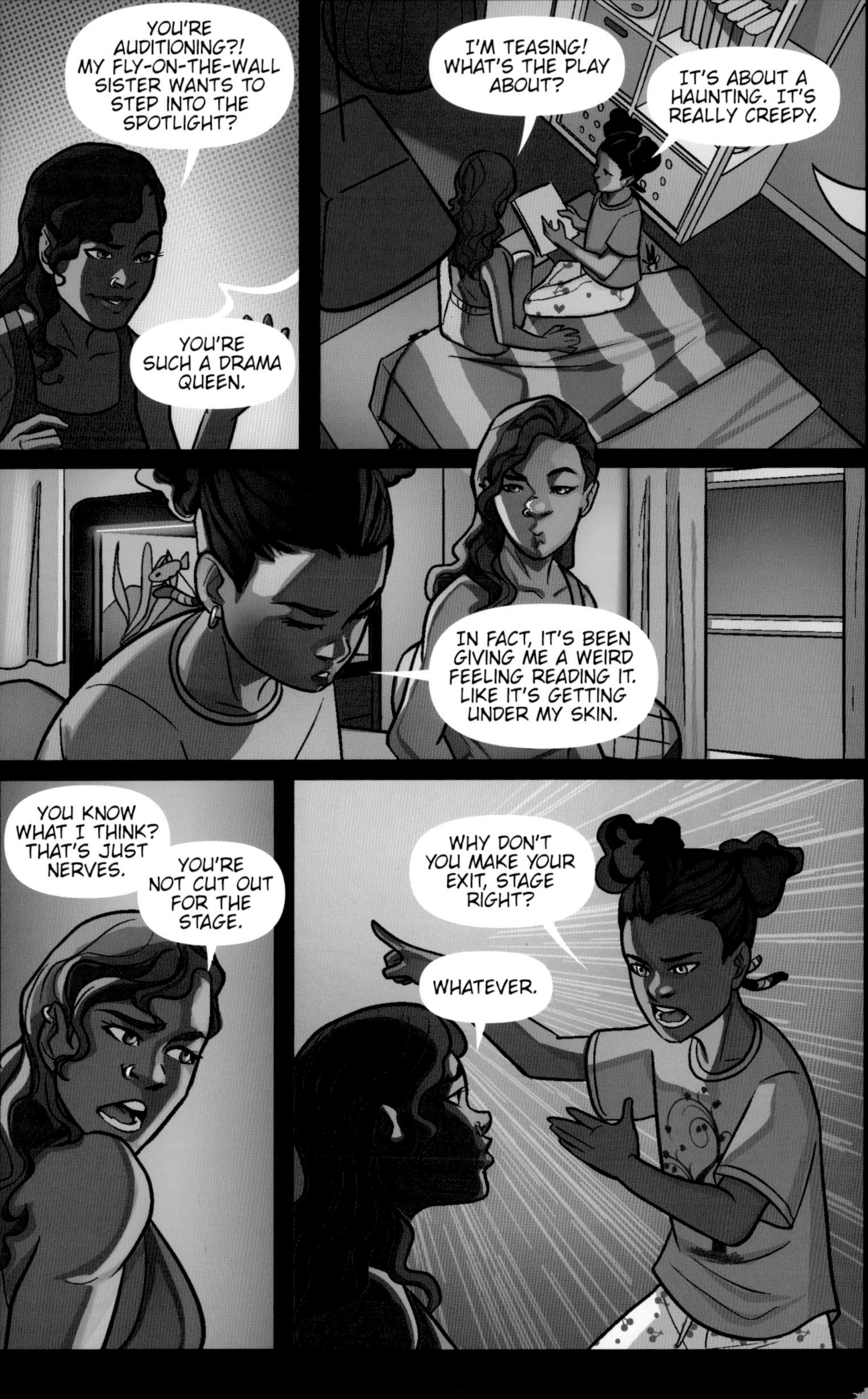
YOU'RE AUDITIONING?! MY FLY-ON-THE-WALL SISTER WANTS TO STEP INTO THE SPOTLIGHT?
YOU'RE SUCH A DRAMA QUEEN.
I'M TEASING! WHAT'S THE PLAY ABOUT?
IT'S ABOUT A HAUNTING. IT'S REALLY CREEPY.
IN FACT, IT'S BEEN GIVING ME A WEIRD FEELING READING IT. LIKE IT'S GETTING UNDER MY SKIN.
YOU KNOW WHAT I THINK? THAT'S JUST NERVES.
YOU'RE NOT CUT OUT FOR THE STAGE.
WHY DON'T YOU MAKE YOUR EXIT, STAGE RIGHT?
WHATEVER.

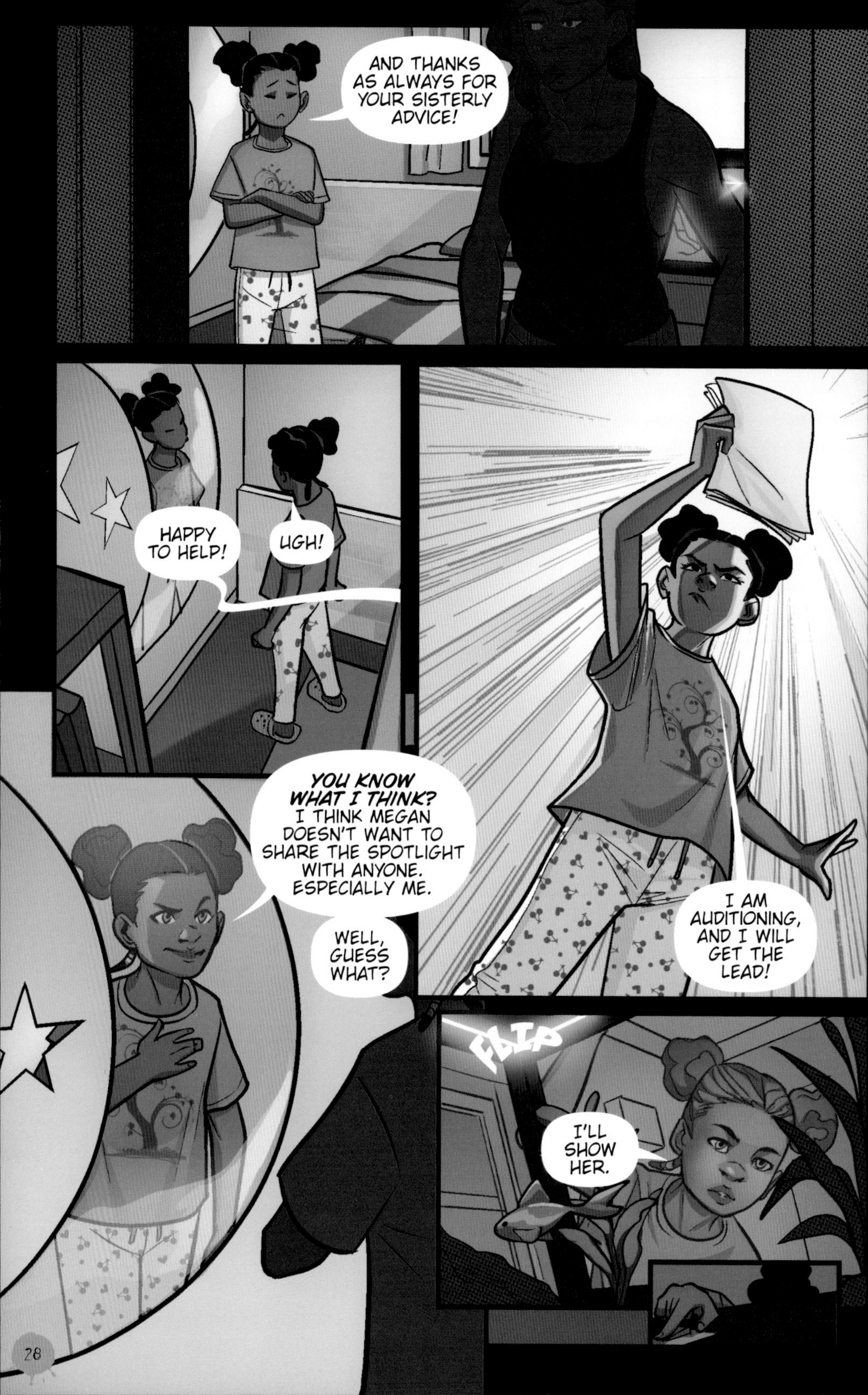
AND THANKS AS ALWAYS FOR YOUR SISTERLY ADVICE!
HAPPY TO HELP!
UGH!
YOU KNOW WHAT I THINK? I THINK MEGAN DOESN'T WANT TO SHARE THE SPOTLIGHT WITH ANYONE. ESPECIALLY ME.
WELL, GUESS WHAT?
I AM AUDITIONING, AND I WILL GET THE LEAD!
FLIP
I'LL SHOW HER.

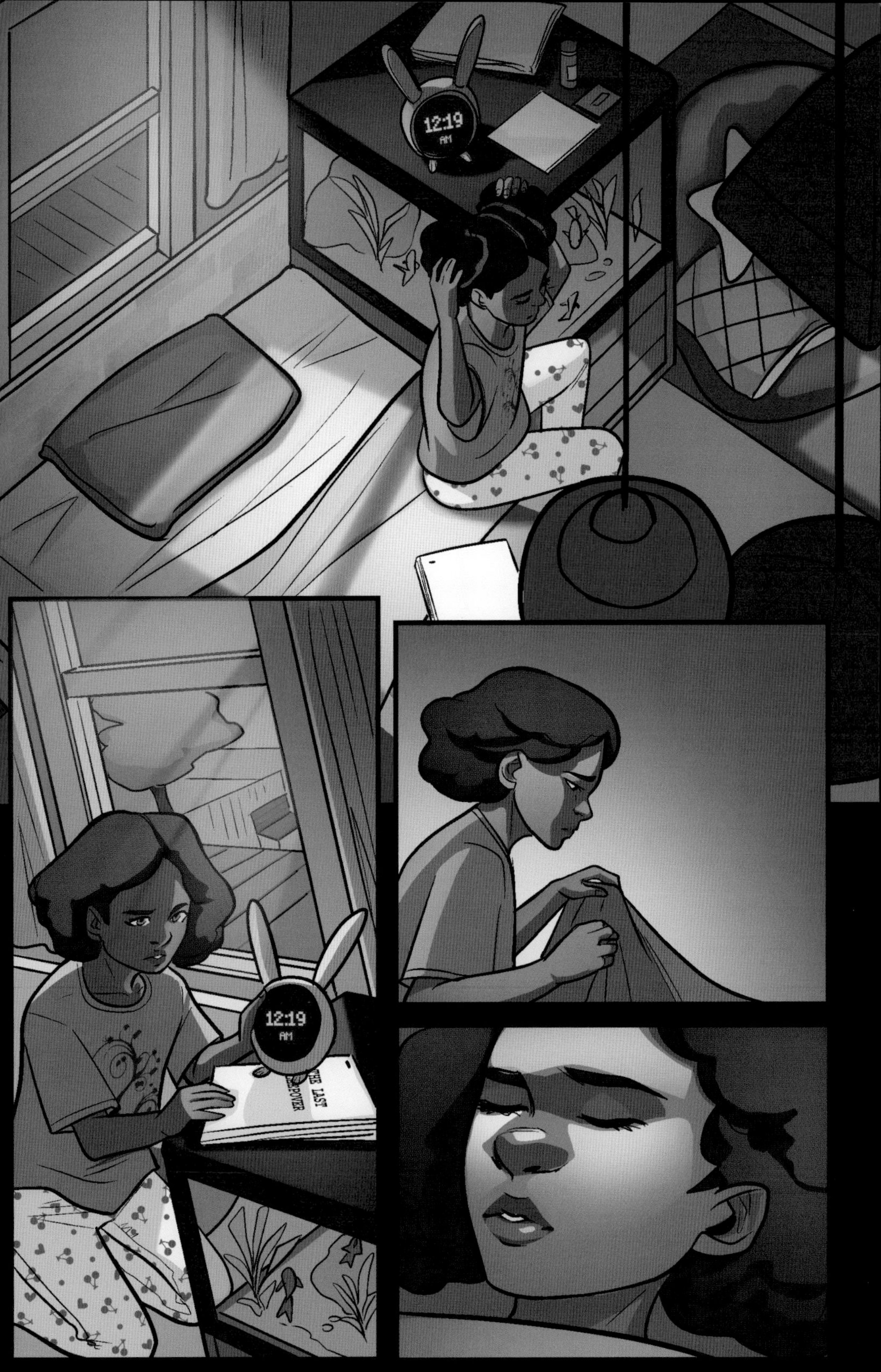
12:19
AM
12:19
AM
THE LAST

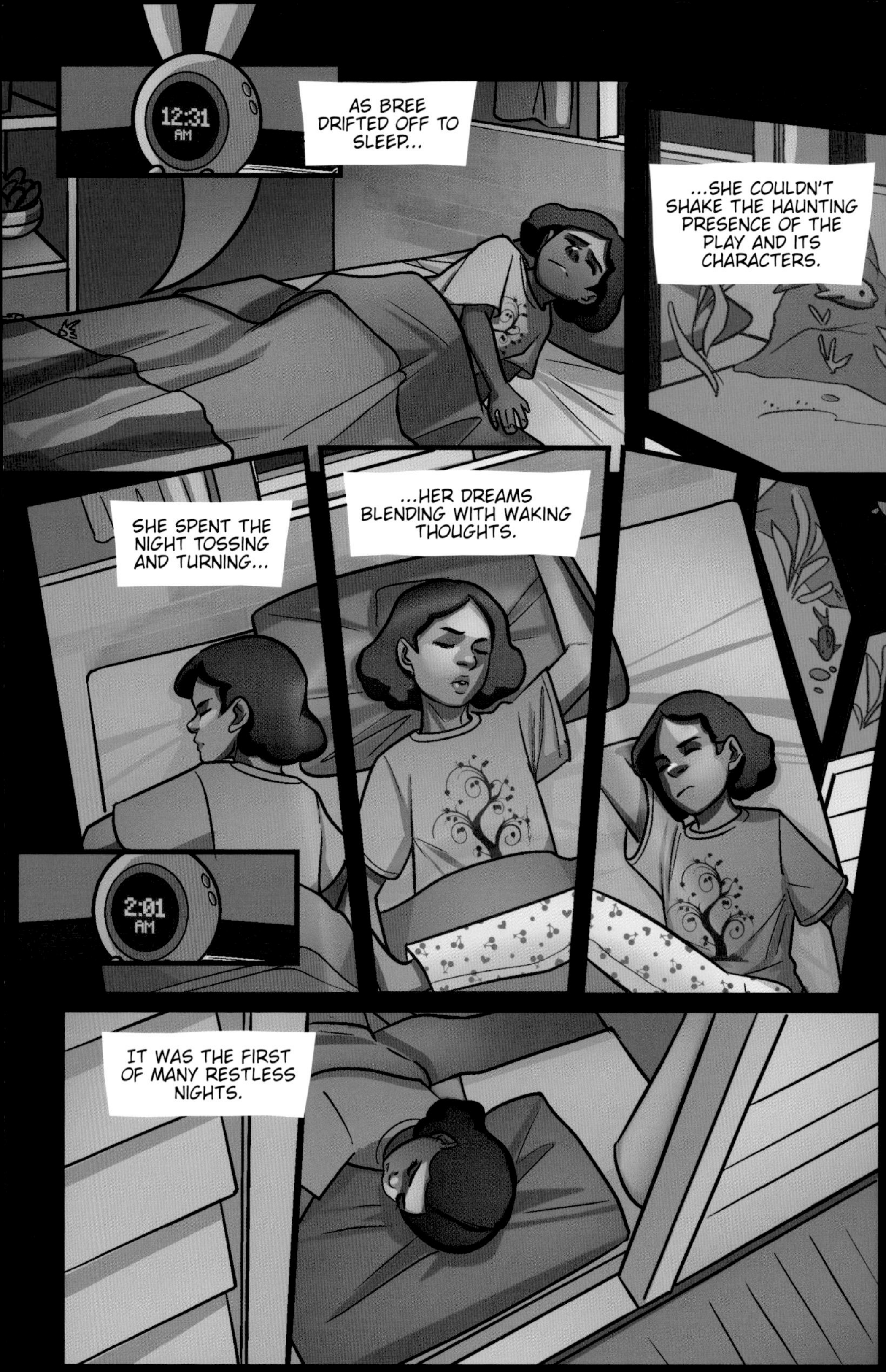
12:31 AM
AS BREE DRIFTED OFF TO SLEEP...
...SHE COULDN'T SHAKE THE HAUNTING PRESENCE OF THE PLAY AND ITS CHARACTERS.
SHE SPENT THE NIGHT TOSSING AND TURNING...
2:01 AM
...HER DREAMS BLENDING WITH WAKING THOUGHTS.
IT WAS THE FIRST OF MANY RESTLESS NIGHTS.

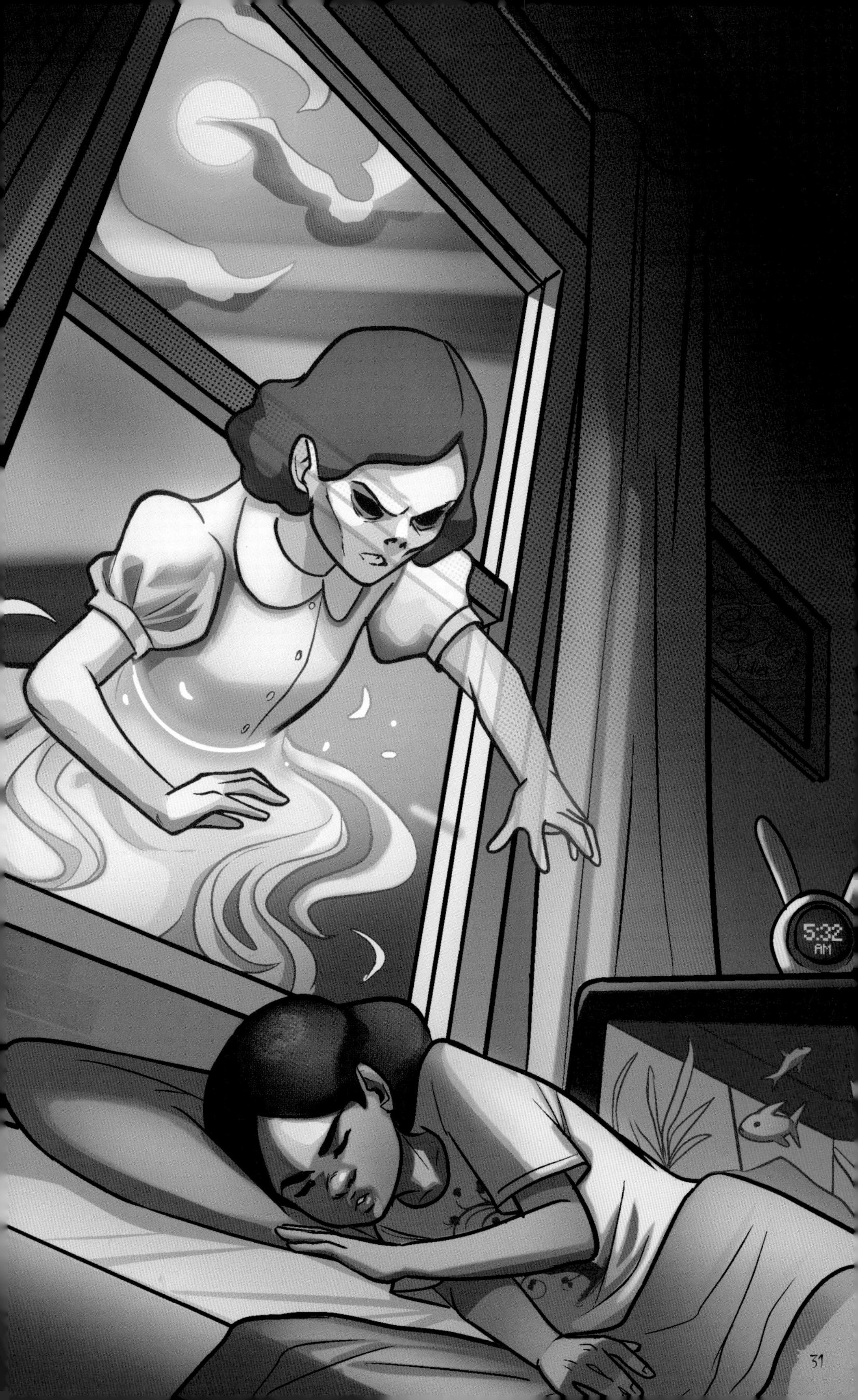
5:32
AM

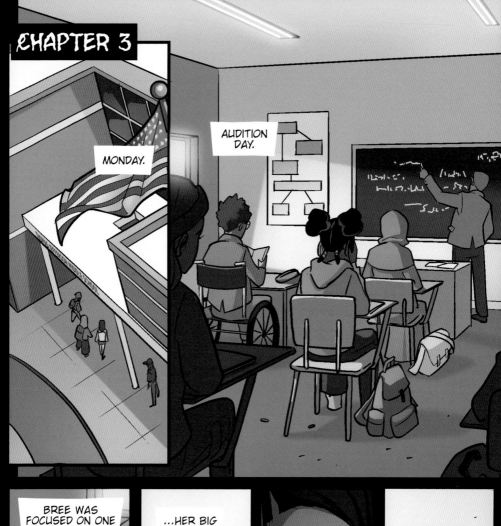

CHAPTER 3

MONDAY.

AUDITION DAY.

BREE WAS FOCUSED ON ONE THING AND ONE THING ONLY...

...HER BIG CHANCE.

RII

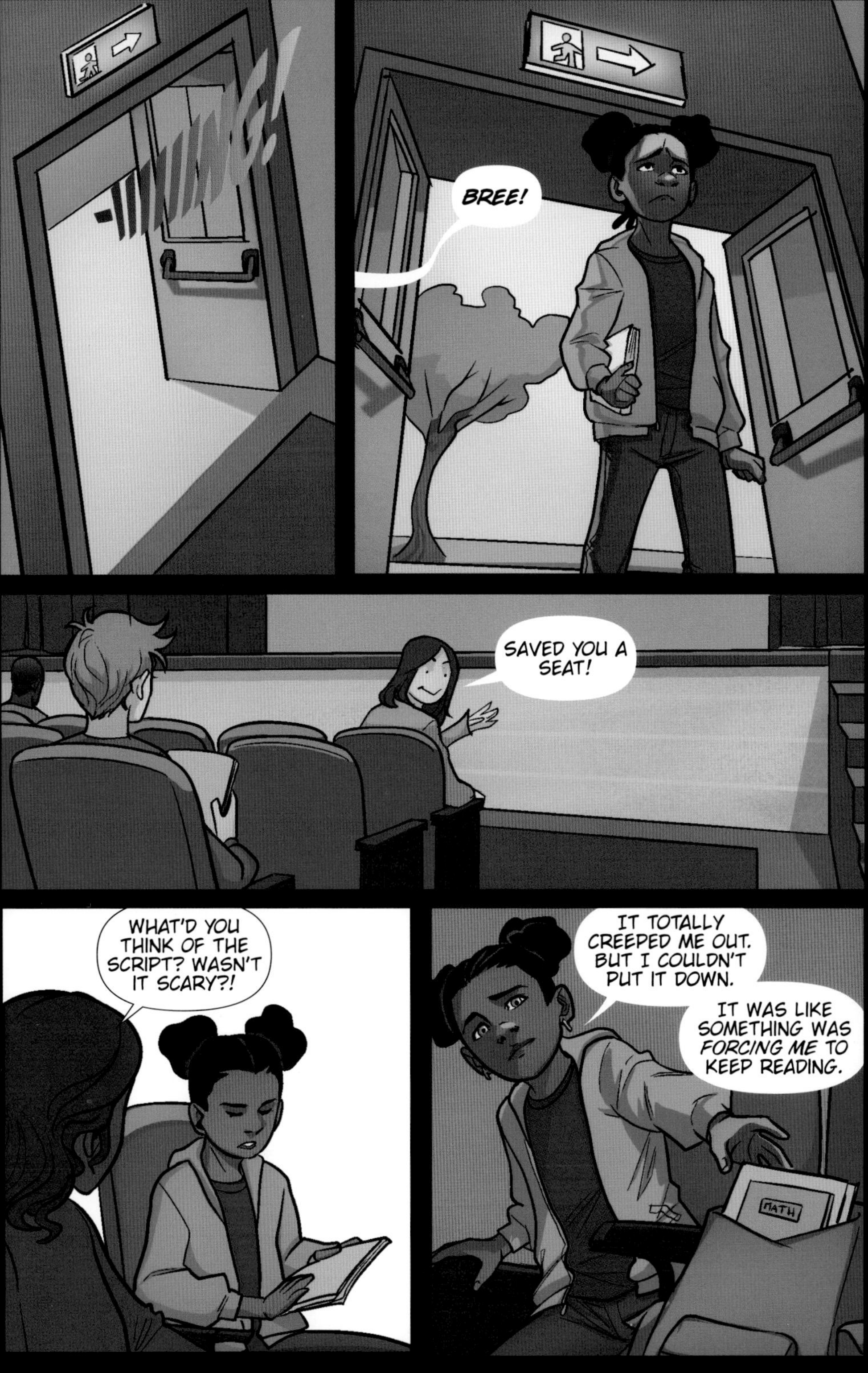
-IIIIIUUNG!
BREE!
SAVED YOU A SEAT!
WHAT'D YOU THINK OF THE SCRIPT? WASN'T IT SCARY?!
IT TOTALLY CREEPED ME OUT. BUT I COULDN'T PUT IT DOWN.
IT WAS LIKE SOMETHING WAS *FORCING ME* TO KEEP READING.
MATH

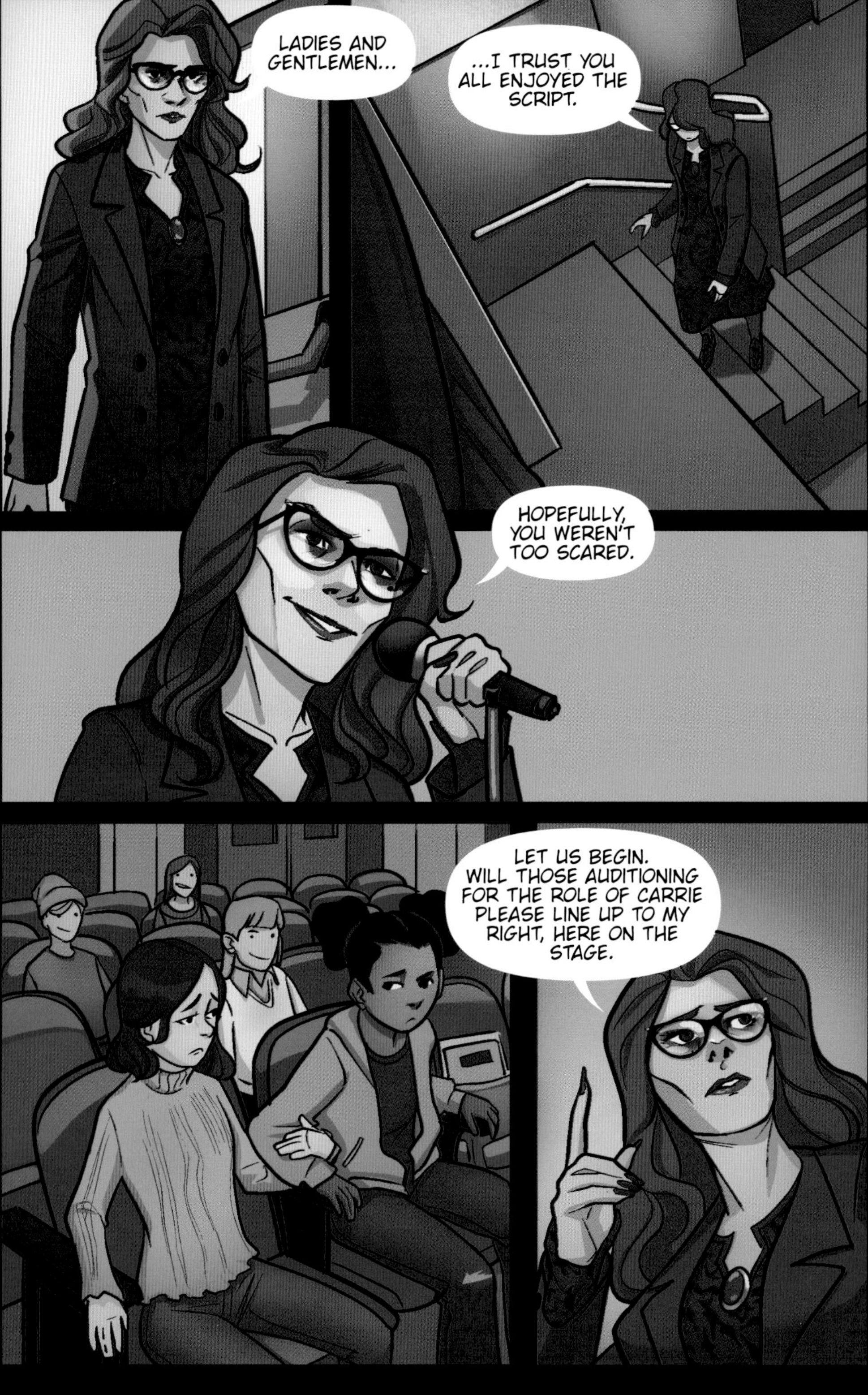
LADIES AND GENTLEMEN...
...I TRUST YOU ALL ENJOYED THE SCRIPT.
HOPEFULLY, YOU WEREN'T TOO SCARED.
LET US BEGIN. WILL THOSE AUDITIONING FOR THE ROLE OF CARRIE PLEASE LINE UP TO MY RIGHT, HERE ON THE STAGE.

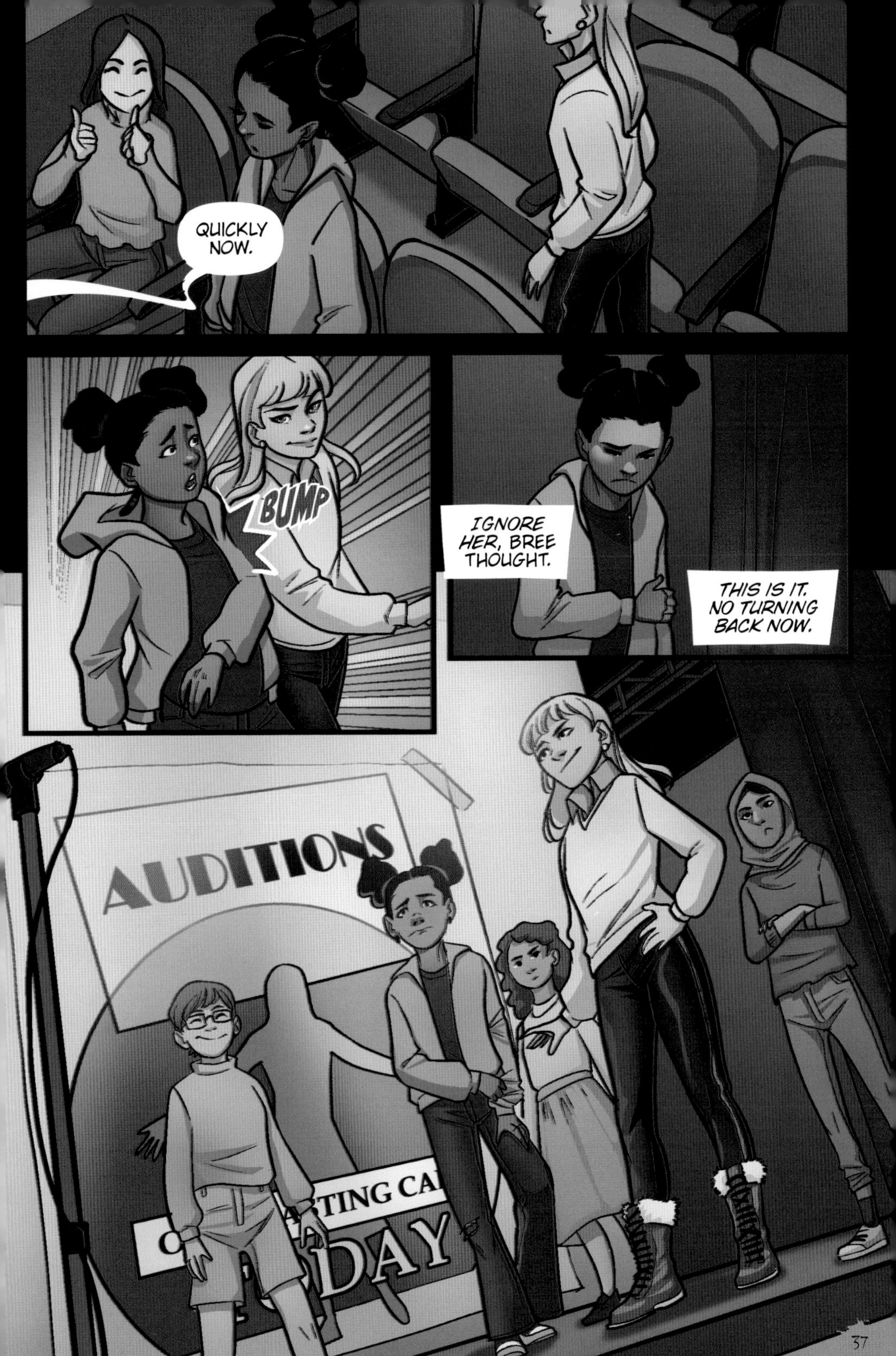
QUICKLY NOW.
BUMP
IGNORE HER, BREE THOUGHT.
THIS IS IT. NO TURNING BACK NOW.
AUDITIONS

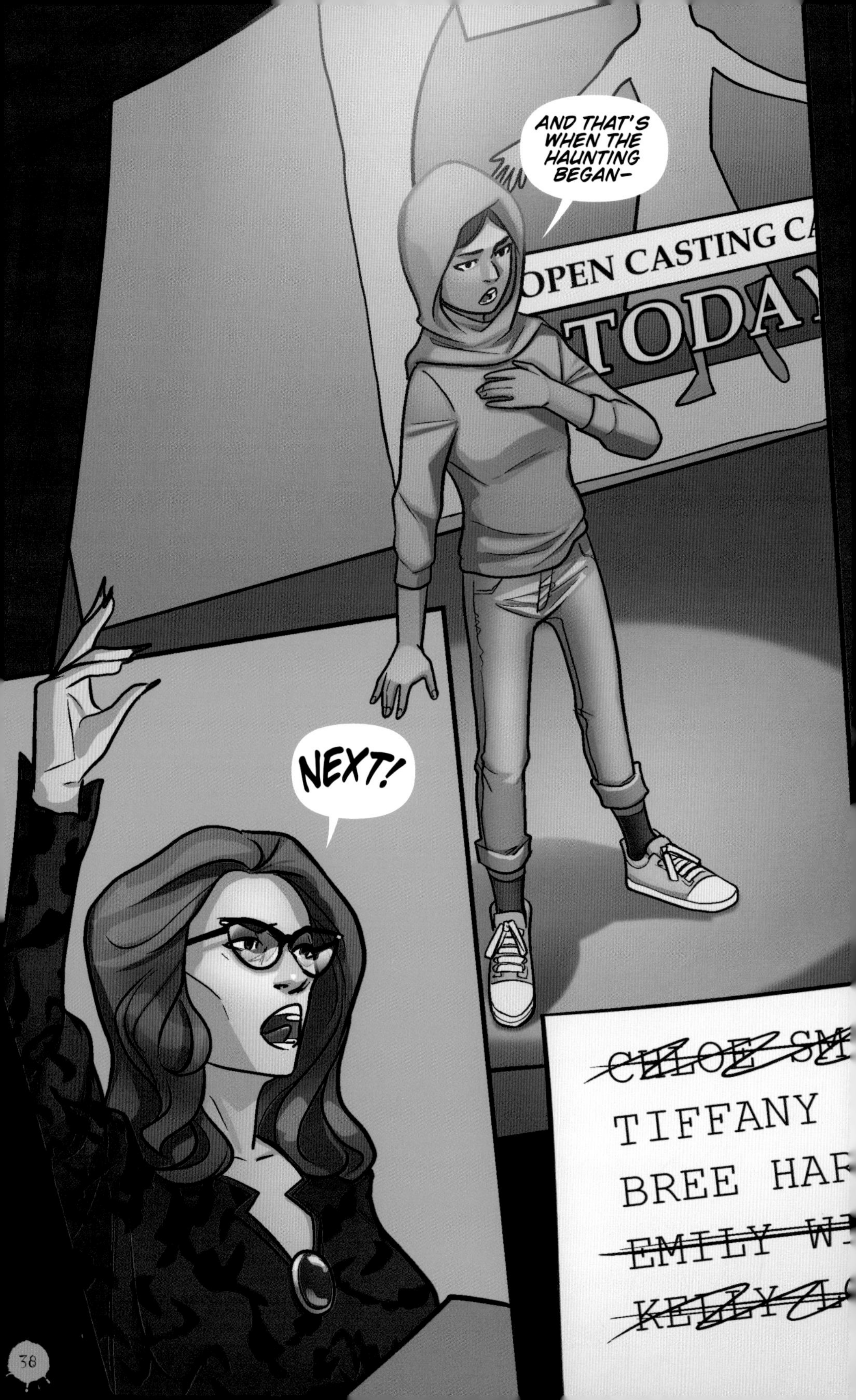
AND THAT'S WHEN THE HAUNTING BEGAN–
OPEN CASTING
NEXT!
TIFFANY
BREE

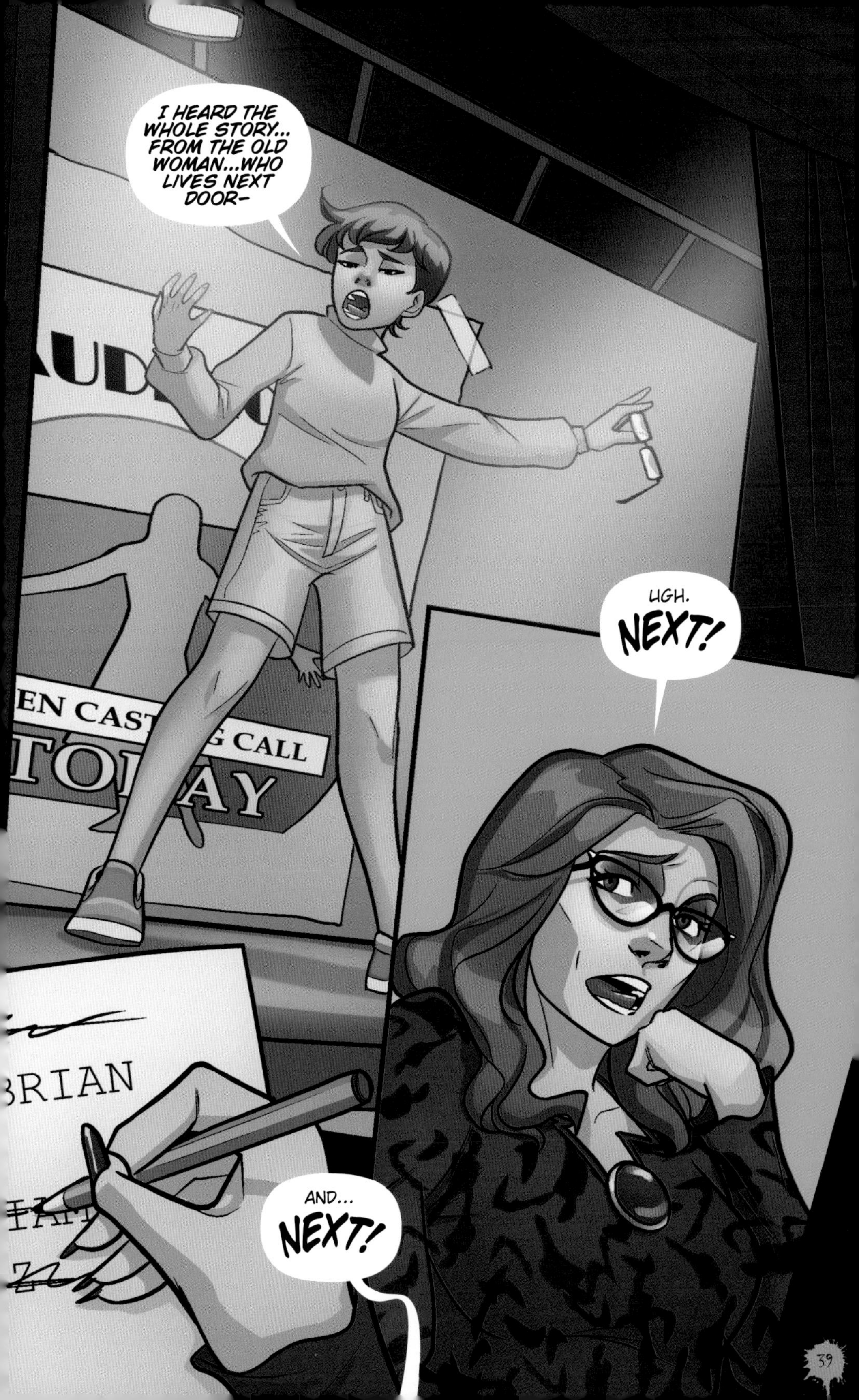
I HEARD THE WHOLE STORY... FROM THE OLD WOMAN...WHO LIVES NEXT DOOR-
UGH. NEXT!
BRIAN
AND... NEXT!

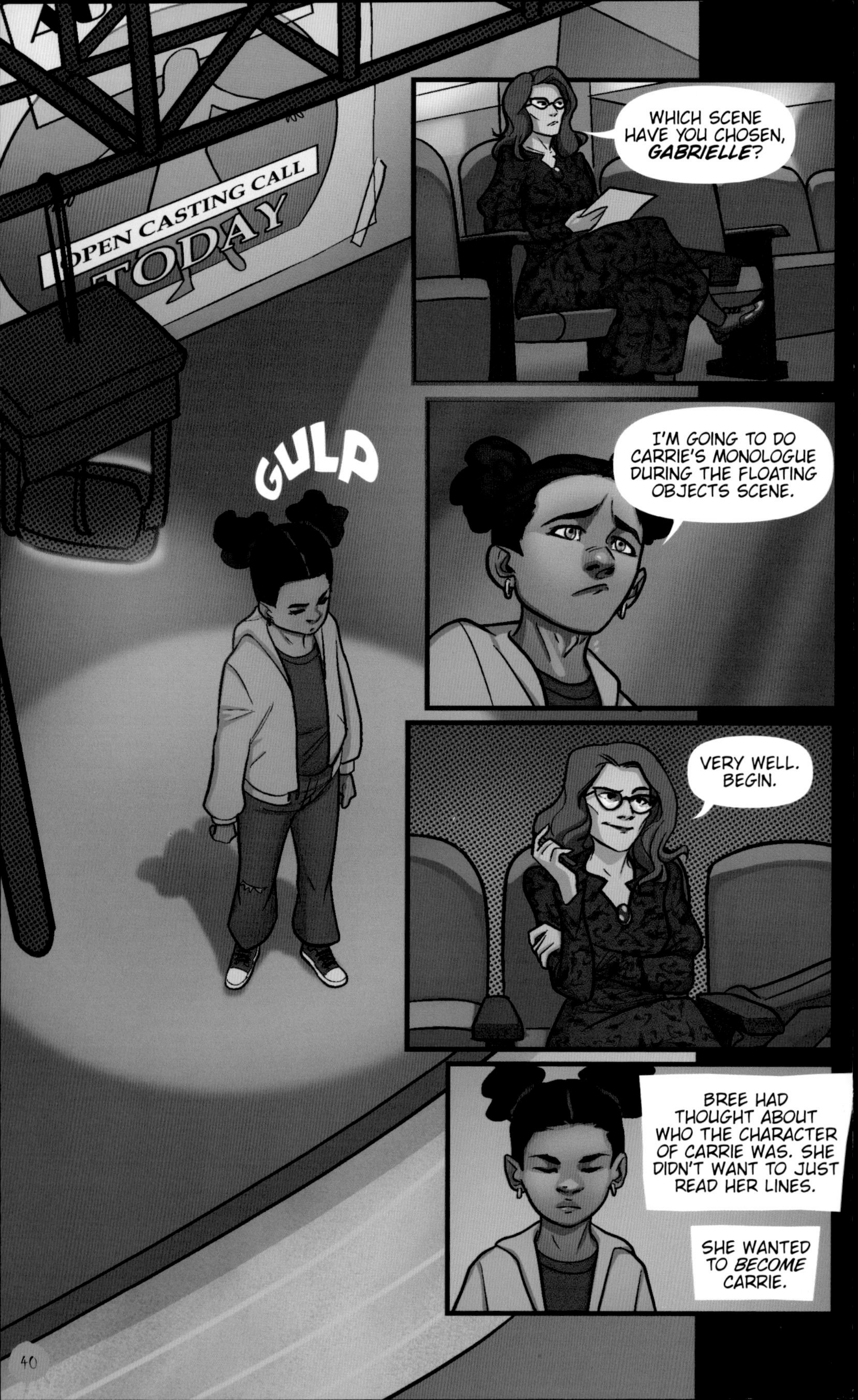
OPEN CASTING CALL
TODAY
WHICH SCENE HAVE YOU CHOSEN, *GABRIELLE*?
GULP
I'M GOING TO DO CARRIE'S MONOLOGUE DURING THE FLOATING OBJECTS SCENE.
VERY WELL. BEGIN.
BREE HAD THOUGHT ABOUT WHO THE CHARACTER OF CARRIE WAS. SHE DIDN'T WANT TO JUST READ HER LINES.
SHE WANTED TO *BECOME* CARRIE.

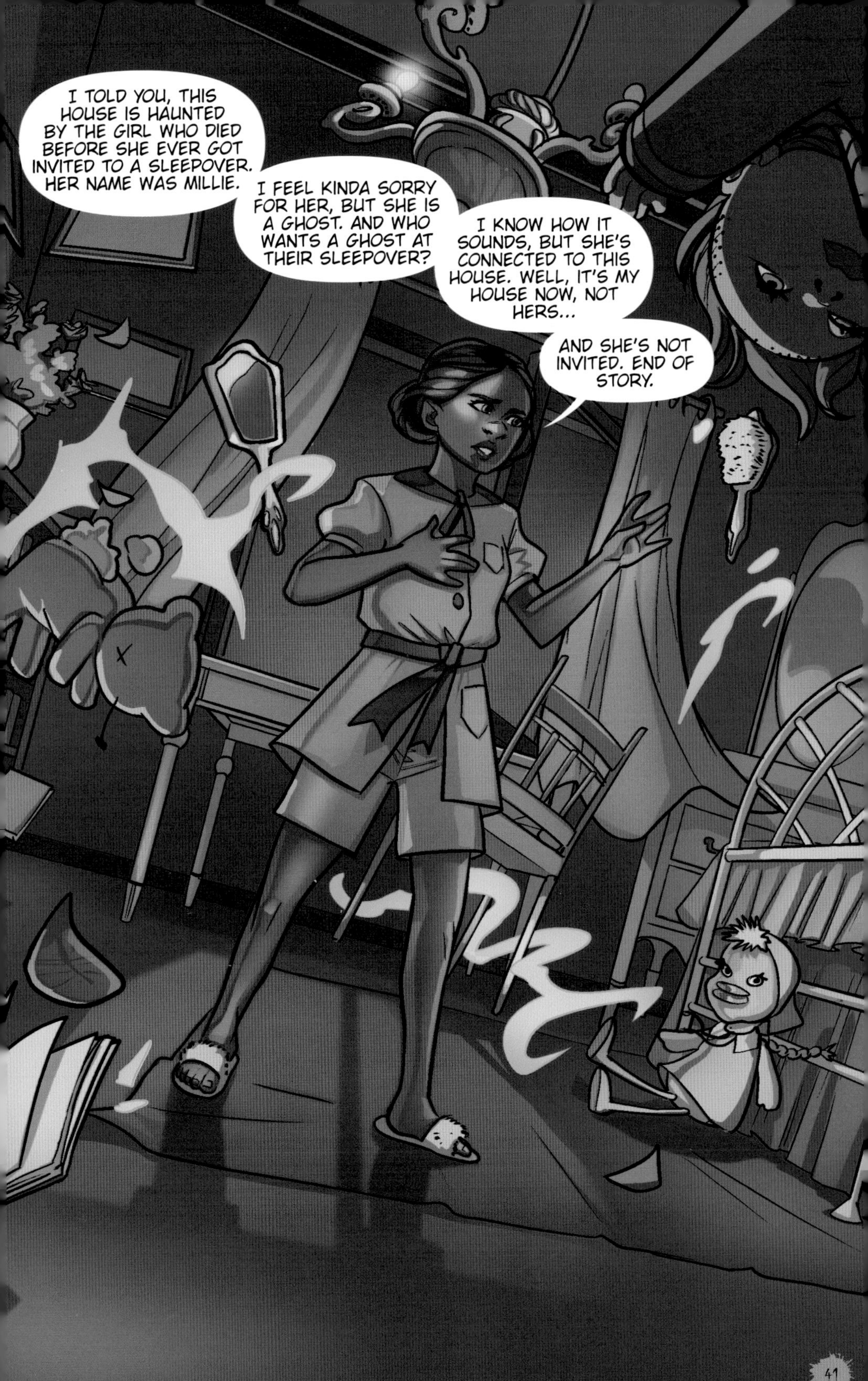
I TOLD YOU, THIS HOUSE IS HAUNTED BY THE GIRL WHO DIED BEFORE SHE EVER GOT INVITED TO A SLEEPOVER. HER NAME WAS MILLIE.
I FEEL KINDA SORRY FOR HER, BUT SHE IS A GHOST. AND WHO WANTS A GHOST AT THEIR SLEEPOVER?
I KNOW HOW IT SOUNDS, BUT SHE'S CONNECTED TO THIS HOUSE. WELL, IT'S MY HOUSE NOW, NOT HERS...
AND SHE'S NOT INVITED. END OF STORY.

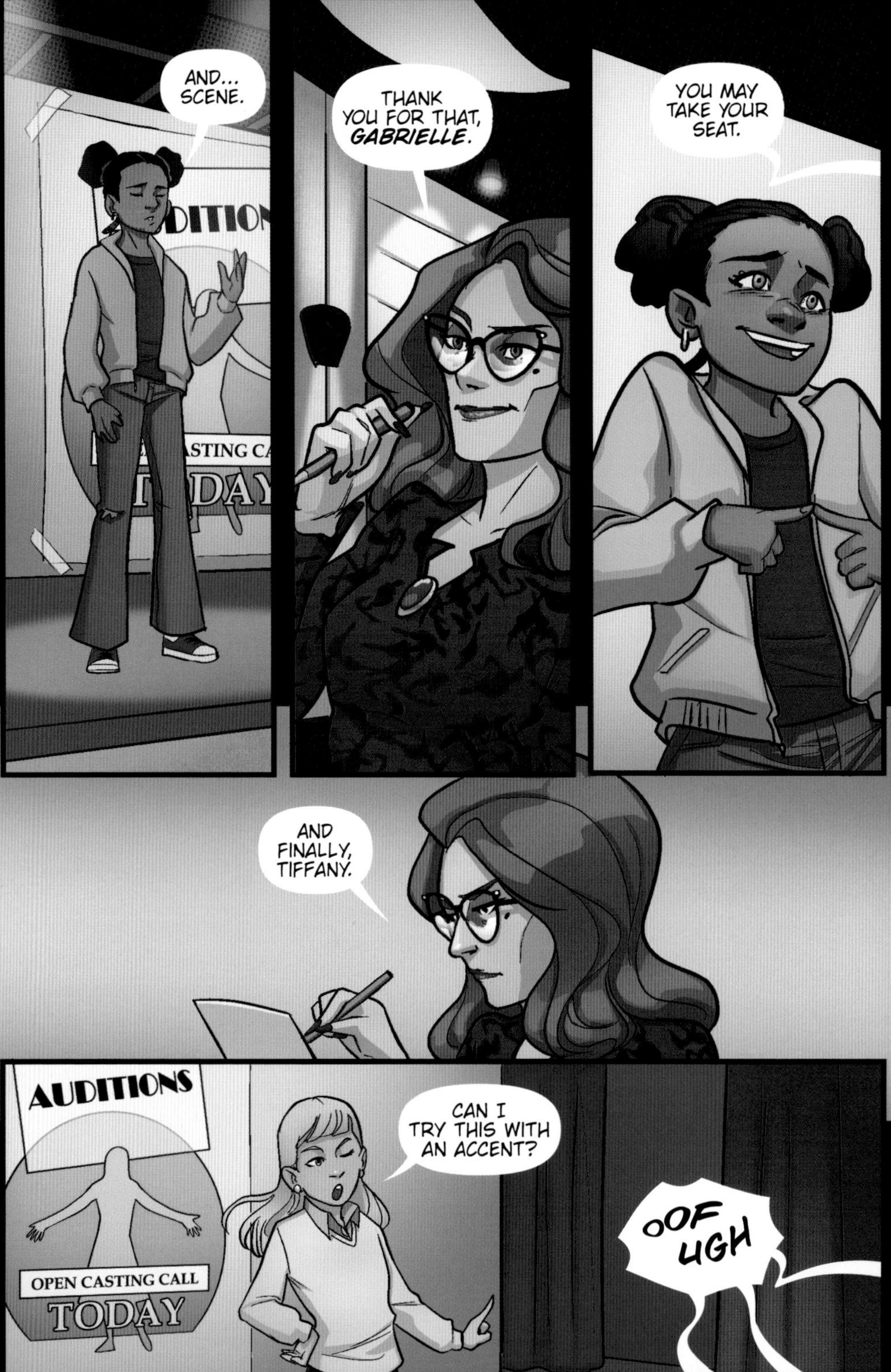
AND... SCENE.
THANK YOU FOR THAT, GABRIELLE.
YOU MAY TAKE YOUR SEAT.
AND FINALLY, TIFFANY.
AUDITIONS
OPEN CASTING CALL
TODAY
CAN I TRY THIS WITH AN ACCENT?
OOF UGH

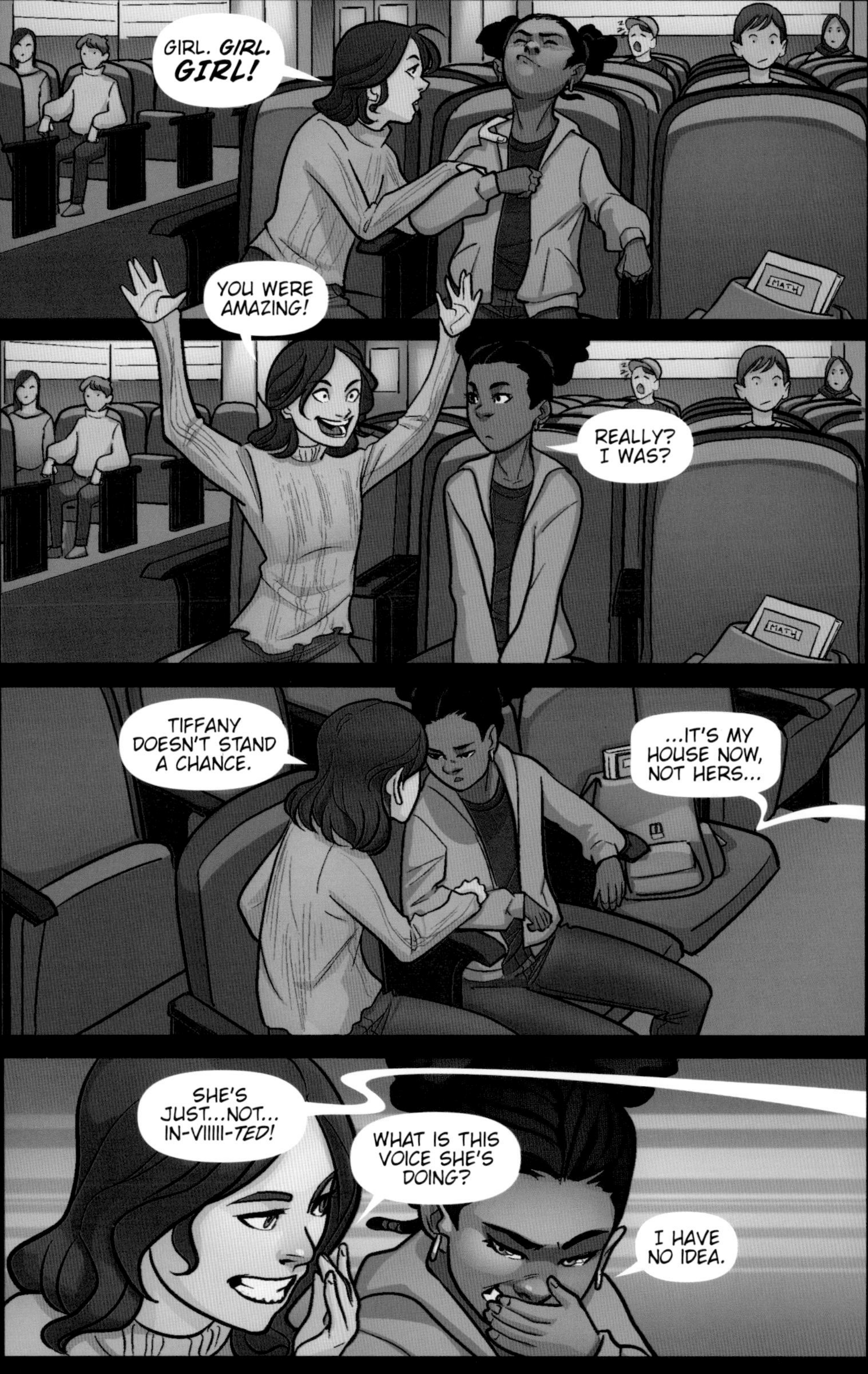
GIRL. GIRL. GIRL!
YOU WERE AMAZING!
REALLY? I WAS?
MATH
TIFFANY DOESN'T STAND A CHANCE.
...IT'S MY HOUSE NOW, NOT HERS...
SHE'S JUST...NOT... IN-VIIIII-TED!
WHAT IS THIS VOICE SHE'S DOING?
I HAVE NO IDEA.

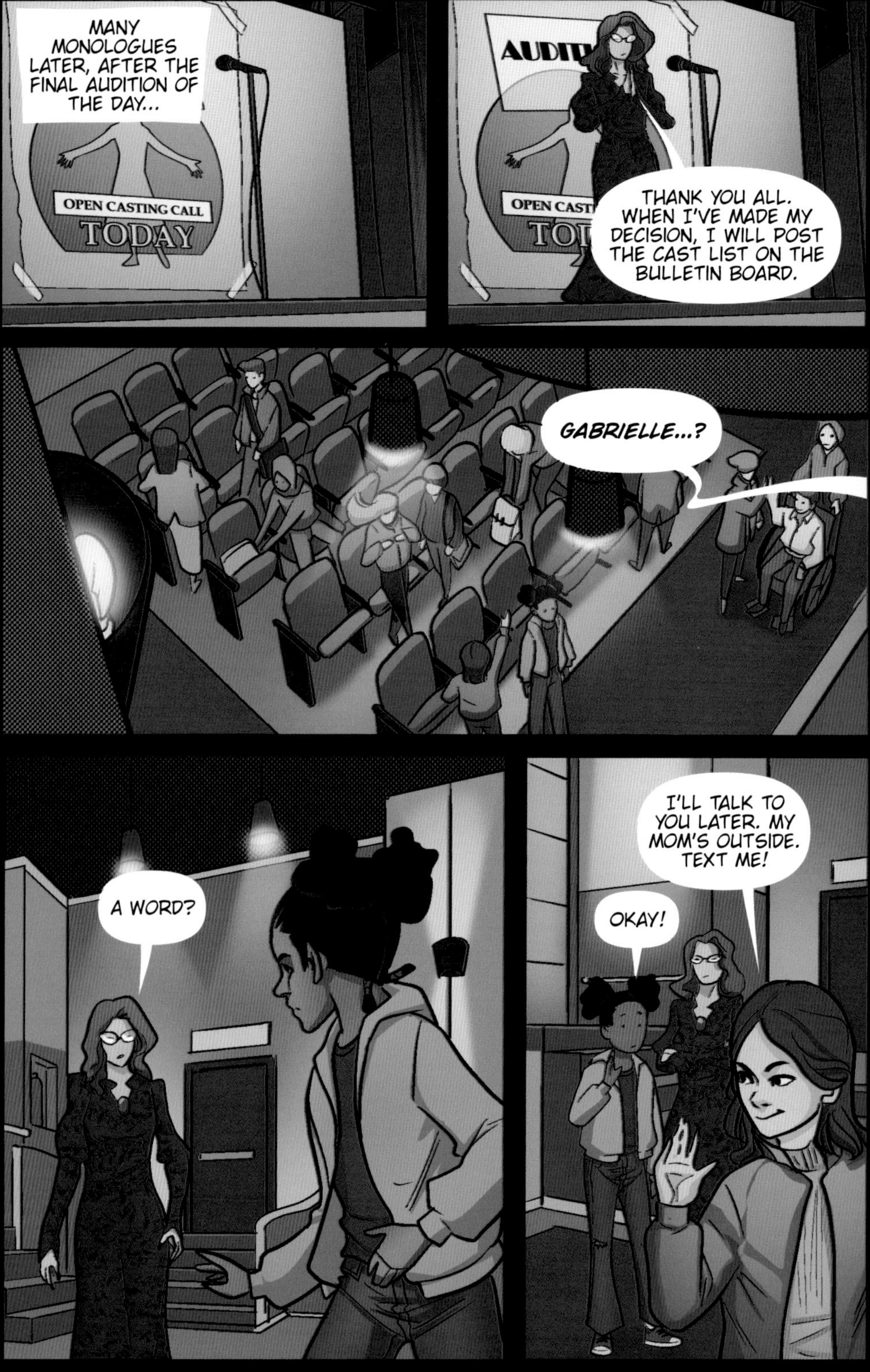
MANY MONOLOGUES LATER, AFTER THE FINAL AUDITION OF THE DAY...
OPEN CASTING CALL
TODAY
AUDITI
THANK YOU ALL. WHEN I'VE MADE MY DECISION, I WILL POST THE CAST LIST ON THE BULLETIN BOARD.
GABRIELLE...?
A WORD?
I'LL TALK TO YOU LATER. MY MOM'S OUTSIDE. TEXT ME!
OKAY!

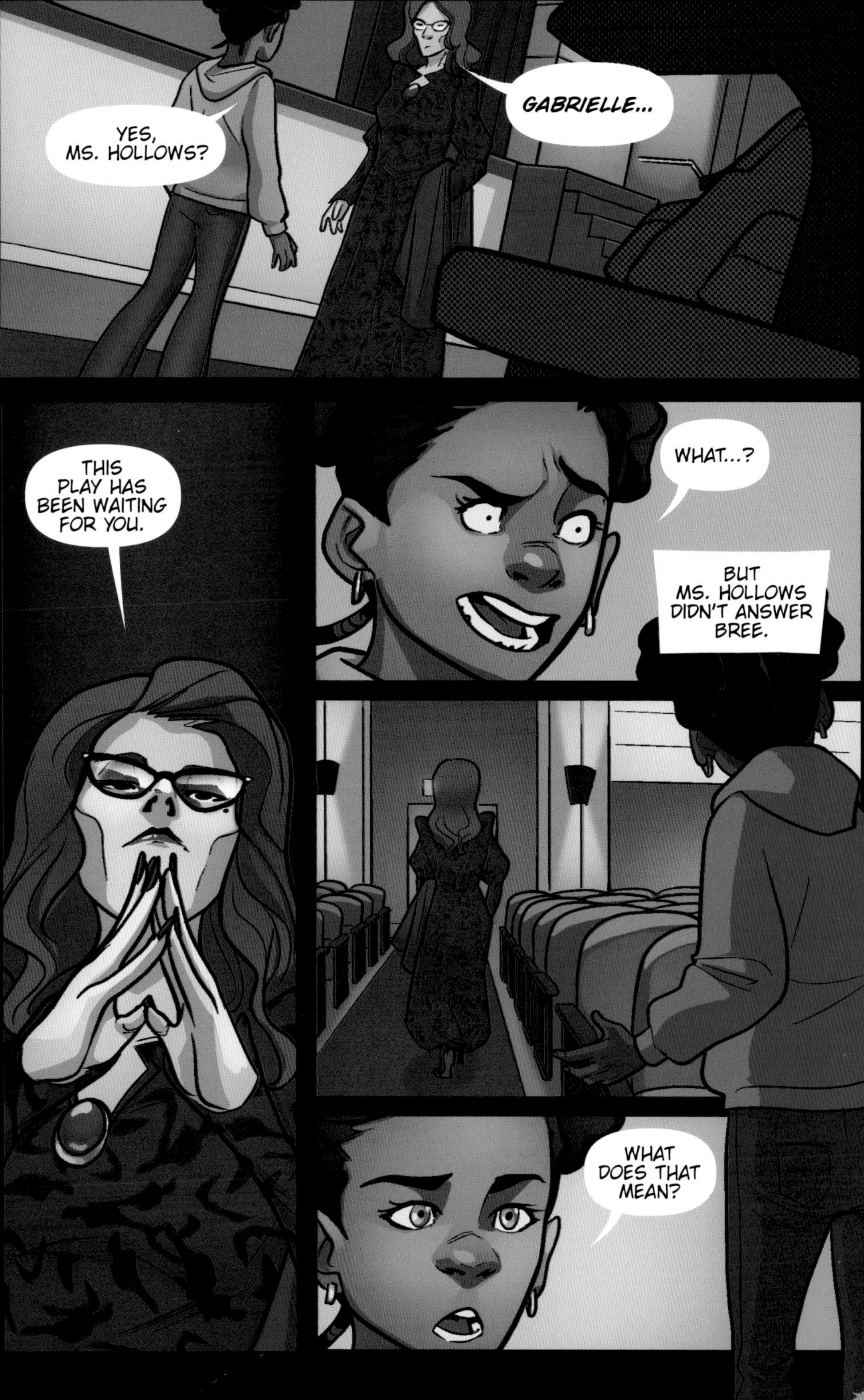
GABRIELLE...
YES, MS. HOLLOWS?
THIS PLAY HAS BEEN WAITING FOR YOU.
WHAT...?
BUT MS. HOLLOWS DIDN'T ANSWER BREE.
WHAT DOES THAT MEAN?

CHAPTER 4

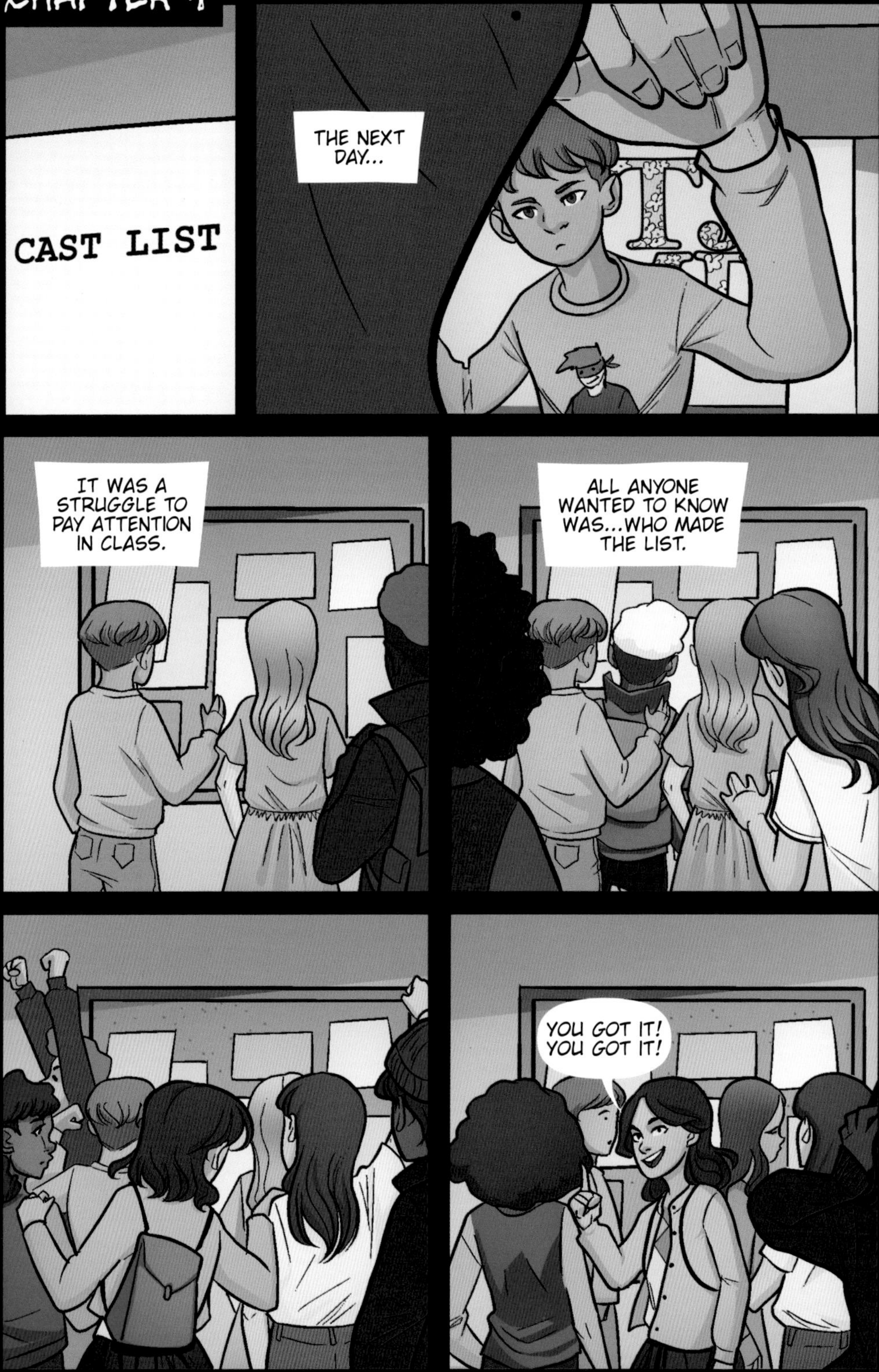
CAST LIST
THE NEXT DAY...
IT WAS A STRUGGLE TO PAY ATTENTION IN CLASS.
ALL ANYONE WANTED TO KNOW WAS...WHO MADE THE LIST.
YOU GOT IT! YOU GOT IT!

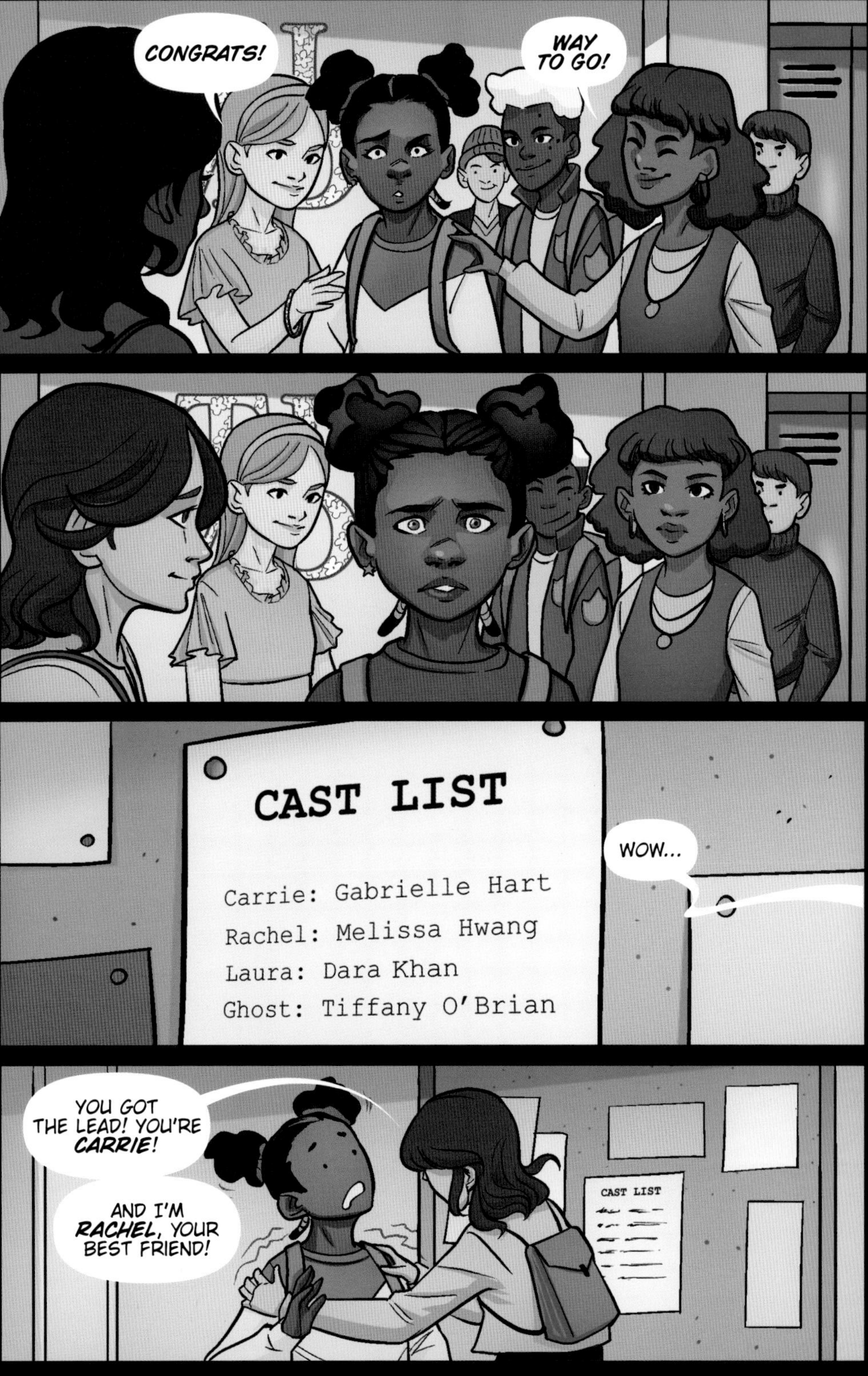
CONGRATS!
WAY TO GO!
CAST LIST
Carrie: Gabrielle Hart
Rachel: Melissa Hwang
Laura: Dara Khan
Ghost: Tiffany O'Brian
WOW...
YOU GOT THE LEAD! YOU'RE *CARRIE*!
AND I'M *RACHEL*, YOUR BEST FRIEND!
CAST LIST

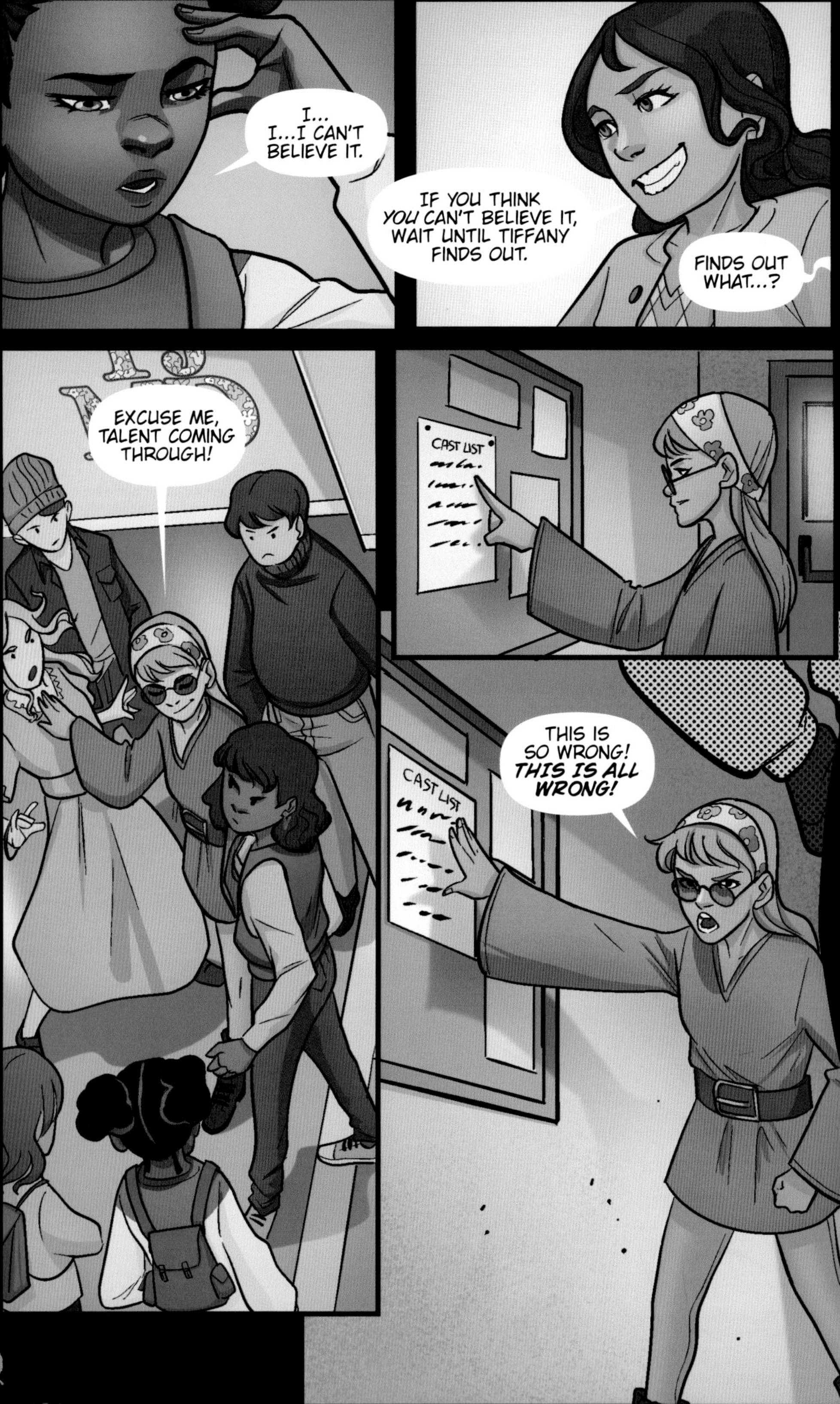

I...
I...I CAN'T BELIEVE IT.
IF YOU THINK *YOU* CAN'T BELIEVE IT, WAIT UNTIL TIFFANY FINDS OUT.
FINDS OUT WHAT...?
EXCUSE ME, TALENT COMING THROUGH!
CAST LIST
CAST LIST
THIS IS SO WRONG! **THIS IS ALL WRONG!**

WHAT'S WRONG ABOUT IT? YOU AUDITIONED, SHE AUDITIONED.

SHE GOT THE PART.

BUT I AM SUCH A BETTER ACTOR! I HAVE TO BE IN THIS PLAY.

YOU *ARE* IN THE PLAY.

YOU PLAY THE GIRL WHO HAUNTS THE SLEEPOVER.

LOOKS LIKE *YOU'RE* MORE SUITED TO PLAY THE GHOST. HA!

CAST LIST

e: Gabrielle Hart
: Melissa Hwang
ra: Dara Marinelli
Ghost: Tiffany O'Brian

SEE YOU AT REHEARSALS, TIFF!

LIS, DON'T! THE MORE YOU UPSET HER, THE MORE SHE'LL TAKE IT OUT ON ME.

WHAT? YOU WON THAT ROLE FAIR AND SQUARE.

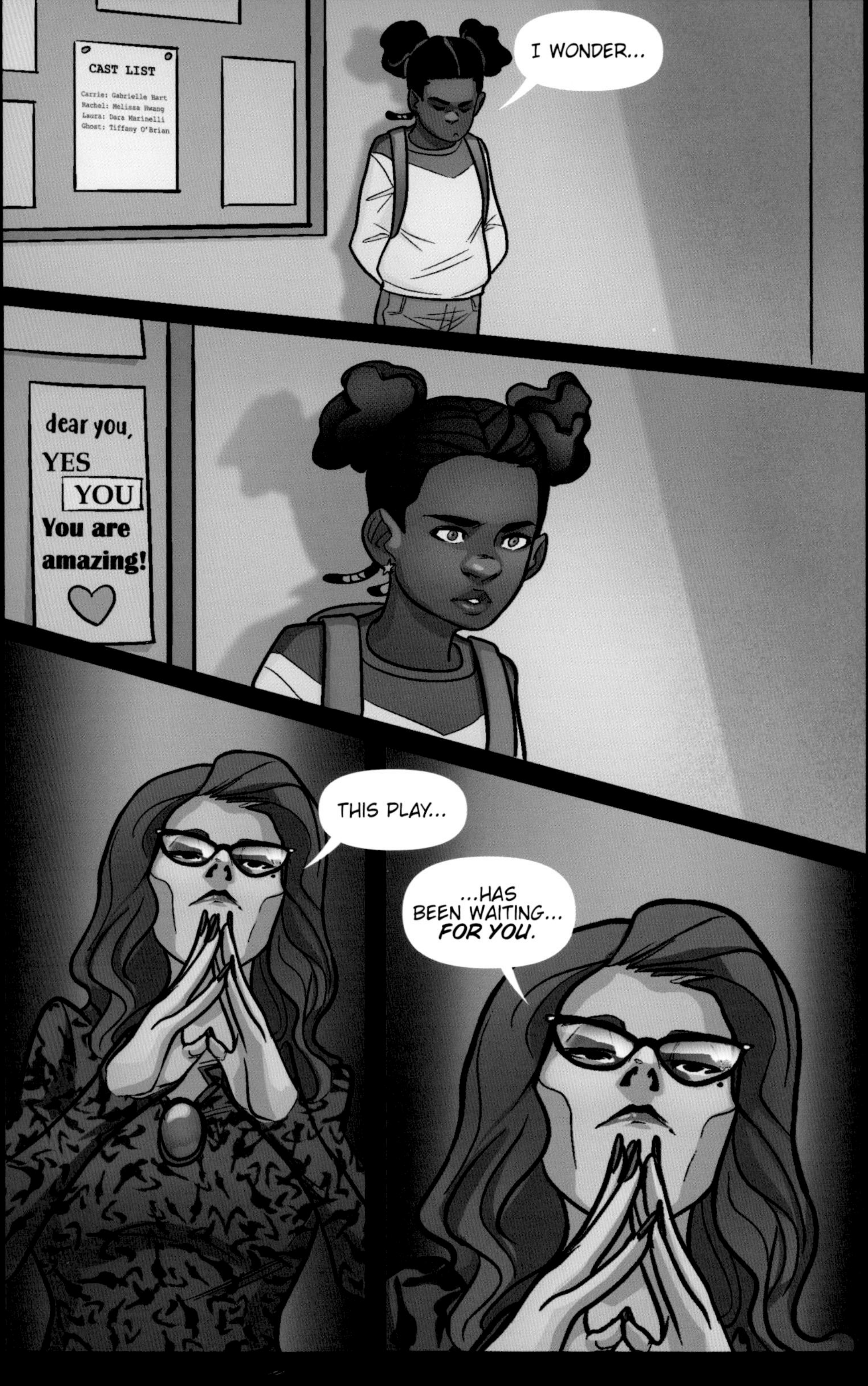
CAST LIST
Carrie: Gabrielle Hart
Rachel: Melissa Hwang
Laura: Dara Marinelli
Ghost: Tiffany O'Brian
I WONDER...
dear you,
YES
YOU
You are amazing!
THIS PLAY...
...HAS BEEN WAITING... FOR YOU.

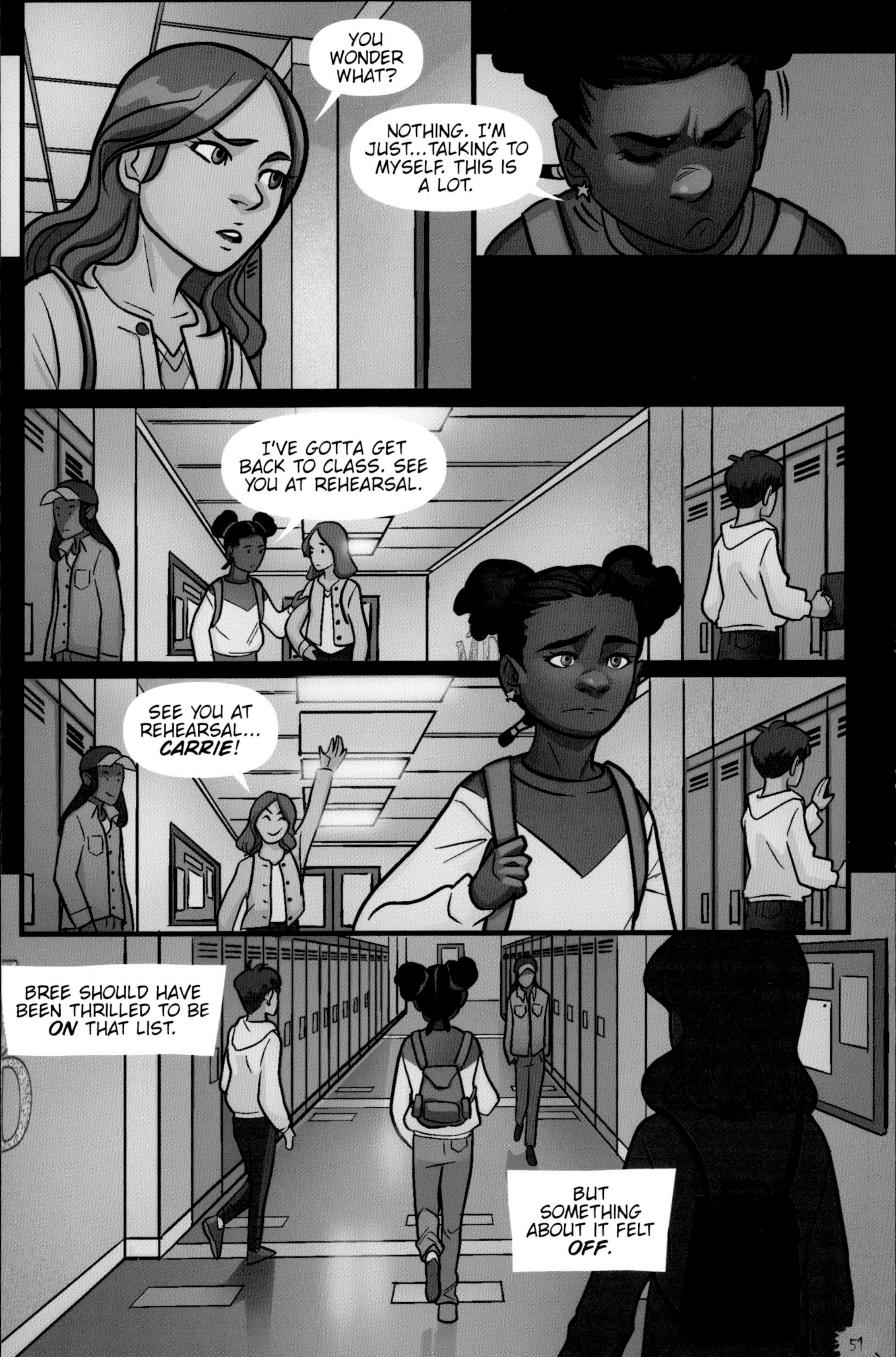
YOU WONDER WHAT?
NOTHING. I'M JUST...TALKING TO MYSELF. THIS IS A LOT.
I'VE GOTTA GET BACK TO CLASS. SEE YOU AT REHEARSAL.
SEE YOU AT REHEARSAL... ***CARRIE***!
BREE SHOULD HAVE BEEN THRILLED TO BE ***ON*** THAT LIST.
BUT SOMETHING ABOUT IT FELT ***OFF***.

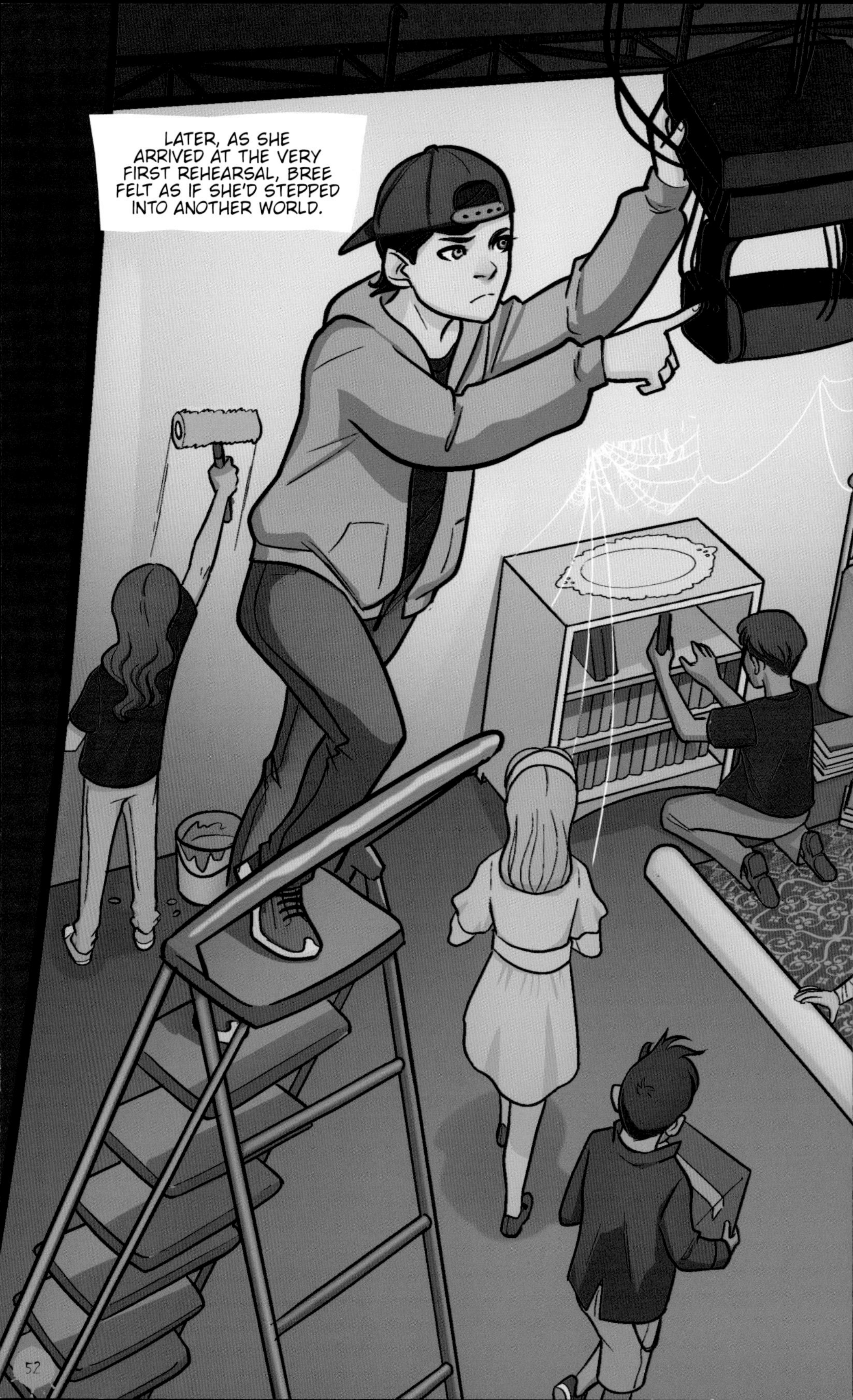
LATER, AS SHE ARRIVED AT THE VERY FIRST REHEARSAL, BREE FELT AS IF SHE'D STEPPED INTO ANOTHER WORLD.

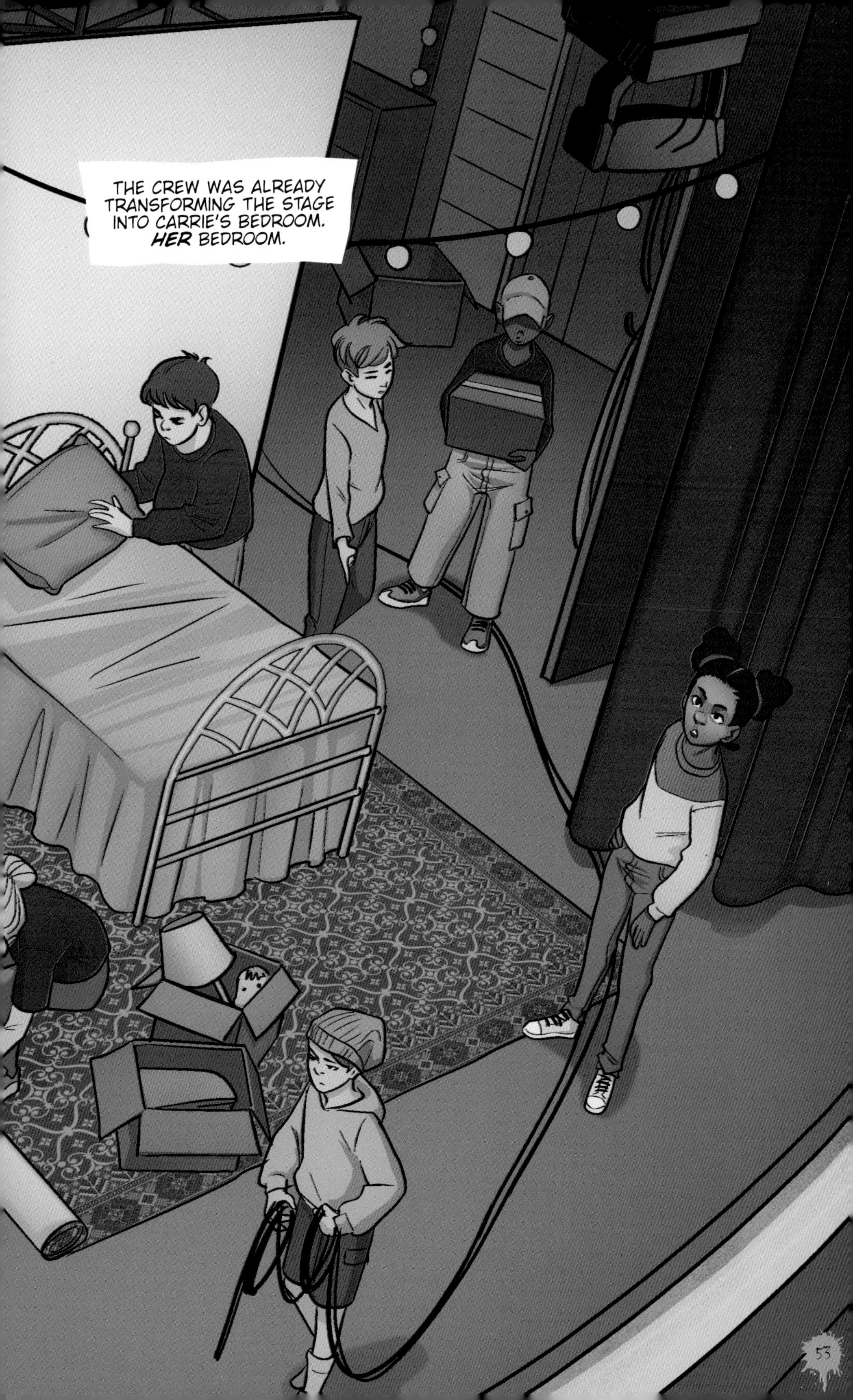
THE CREW WAS ALREADY TRANSFORMING THE STAGE INTO CARRIE'S BEDROOM. *HER* BEDROOM.

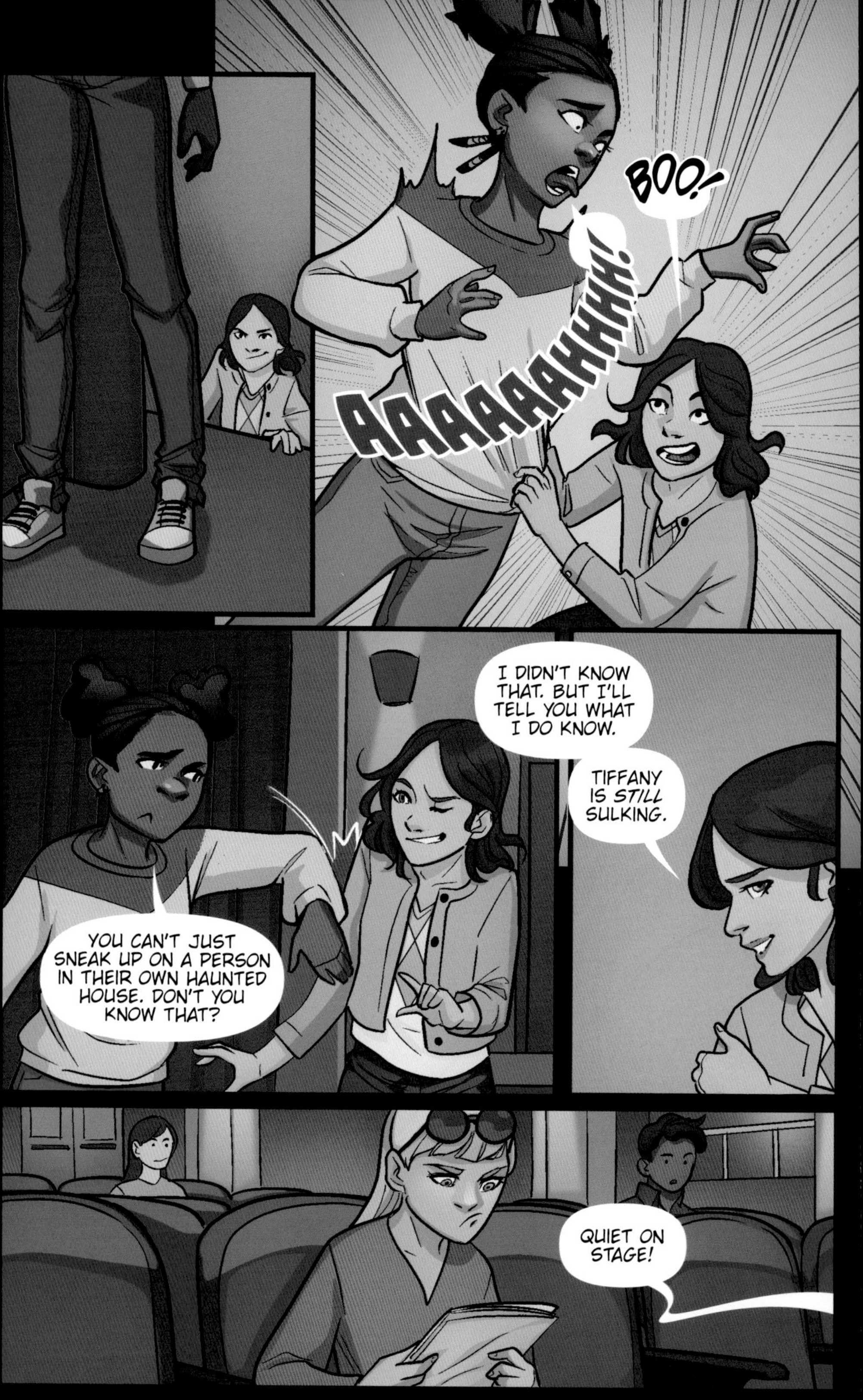
BOO!
AAAAAAHHHH!
YOU CAN'T JUST SNEAK UP ON A PERSON IN THEIR OWN HAUNTED HOUSE. DON'T YOU KNOW THAT?
I DIDN'T KNOW THAT. BUT I'LL TELL YOU WHAT I DO KNOW.
TIFFANY IS *STILL* SULKING.
QUIET ON STAGE!

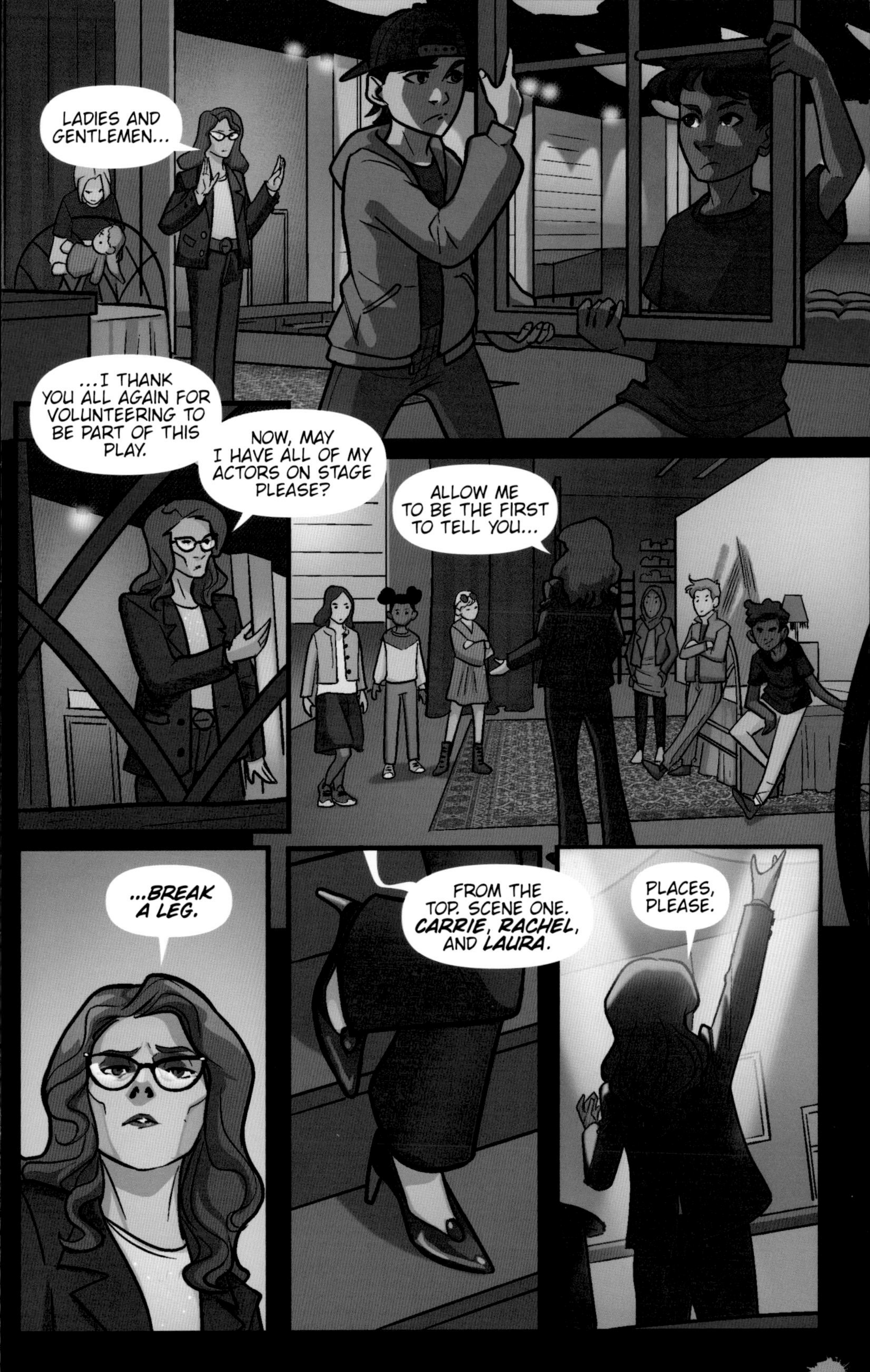
LADIES AND GENTLEMEN...
...I THANK YOU ALL AGAIN FOR VOLUNTEERING TO BE PART OF THIS PLAY.
NOW, MAY I HAVE ALL OF MY ACTORS ON STAGE PLEASE?
ALLOW ME TO BE THE FIRST TO TELL YOU...
...BREAK A LEG.
FROM THE TOP. SCENE ONE. CARRIE, RACHEL, AND LAURA.
PLACES, PLEASE.

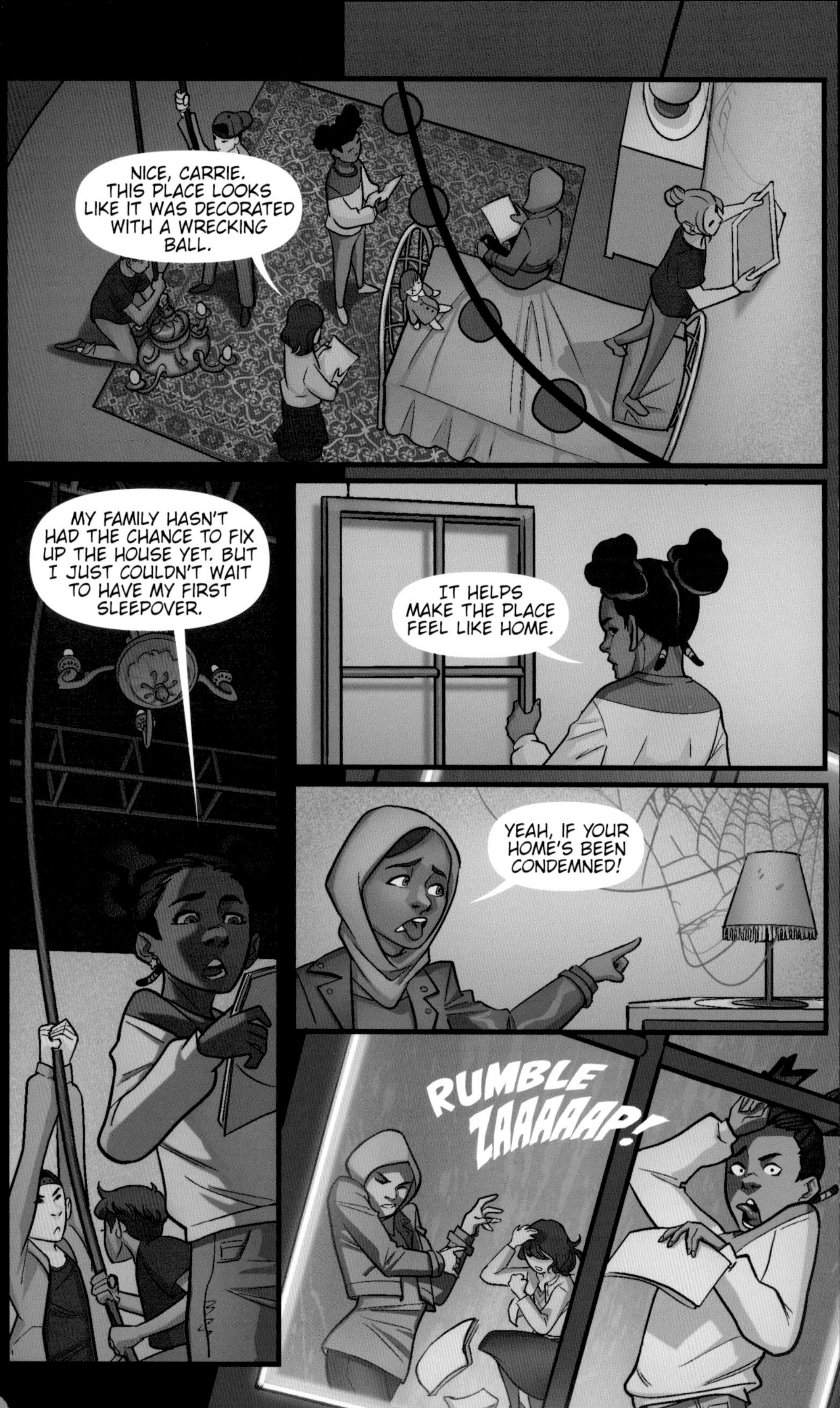
NICE, CARRIE. THIS PLACE LOOKS LIKE IT WAS DECORATED WITH A WRECKING BALL.
MY FAMILY HASN'T HAD THE CHANCE TO FIX UP THE HOUSE YET. BUT I JUST COULDN'T WAIT TO HAVE MY FIRST SLEEPOVER.
IT HELPS MAKE THE PLACE FEEL LIKE HOME.
YEAH, IF YOUR HOME'S BEEN CONDEMNED!
RUMBLE
ZAAAAAP!

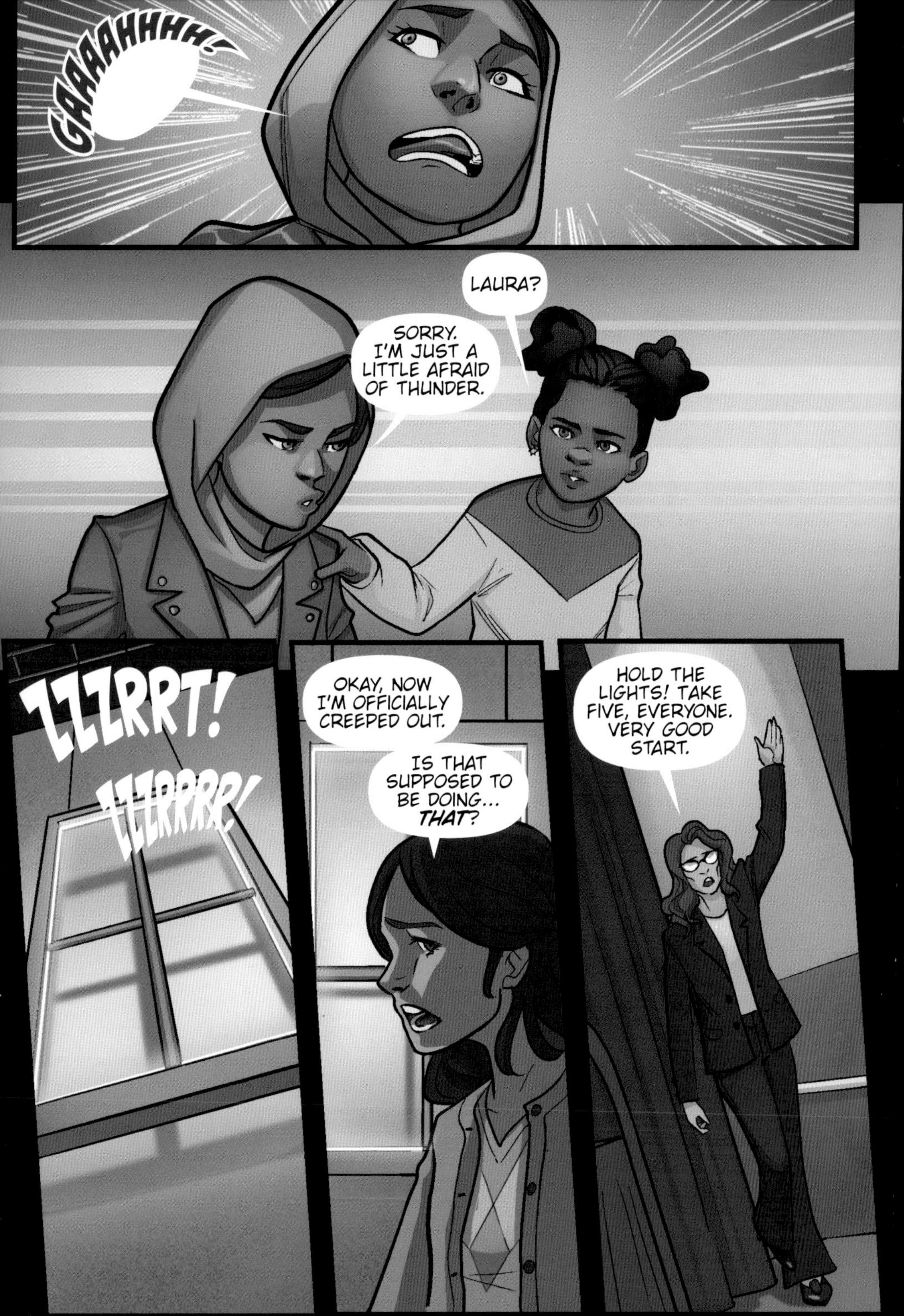
GAAAAHHHH!
LAURA?
SORRY. I'M JUST A LITTLE AFRAID OF THUNDER.
ZZZRRT!
ZZZRRRR!
OKAY, NOW I'M OFFICIALLY CREEPED OUT.
IS THAT SUPPOSED TO BE DOING... *THAT*?
HOLD THE LIGHTS! TAKE FIVE, EVERYONE. VERY GOOD START.

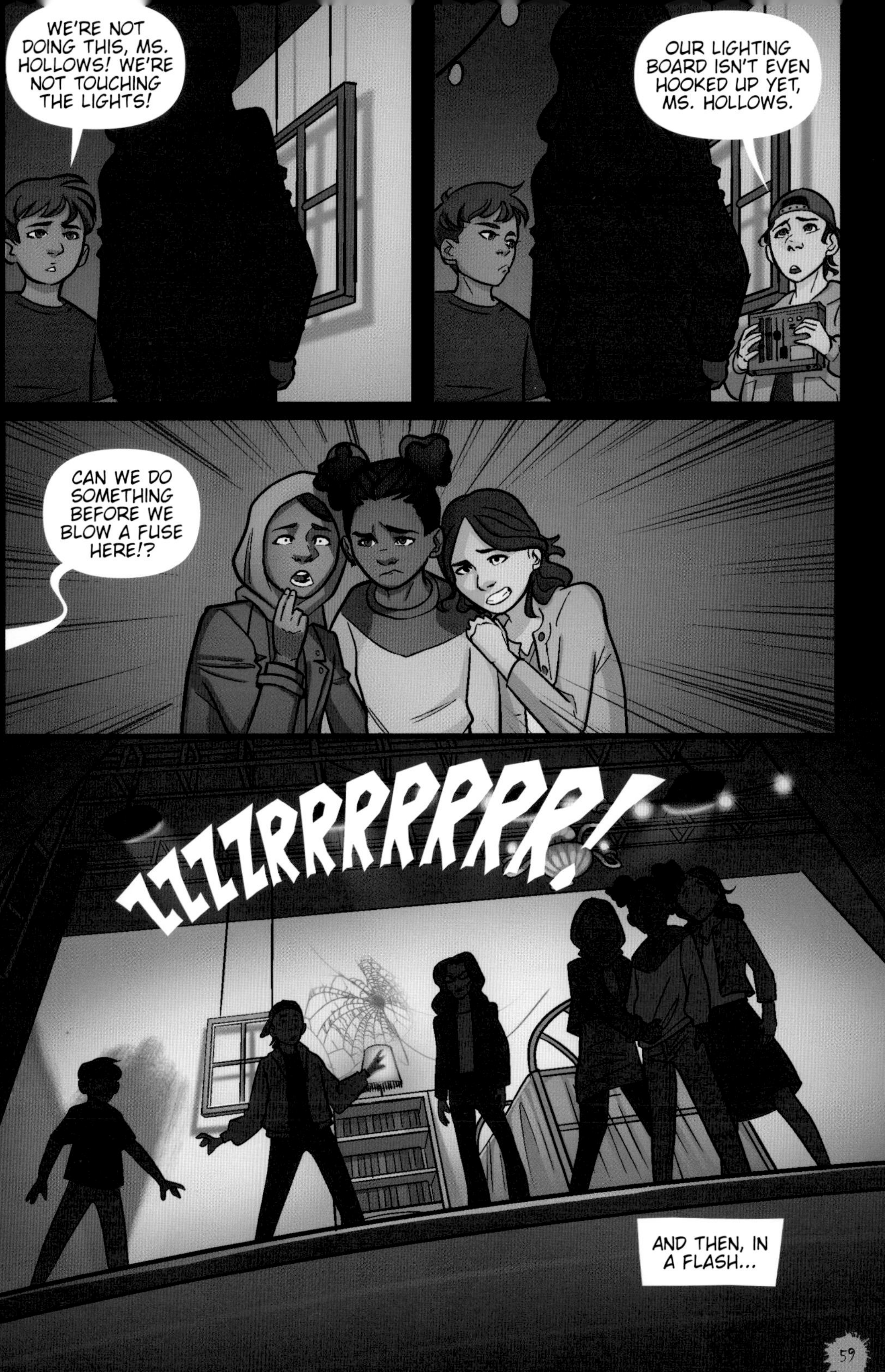
WE'RE NOT DOING THIS, MS. HOLLOWS! WE'RE NOT TOUCHING THE LIGHTS!
OUR LIGHTING BOARD ISN'T EVEN HOOKED UP YET, MS. HOLLOWS.
CAN WE DO SOMETHING BEFORE WE BLOW A FUSE HERE!?
ZZZZRRRRRRR!
AND THEN, IN A FLASH...

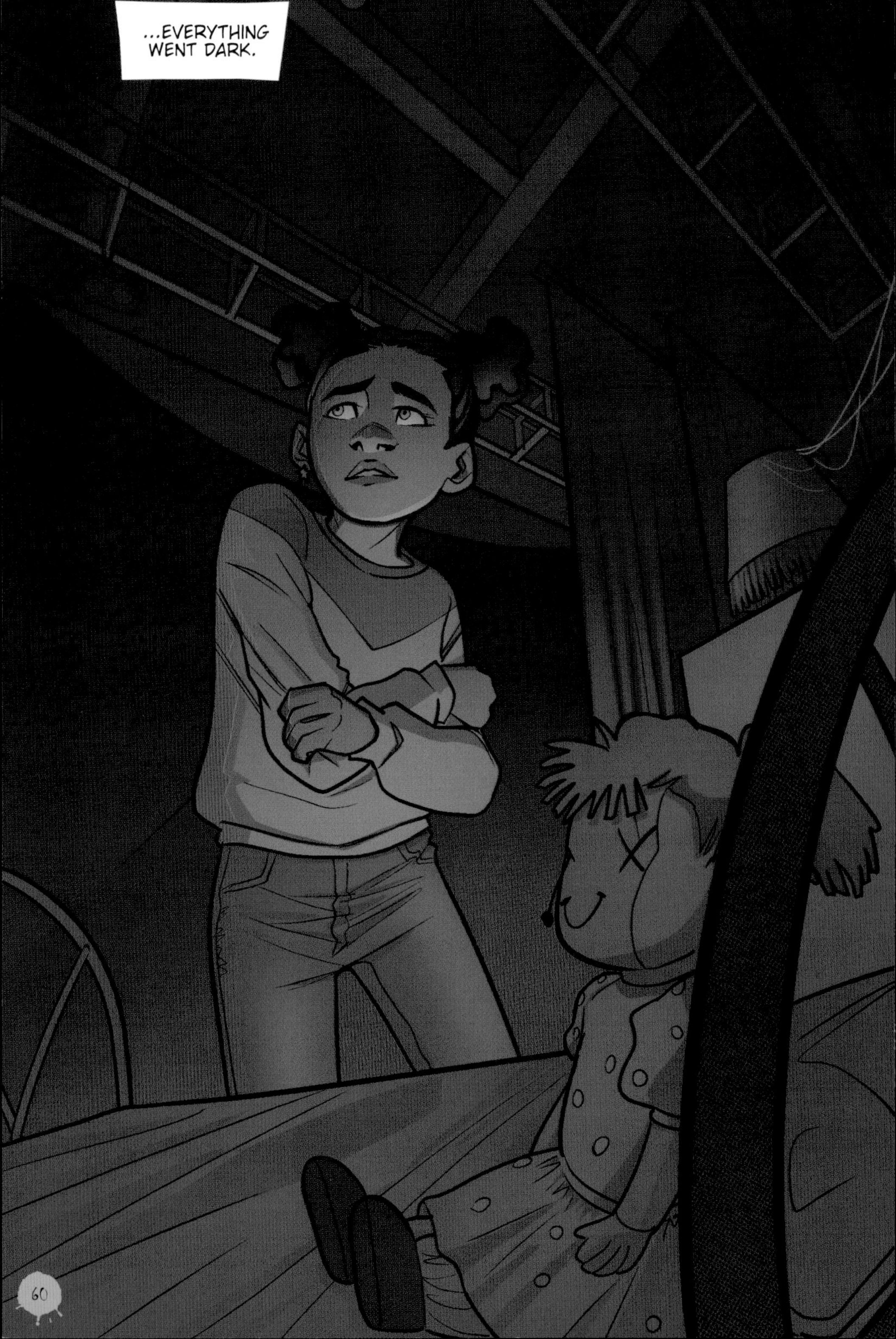
...EVERYTHING WENT DARK.

CHAPTER 5

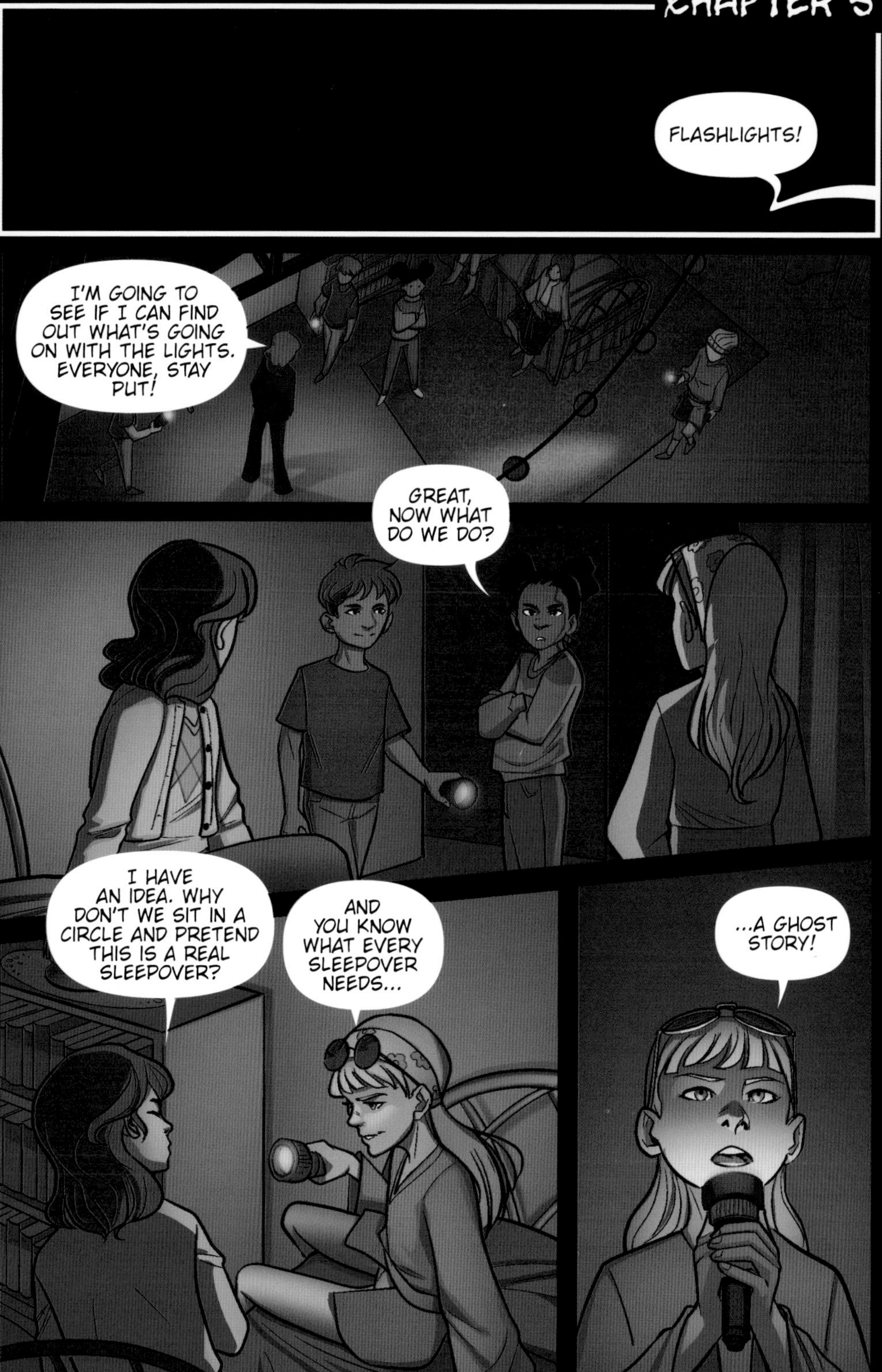
FLASHLIGHTS!
I'M GOING TO SEE IF I CAN FIND OUT WHAT'S GOING ON WITH THE LIGHTS. EVERYONE, STAY PUT!
GREAT, NOW WHAT DO WE DO?
I HAVE AN IDEA. WHY DON'T WE SIT IN A CIRCLE AND PRETEND THIS IS A REAL SLEEPOVER?
AND YOU KNOW WHAT EVERY SLEEPOVER NEEDS...
...A GHOST STORY!

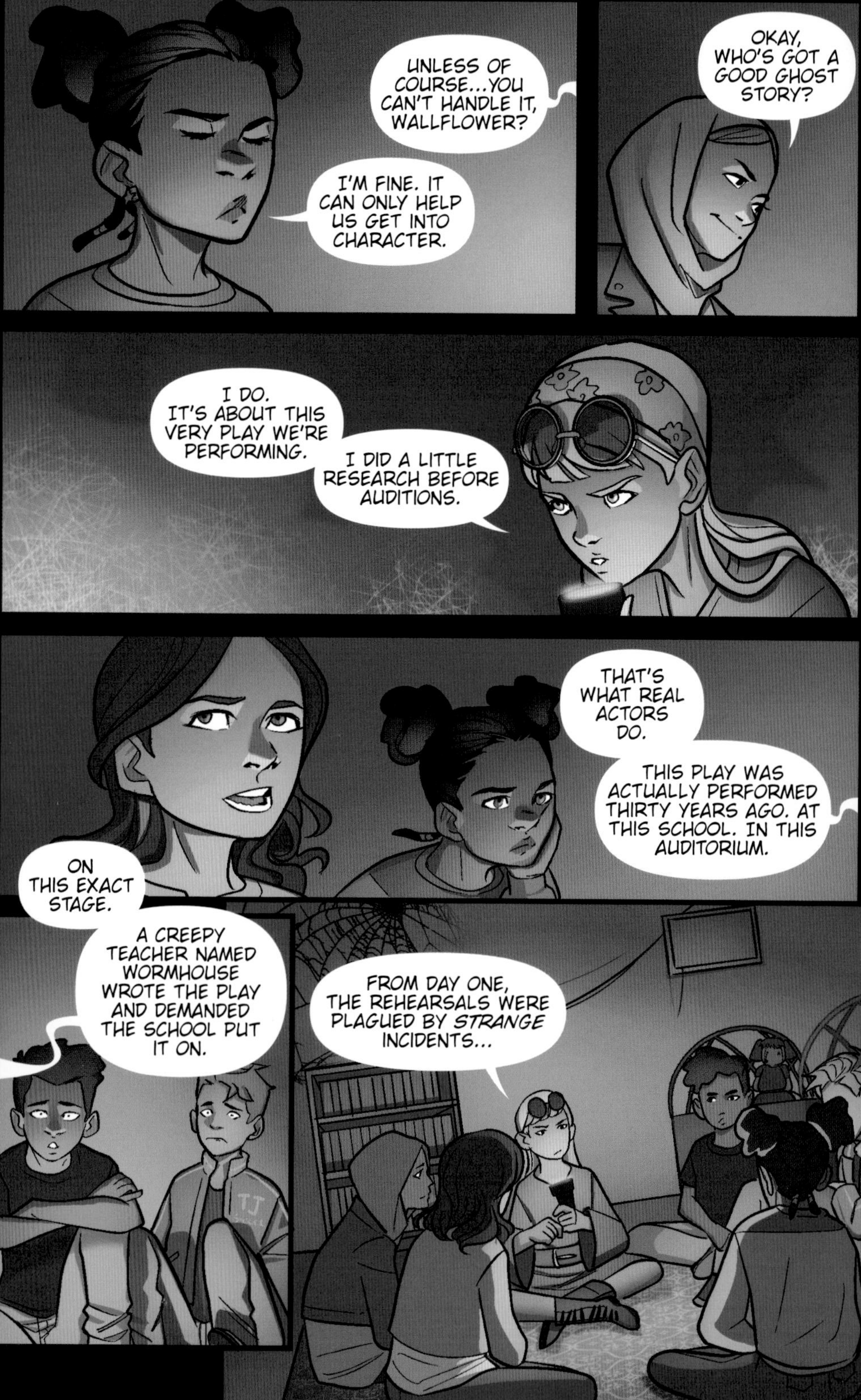
UNLESS OF COURSE...YOU CAN'T HANDLE IT, WALLFLOWER?
I'M FINE. IT CAN ONLY HELP US GET INTO CHARACTER.
OKAY, WHO'S GOT A GOOD GHOST STORY?
I DO. IT'S ABOUT THIS VERY PLAY WE'RE PERFORMING.
I DID A LITTLE RESEARCH BEFORE AUDITIONS.
THAT'S WHAT REAL ACTORS DO.
THIS PLAY WAS ACTUALLY PERFORMED THIRTY YEARS AGO. AT THIS SCHOOL. IN THIS AUDITORIUM.
ON THIS EXACT STAGE.
A CREEPY TEACHER NAMED WORMHOUSE WROTE THE PLAY AND DEMANDED THE SCHOOL PUT IT ON.
FROM DAY ONE, THE REHEARSALS WERE PLAGUED BY *STRANGE* INCIDENTS...

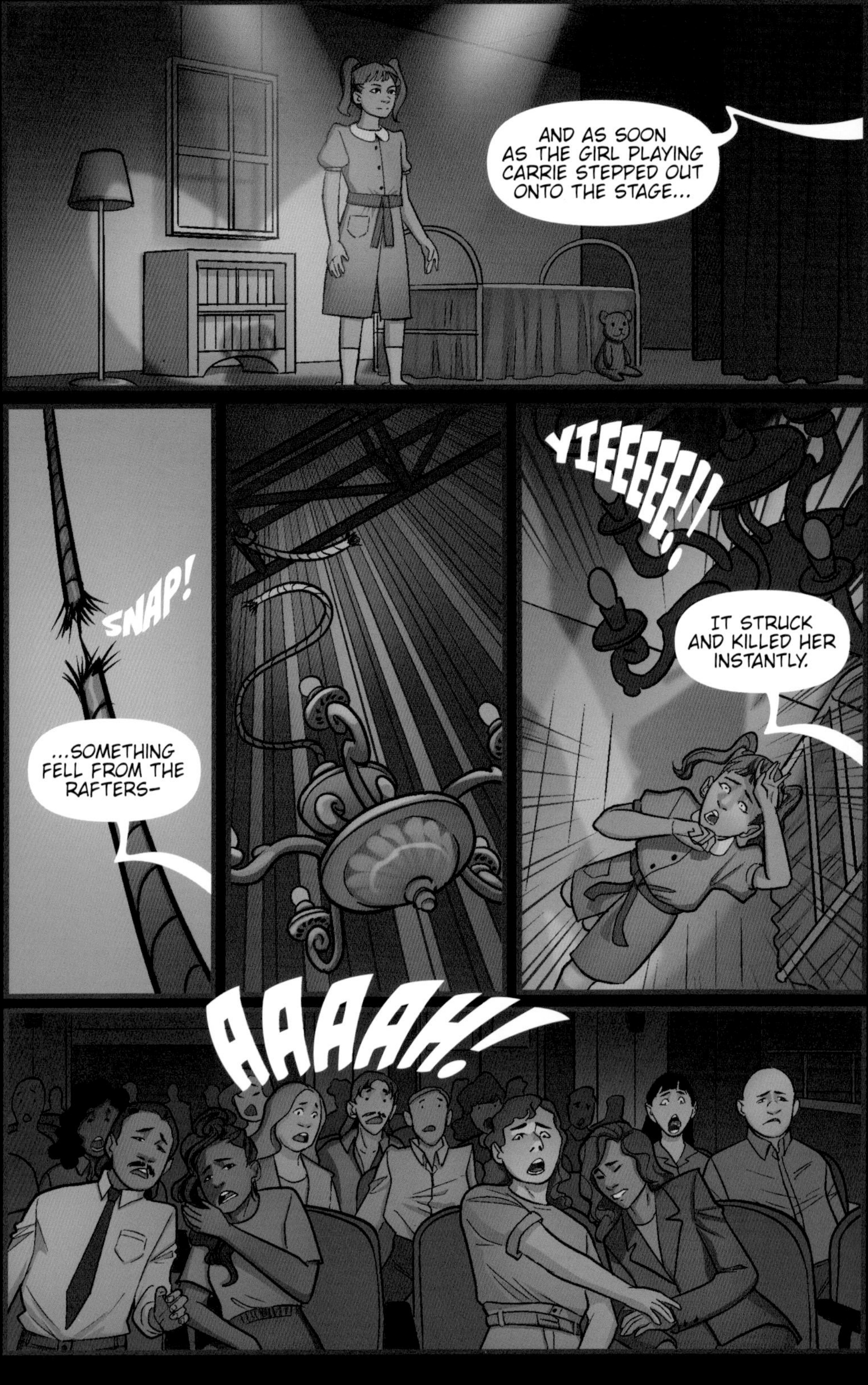

AND AS SOON AS THE GIRL PLAYING CARRIE STEPPED OUT ONTO THE STAGE...
SNAP!
...SOMETHING FELL FROM THE RAFTERS–
YIEEEEE!!
IT STRUCK AND KILLED HER INSTANTLY.
AAAAH!

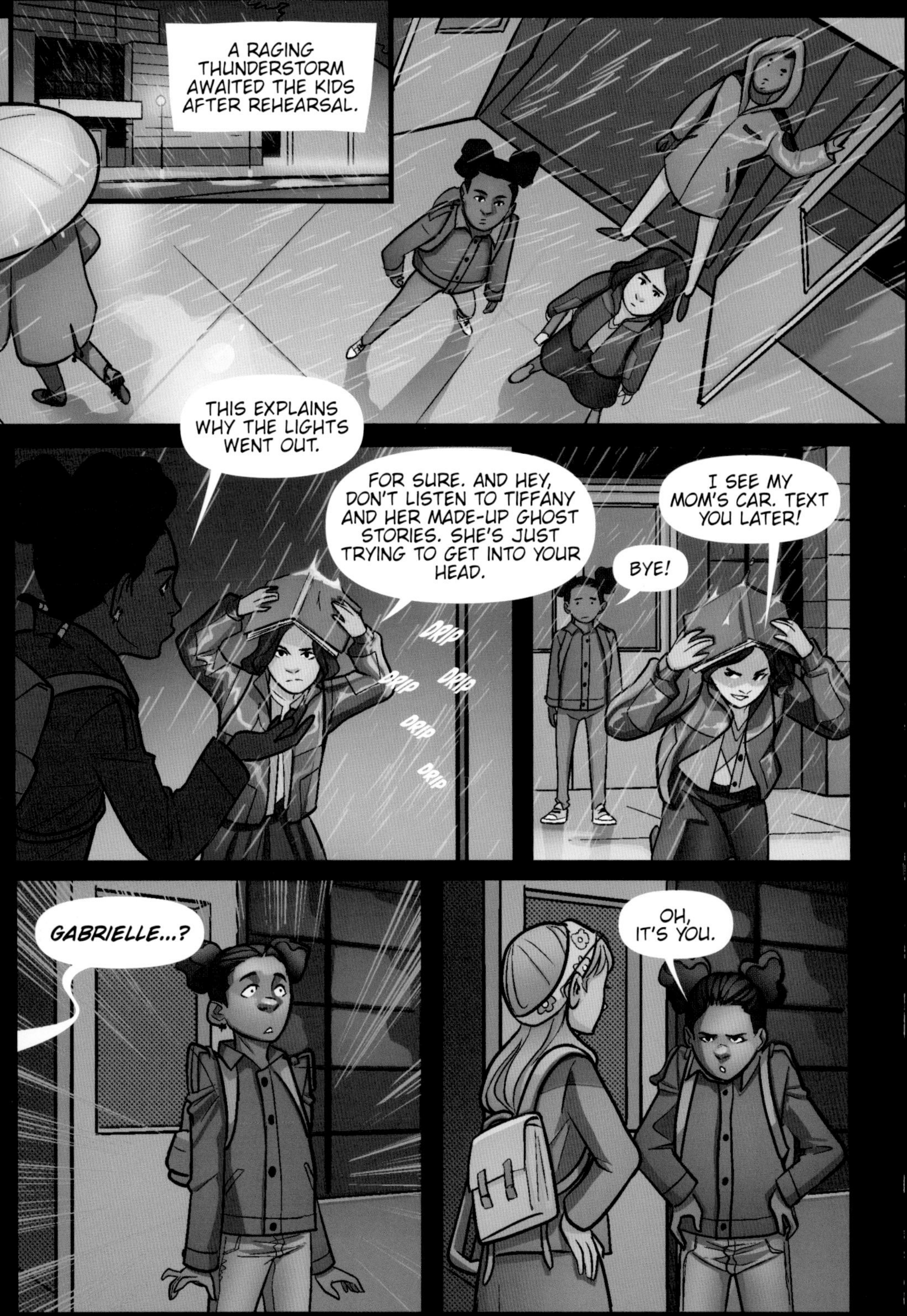
A RAGING THUNDERSTORM AWAITED THE KIDS AFTER REHEARSAL.
THIS EXPLAINS WHY THE LIGHTS WENT OUT.
FOR SURE. AND HEY, DON'T LISTEN TO TIFFANY AND HER MADE-UP GHOST STORIES. SHE'S JUST TRYING TO GET INTO YOUR HEAD.
DRIP
DRIP
DRIP
DRIP
DRIP
I SEE MY MOM'S CAR. TEXT YOU LATER!
BYE!
GABRIELLE...?
OH, IT'S YOU.

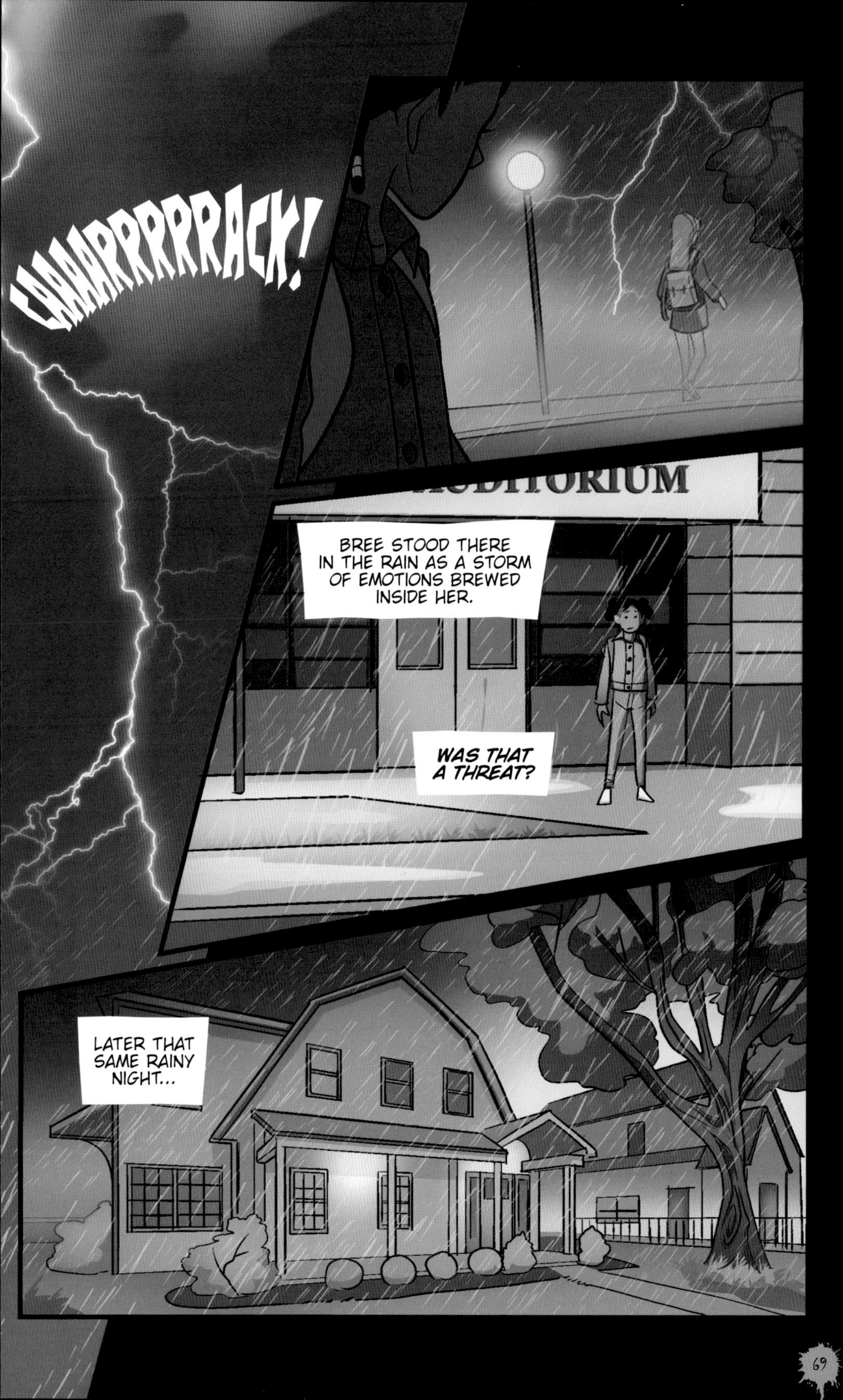
CRAAARRRRRACK!
AUDITORIUM
BREE STOOD THERE IN THE RAIN AS A STORM OF EMOTIONS BREWED INSIDE HER.
WAS THAT A THREAT?
LATER THAT SAME RAINY NIGHT...

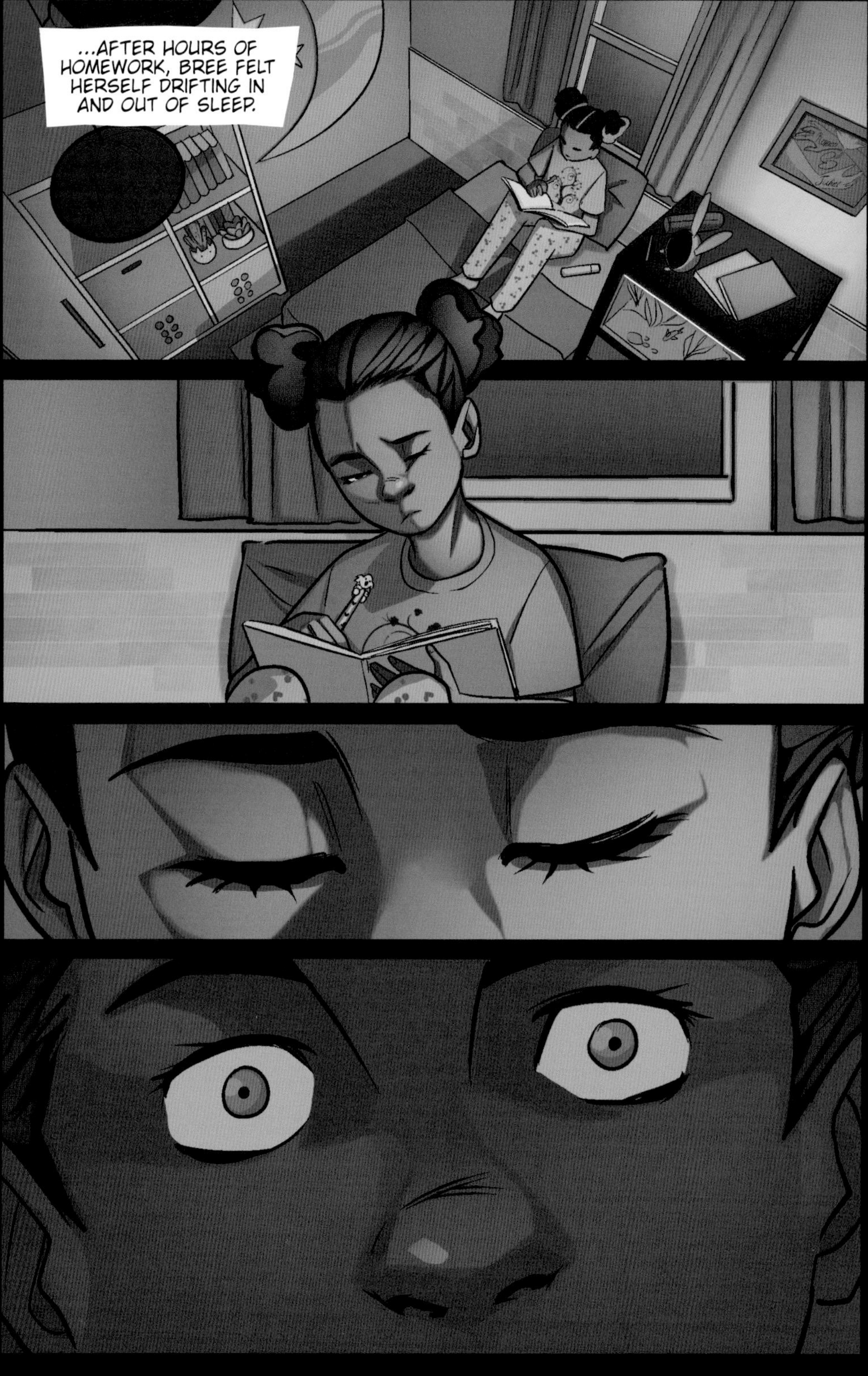
...AFTER HOURS OF HOMEWORK, BREE FELT HERSELF DRIFTING IN AND OUT OF SLEEP.

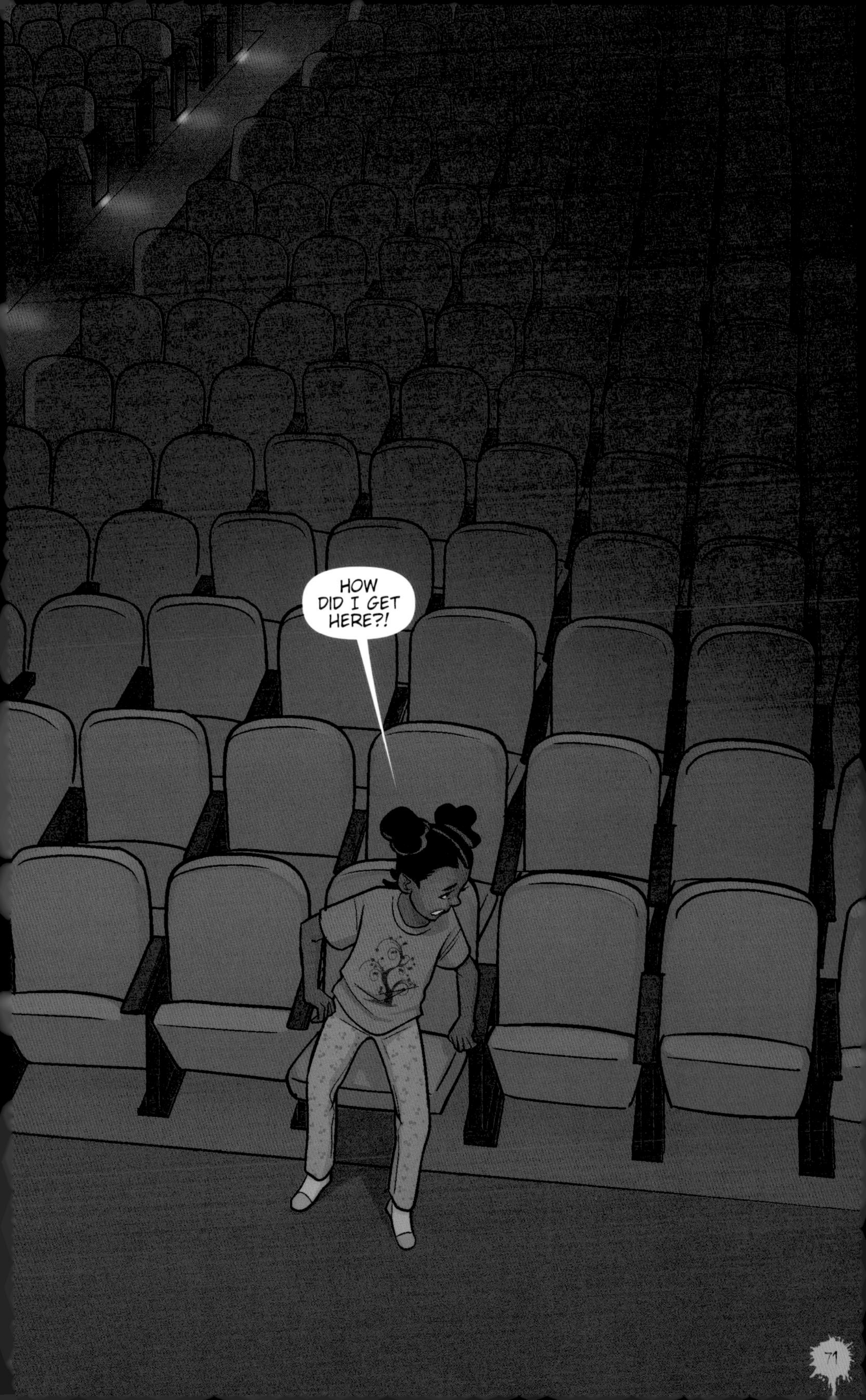
HOW DID I GET HERE?!

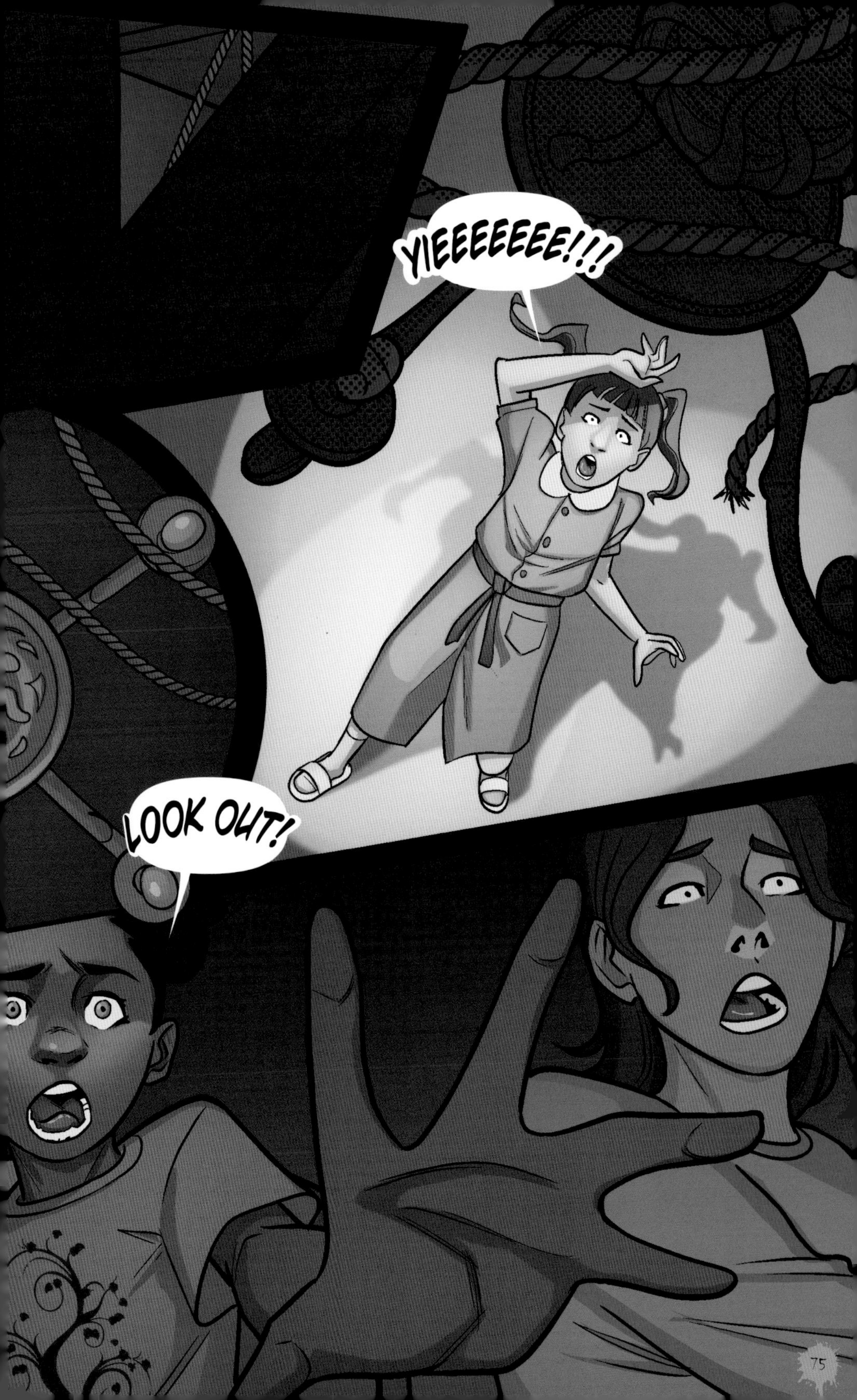
YIEEEEEEE!!!
LOOK OUT!

CHAPTER 6

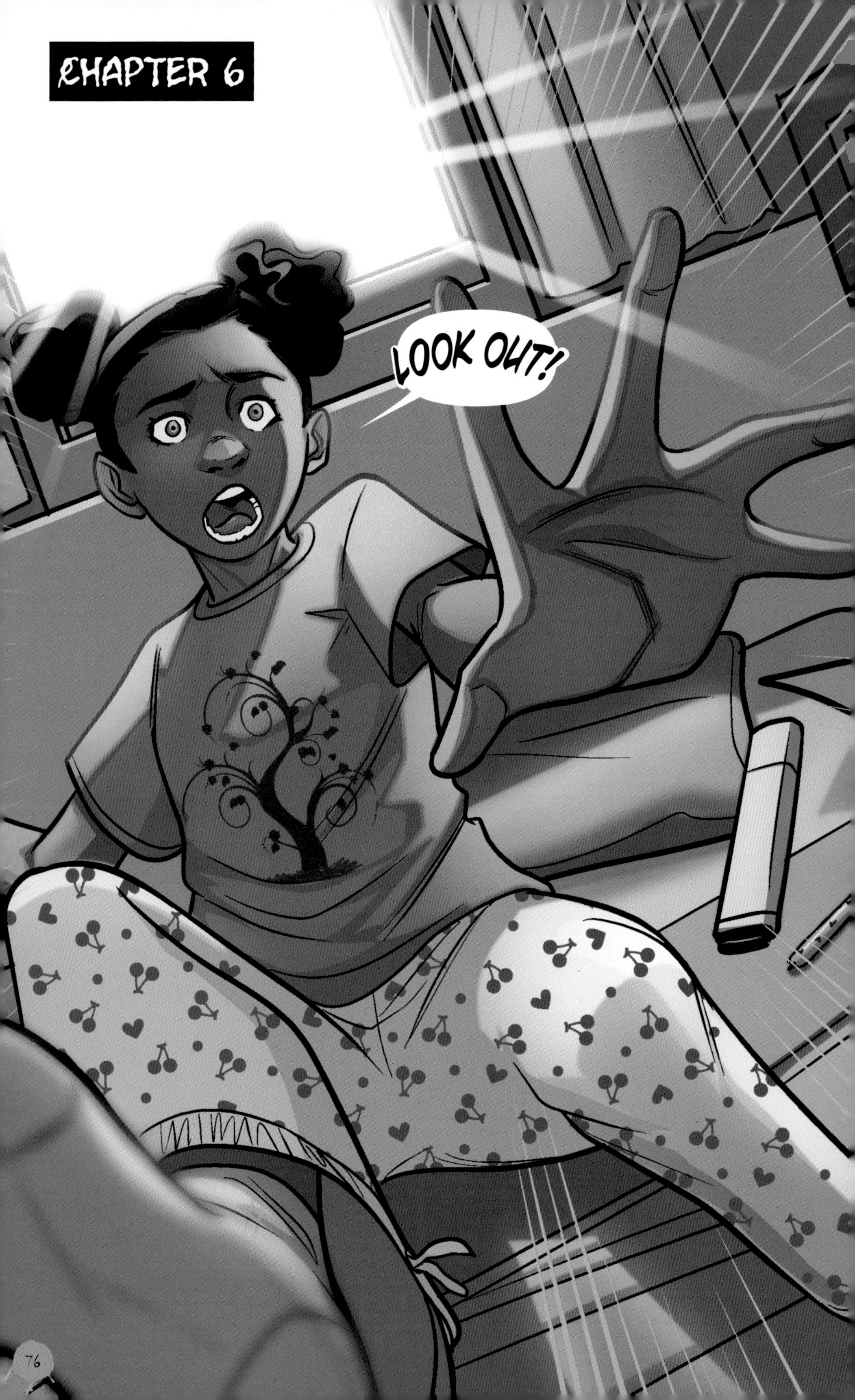
LOOK OUT!

HUFF PUFF HUFF PUFF

BREE'S HEART WAS POUNDING. HER HANDS WERE SHAKING.

SIGH

IT WAS ALL A TERRIBLE DREAM.

YOU OKAY? I HEARD SCREAMING.

KNOCK KNOCK

I...JUST NEED...A MINUTE.

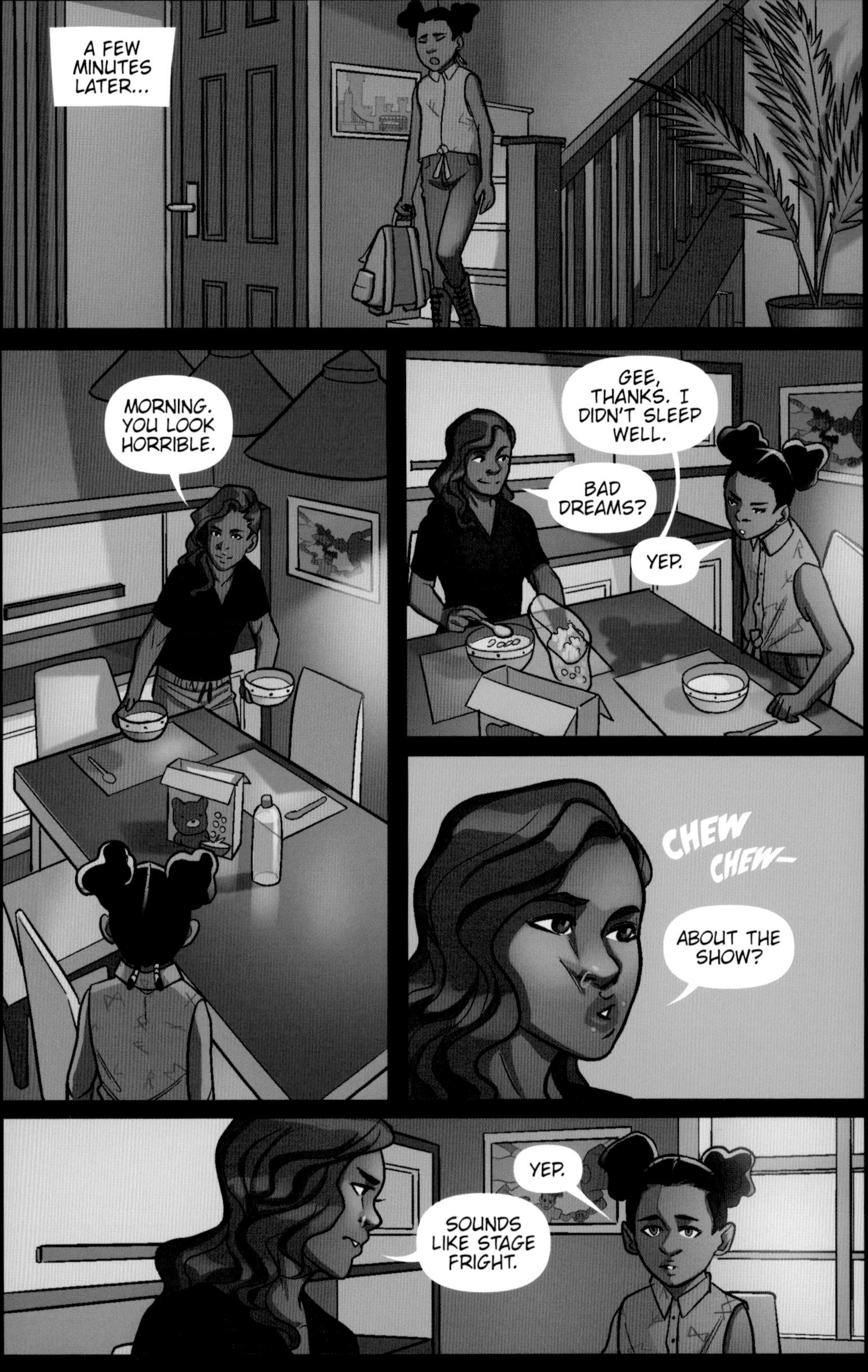
A FEW MINUTES LATER...
MORNING. YOU LOOK HORRIBLE.
GEE, THANKS. I DIDN'T SLEEP WELL.
BAD DREAMS?
YEP.
CHEW CHEW—
ABOUT THE SHOW?
YEP.
SOUNDS LIKE STAGE FRIGHT.

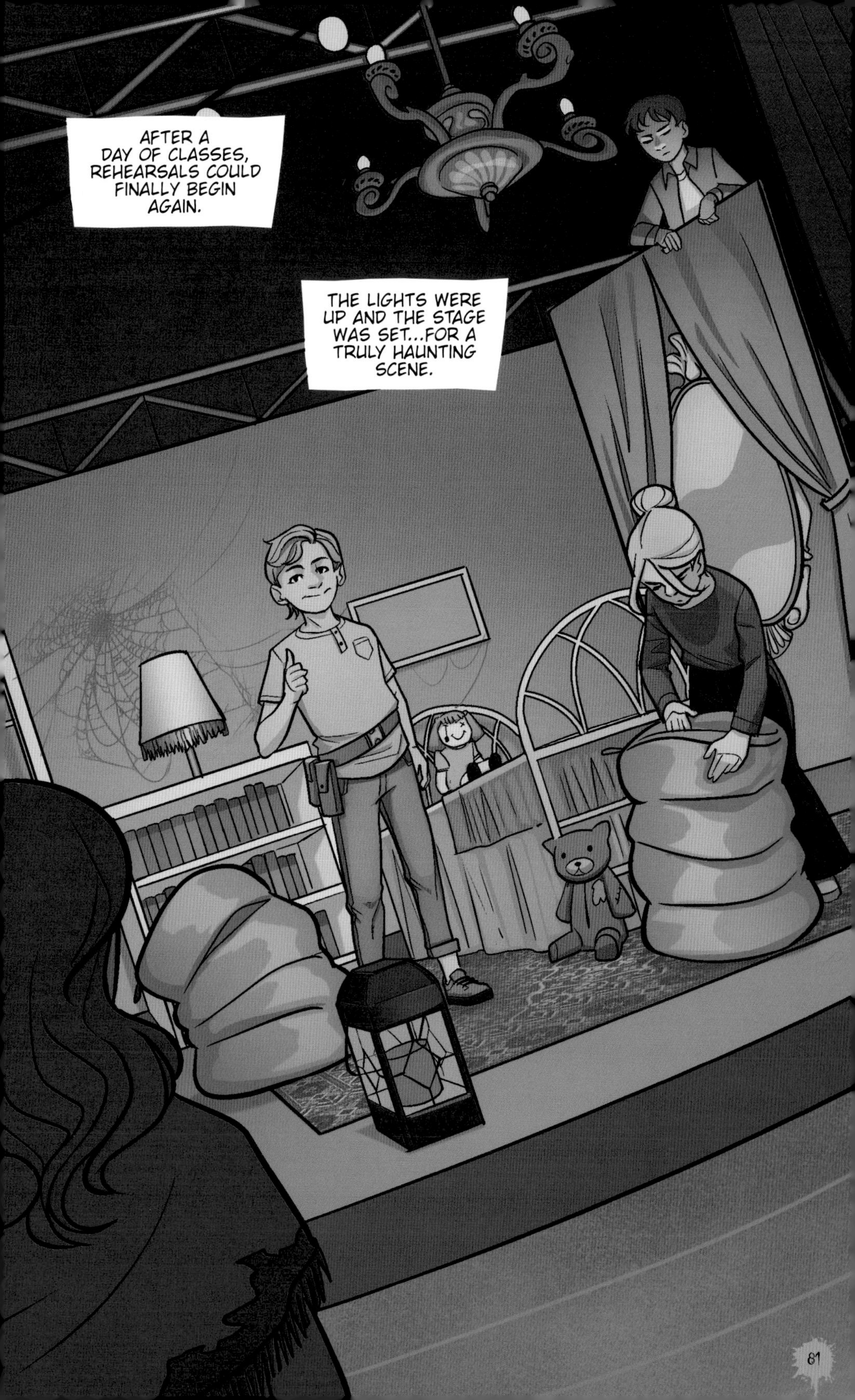
AFTER A DAY OF CLASSES, REHEARSALS COULD FINALLY BEGIN AGAIN.
THE LIGHTS WERE UP AND THE STAGE WAS SET...FOR A TRULY HAUNTING SCENE.

LADIES AND GENTLEMEN...

LOOK, THEY ADDED SLEEPING BAGS! AND LANTERNS! IT LOOKS LIKE A REAL SLEEPOVER.

...LISTEN UP! IT'S TIME TO "DO THE WORK," AS THEY SAY IN THE THEATER.

LET'S RUN THE CARRIE AND RACHEL SCENE, PLEASE. FROM THE TOP!

CARRIE... YOU'RE SUPPOSED TO BE UPSET IN THIS SCENE. SO REALLY SELL IT. I WANT TO SEE YOU PACING. ANXIOUS.

HAVE YOU ACTUALLY SEEN ANYONE?

AND WHAT'S WORSE—

THERE'S A WORSE PART?

I HEAR FOOTSTEPS ALL THE TIME. AND WHEN I TURN AROUND, NO ONE IS THERE!

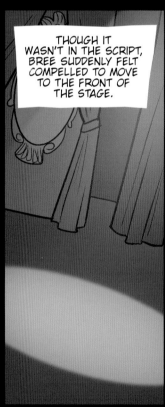

THOUGH IT WASN'T IN THE SCRIPT, BREE SUDDENLY FELT COMPELLED TO MOVE TO THE FRONT OF THE STAGE.

I'M POSITIVE THAT WHOEVER IS FOLLOWING ME...

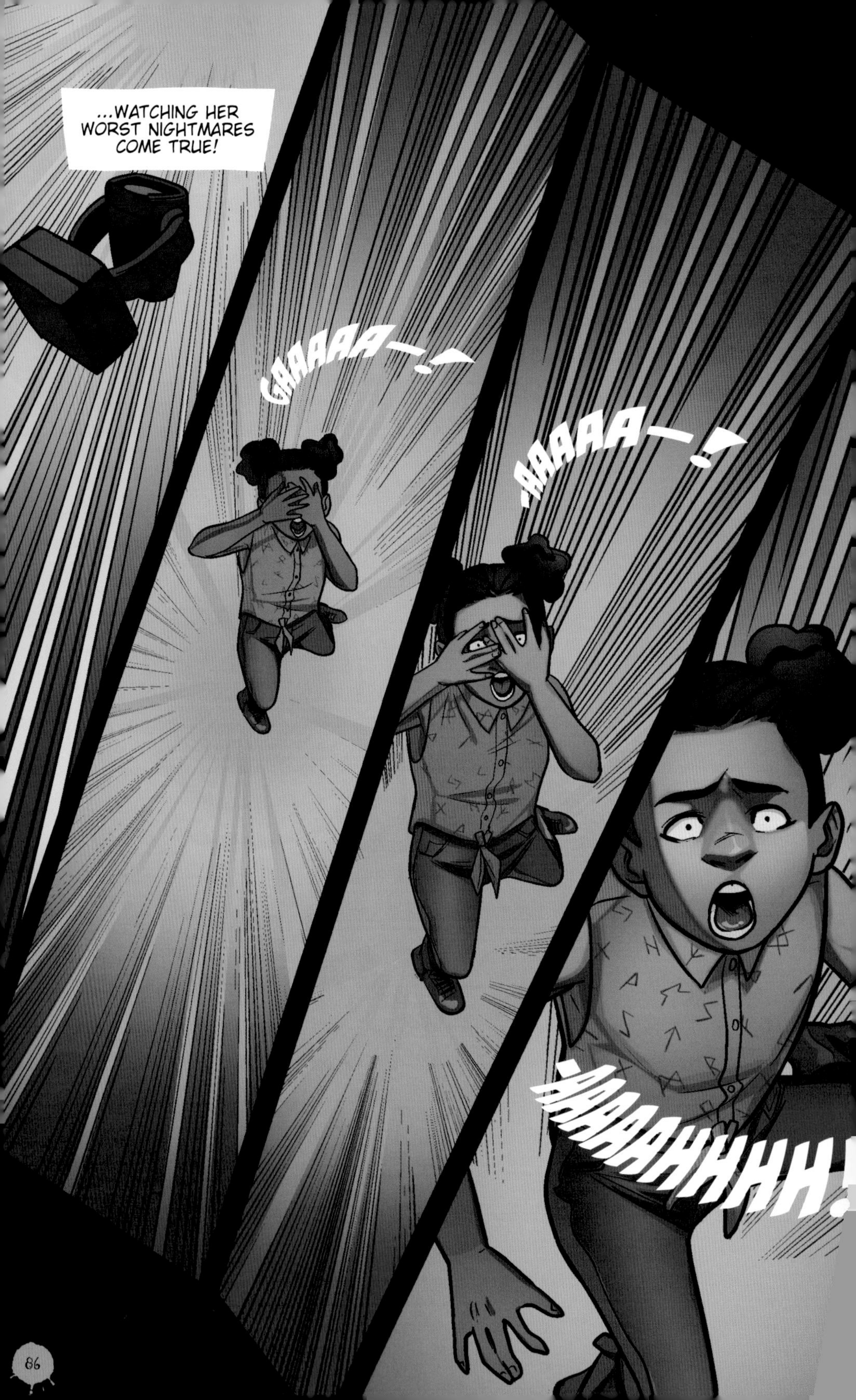
...WATCHING HER
WORST NIGHTMARES
COME TRUE!
GAAAAA—!
AAAAA—!
AAAAAAHHHHH!

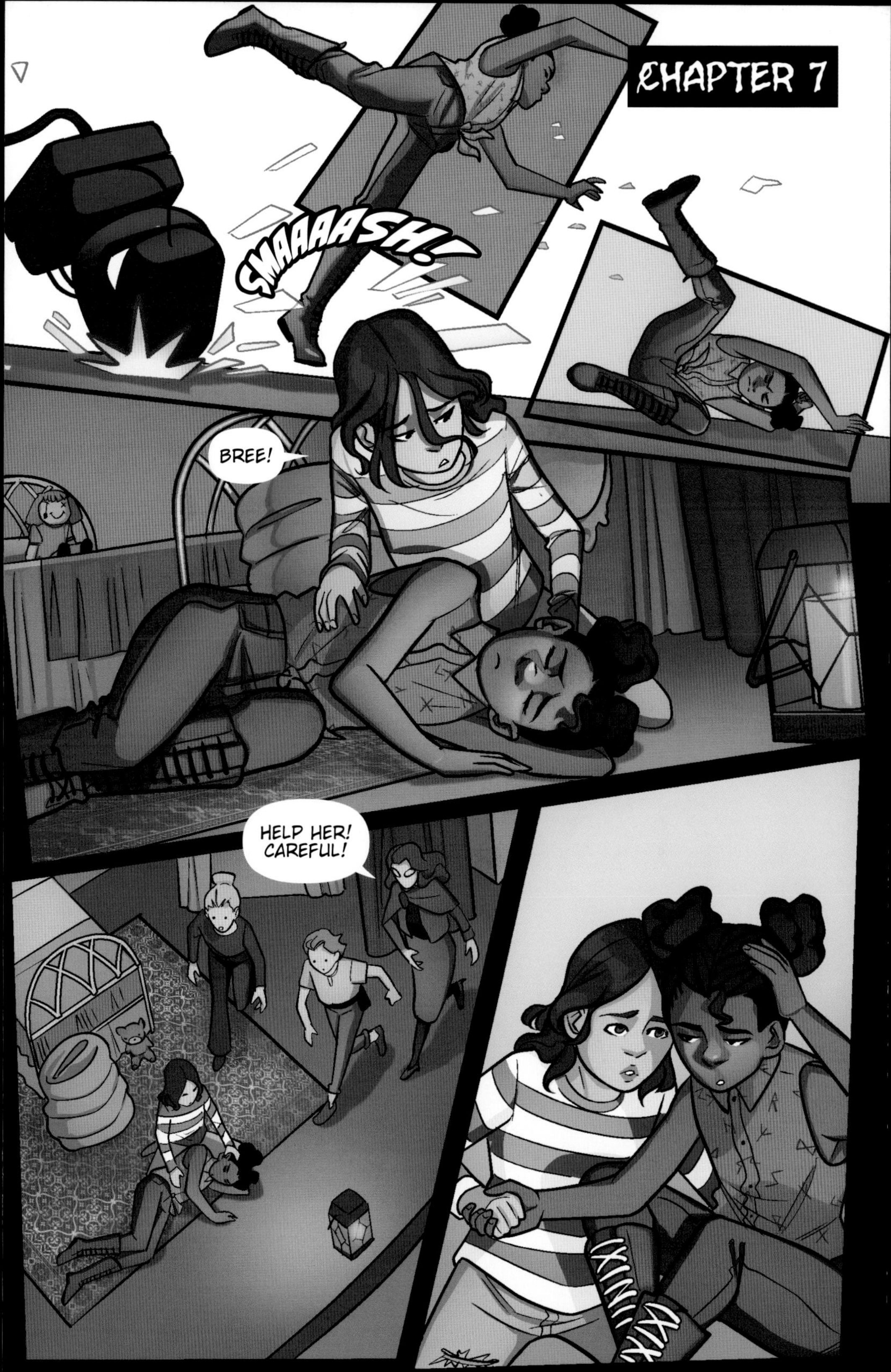
CHAPTER 7
SMAAAASH!
BREE!
HELP HER! CAREFUL!

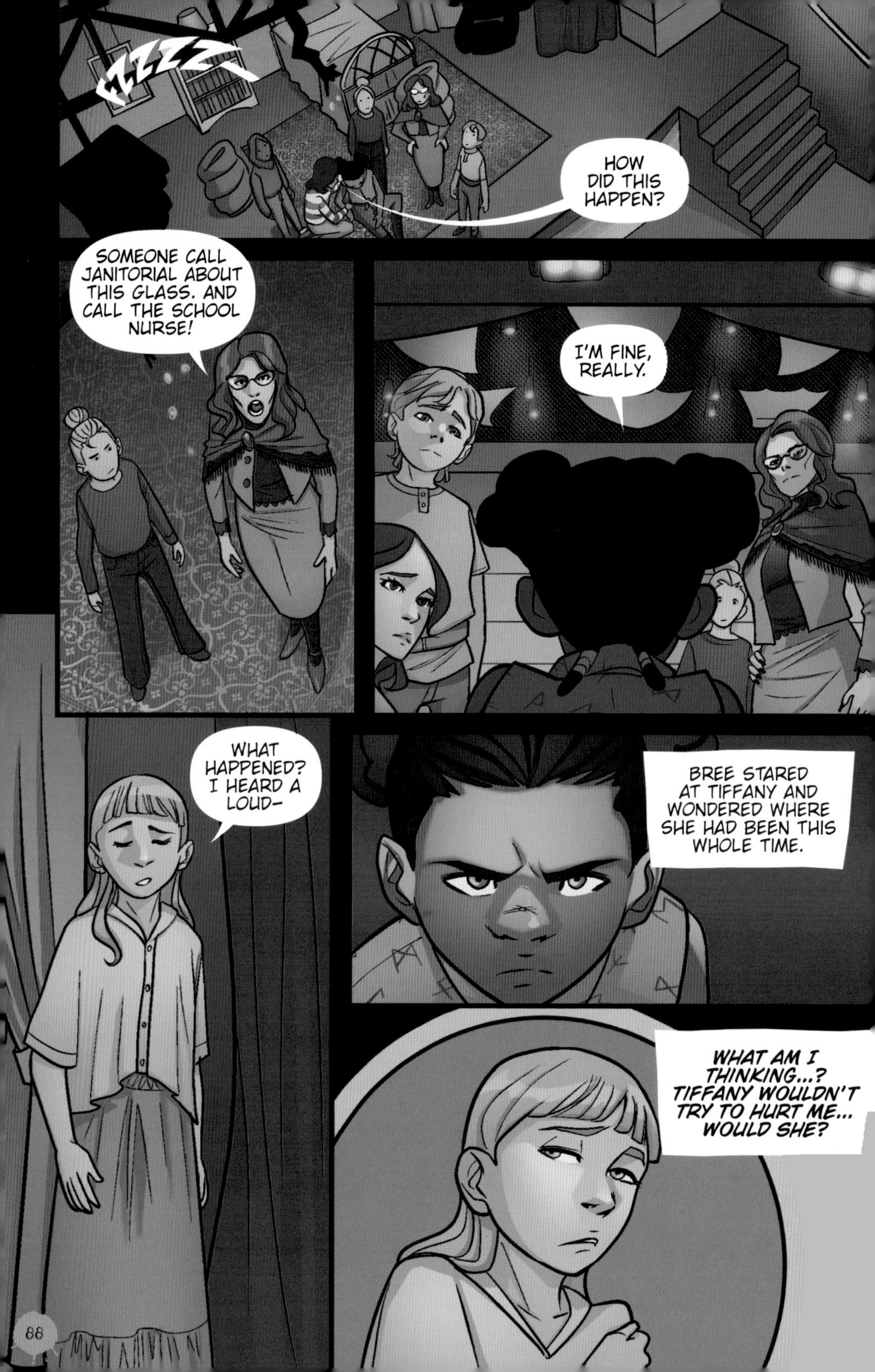
FZZZZZ
HOW DID THIS HAPPEN?
SOMEONE CALL JANITORIAL ABOUT THIS GLASS. AND CALL THE SCHOOL NURSE!
I'M FINE, REALLY.
WHAT HAPPENED? I HEARD A LOUD-
BREE STARED AT TIFFANY AND WONDERED WHERE SHE HAD BEEN THIS WHOLE TIME.
WHAT AM I THINKING...? TIFFANY WOULDN'T TRY TO HURT ME... WOULD SHE?

IT WAS JUST AN ACCIDENT. I'M FINE, EVERYONE.

CAN WE TRY THE SCENE AGAIN? THIS TIME, WITHOUT THE FALLING LIGHT.

HAHAHAHA

BRAVO, *GABRIELLE*. A TRUE PROFESSIONAL. SO BRAVE.

YES, SO BRAVE. GO, BREE.

NOT EVEN OPENING NIGHT, AND ALREADY A STANDING OVATION!

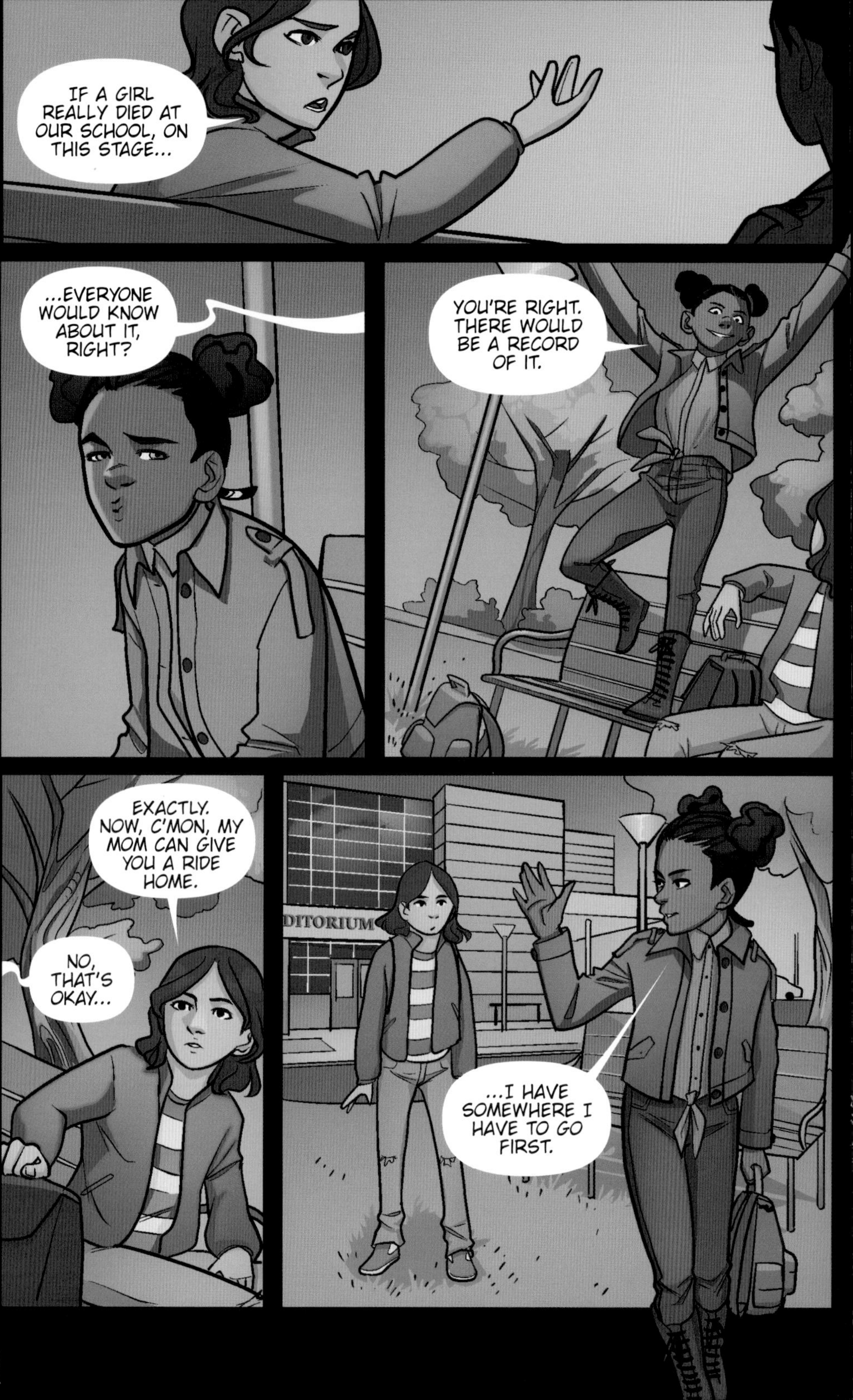
IF A GIRL REALLY DIED AT OUR SCHOOL, ON THIS STAGE...
...EVERYONE WOULD KNOW ABOUT IT, RIGHT?
YOU'RE RIGHT. THERE WOULD BE A RECORD OF IT.
EXACTLY. NOW, C'MON, MY MOM CAN GIVE YOU A RIDE HOME.
NO, THAT'S OKAY...
DITORIUM
...I HAVE SOMEWHERE I HAVE TO GO FIRST.

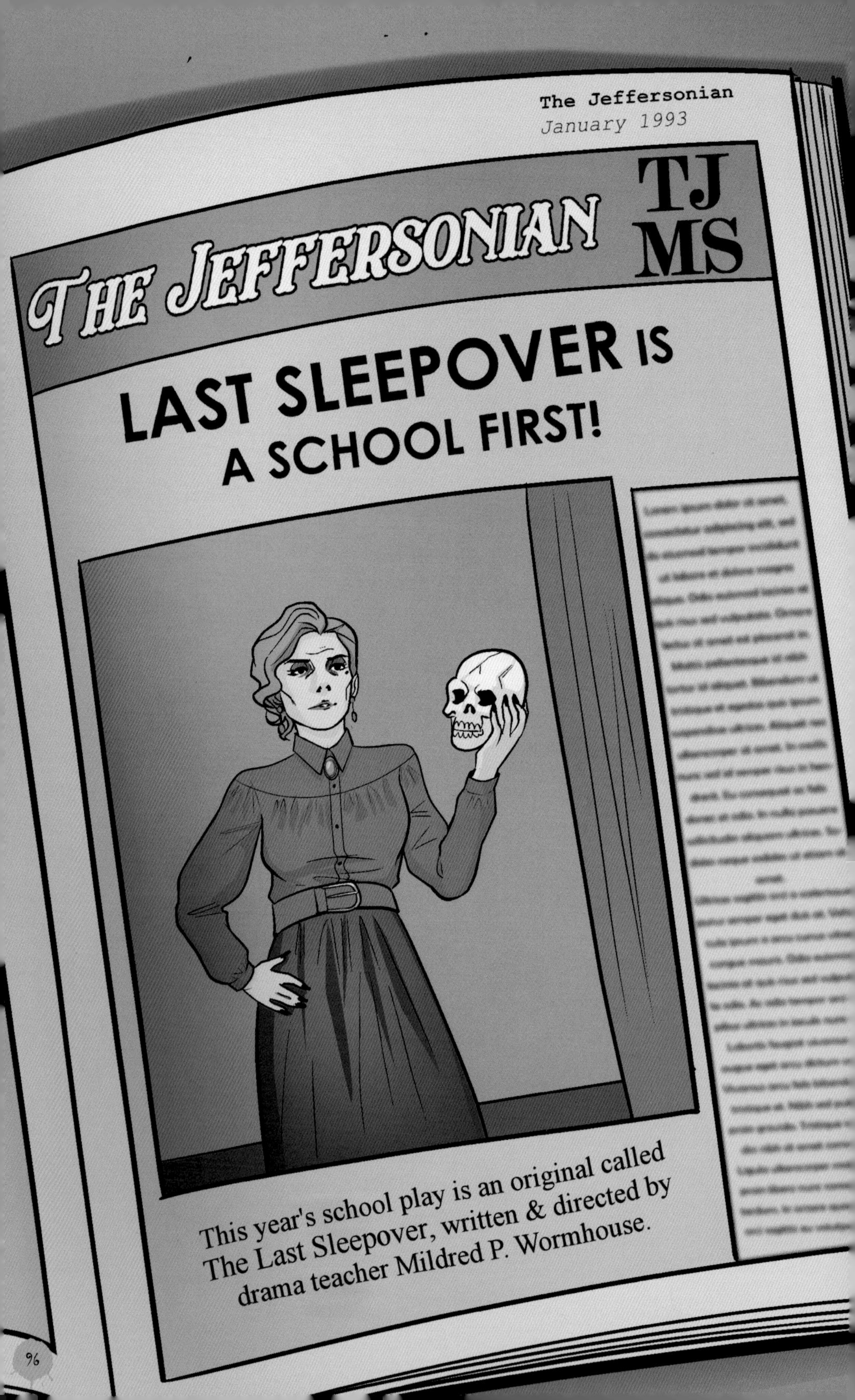
The Jeffersonian
January 1993
THE JEFFERSONIAN
TJ
MS
LAST SLEEPOVER IS
A SCHOOL FIRST!
This year's school play is an original called
The Last Sleepover, written & directed by
drama teacher Mildred P. Wormhouse.

Tragedy struck on opening night of the school play when a stage light fell and killed eighth-grader Gabrielle Ashford.

Gabrielle Ashford

GASP

GABRIELLE! THE GIRL WHO DIED WAS NAMED GABRIELLE.

BREE? WHY DON'T YOU TAKE A QUICK BREATH AND SLOW DOWN...?

DON'T YOU SEE, MR. HARRIS? IT'S ALL SO FREAKY! THE PLAY HASN'T BEEN PERFORMED SINCE THEN. UNTIL NOW.

AND I'M PLAYING THE LEAD.

AND MY NAME IS "GABRIELLE" TOO!

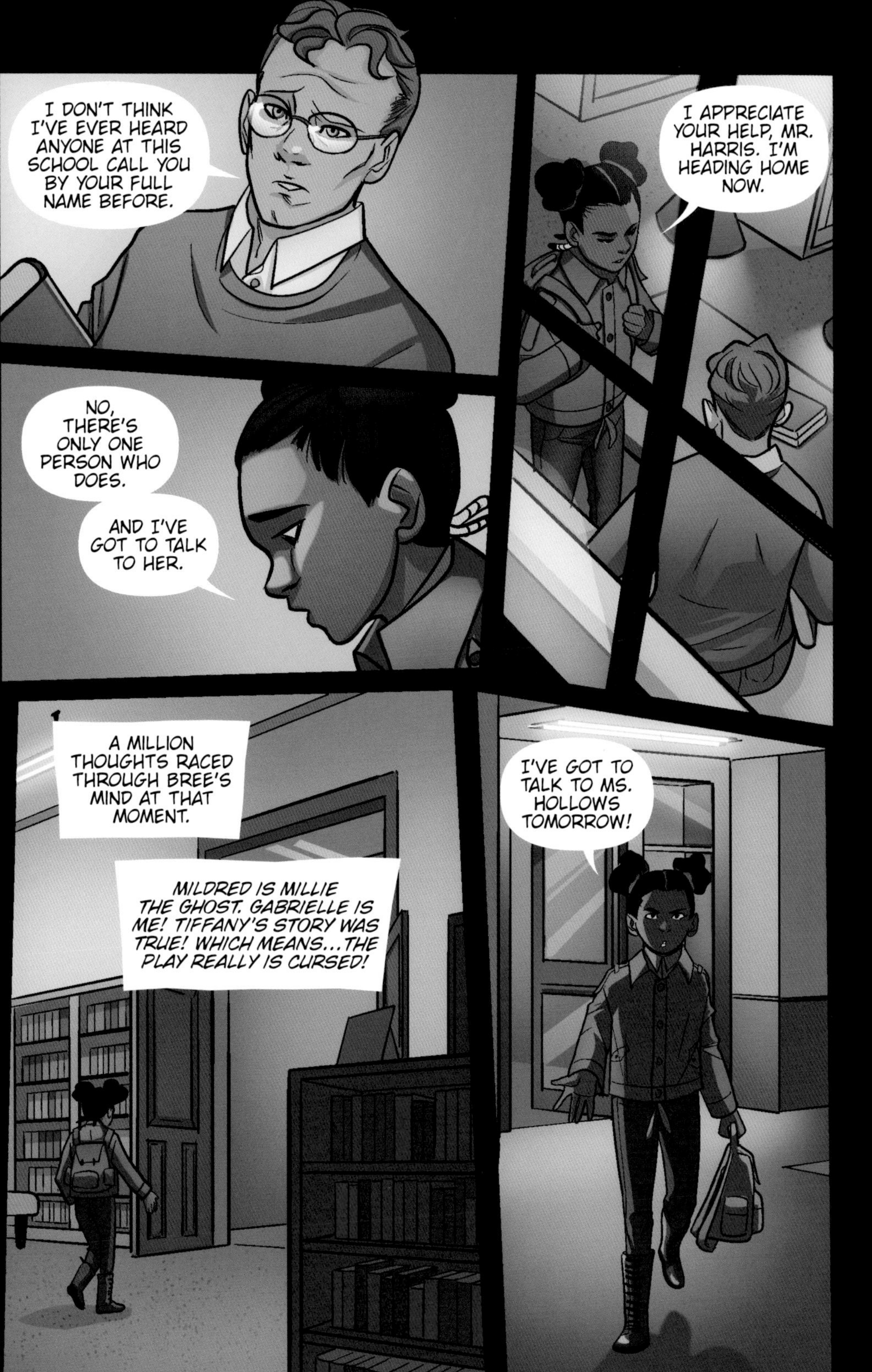
I DON'T THINK I'VE EVER HEARD ANYONE AT THIS SCHOOL CALL YOU BY YOUR FULL NAME BEFORE.
I APPRECIATE YOUR HELP, MR. HARRIS. I'M HEADING HOME NOW.
NO, THERE'S ONLY ONE PERSON WHO DOES.
AND I'VE GOT TO TALK TO HER.
A MILLION THOUGHTS RACED THROUGH BREE'S MIND AT THAT MOMENT.
MILDRED IS MILLIE THE GHOST. GABRIELLE IS ME! TIFFANY'S STORY WAS TRUE! WHICH MEANS...THE PLAY REALLY IS CURSED!
I'VE GOT TO TALK TO MS. HOLLOWS TOMORROW!

BREE STRODE QUICKLY ACROSS THE SCHOOL'S MAIN LAWN.

BUT AS SHE LISTENED TO THE SOUND OF HER OWN FOOTSTEPS...

...SHE SWORE SHE COULD HEAR A SECOND SET OF FOOTSTEPS IN THE GRASS...

THUMP

THUMP

THUMP

THUMP

THUMP

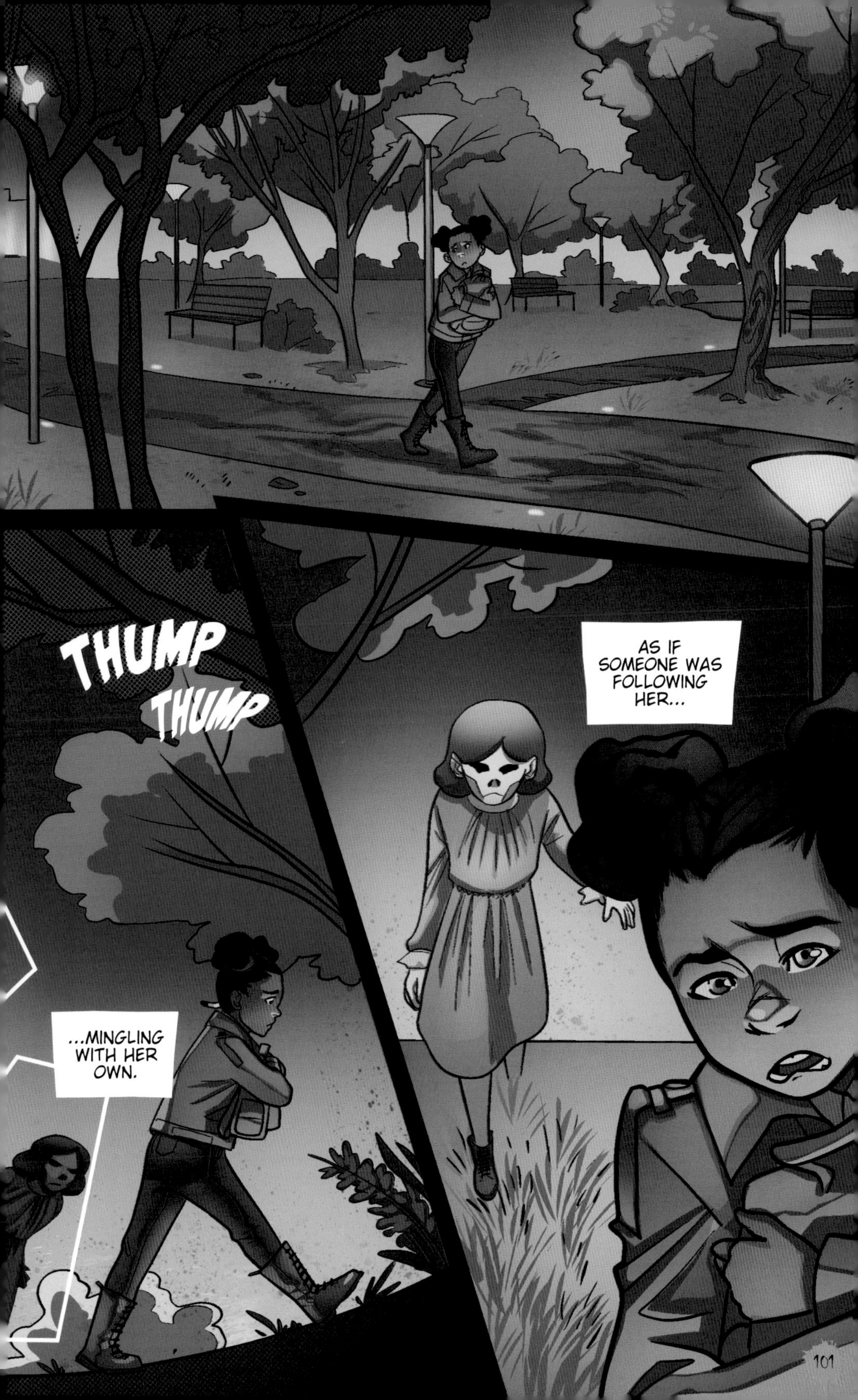
THUMP
THUMP
...MINGLING WITH HER OWN.
AS IF SOMEONE WAS FOLLOWING HER...

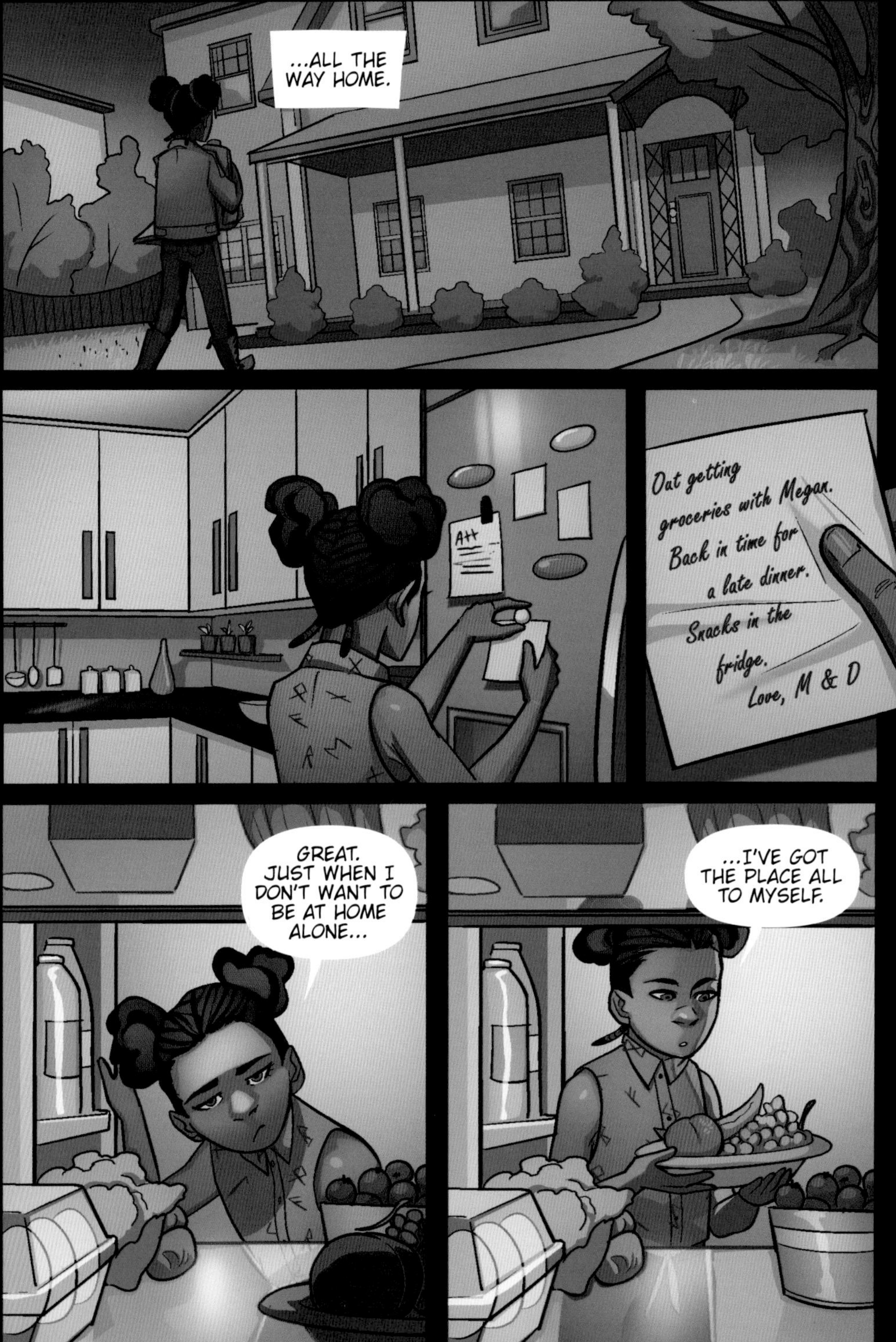
...ALL THE WAY HOME.
Out getting groceries with Megan. Back in time for a late dinner. Snacks in the fridge. Love, M & D
GREAT. JUST WHEN I DON'T WANT TO BE AT HOME ALONE...
...I'VE GOT THE PLACE ALL TO MYSELF.

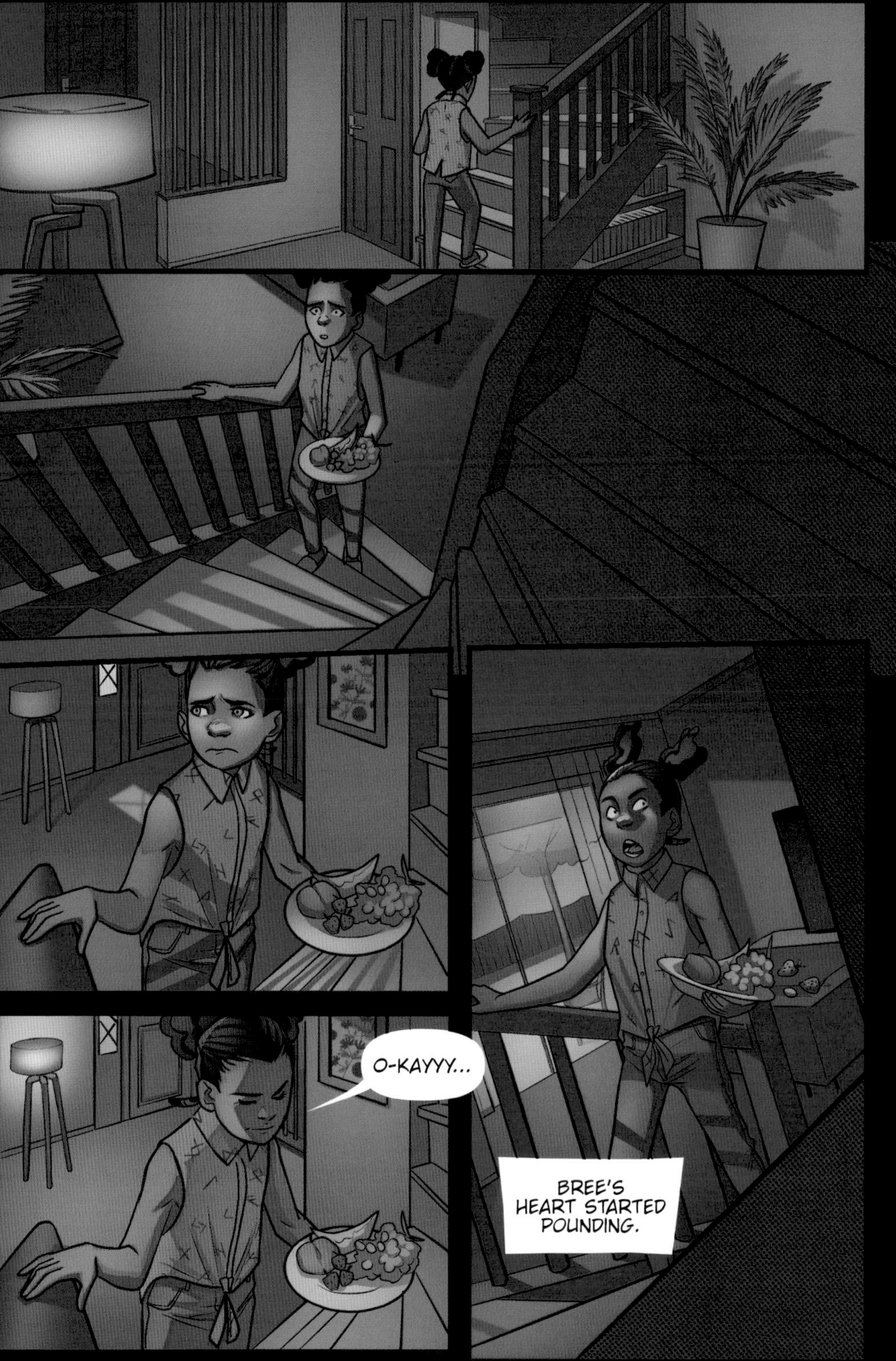
O-KAYYY...
BREE'S HEART STARTED POUNDING.

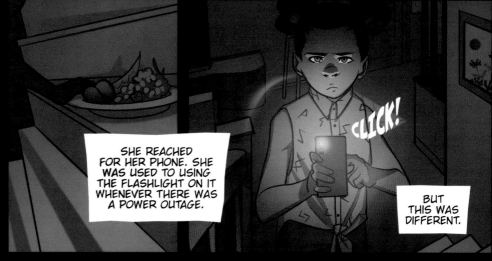

SHE REACHED FOR HER PHONE. SHE WAS USED TO USING THE FLASHLIGHT ON IT WHENEVER THERE WAS A POWER OUTAGE.

CLICK!

BUT THIS WAS DIFFERENT.

SHE NOTICED THAT ALTHOUGH EVERY LIGHT IN THE HOUSE SEEMED TO BE OUT...

...THEY HADN'T ACTUALLY LOST POWER. THE CLOCKS WERE STILL ON AND KEEPING CORRECT TIME.

FLIP
FLIP
FLIP
FLIP

WEIRD.

ONLY THE LIGHTS SEEMED TO BE AFFECTED.

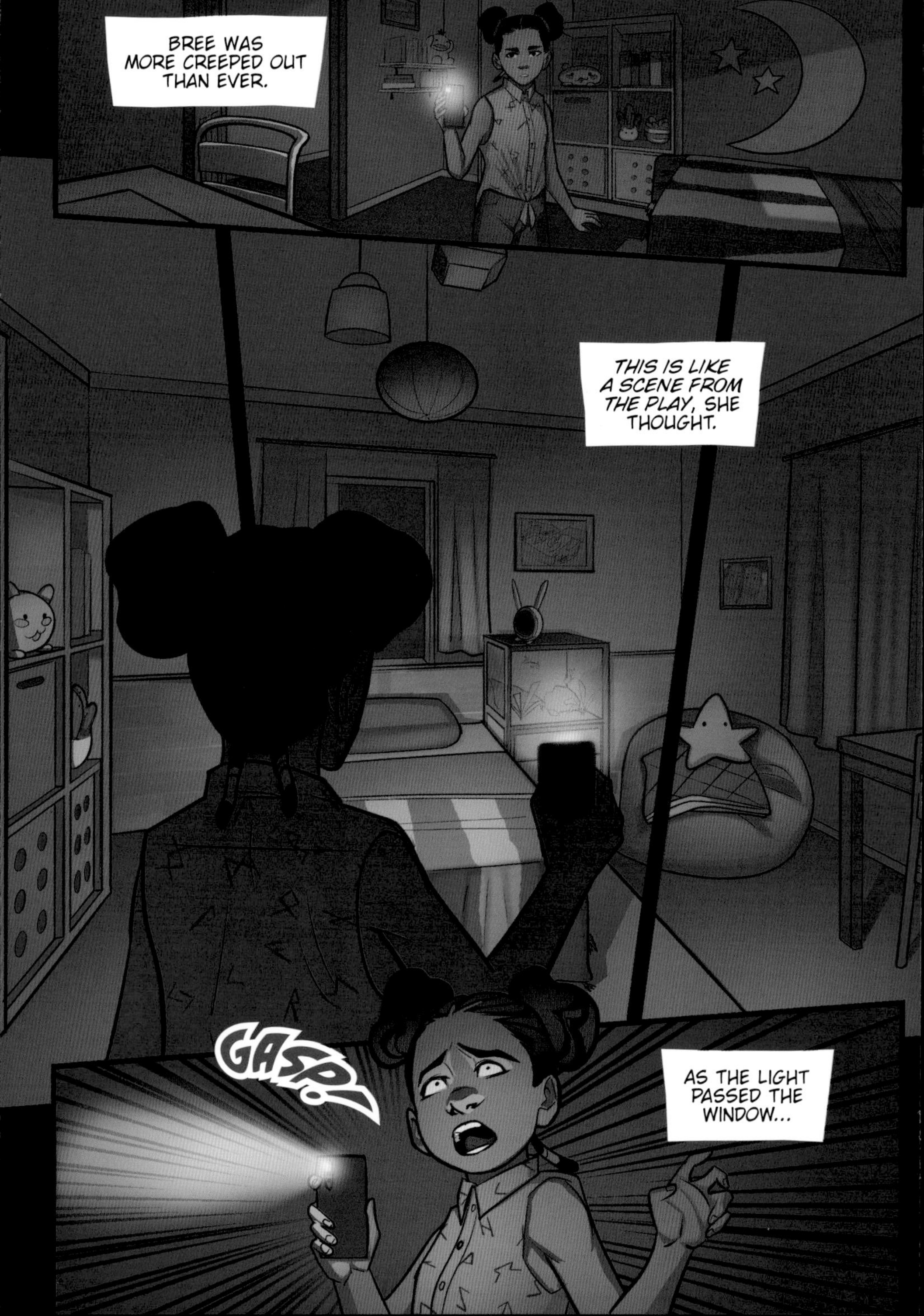
BREE WAS MORE CREEPED OUT THAN EVER.
THIS IS LIKE A SCENE FROM THE PLAY, SHE THOUGHT.
GASP!
AS THE LIGHT PASSED THE WINDOW...

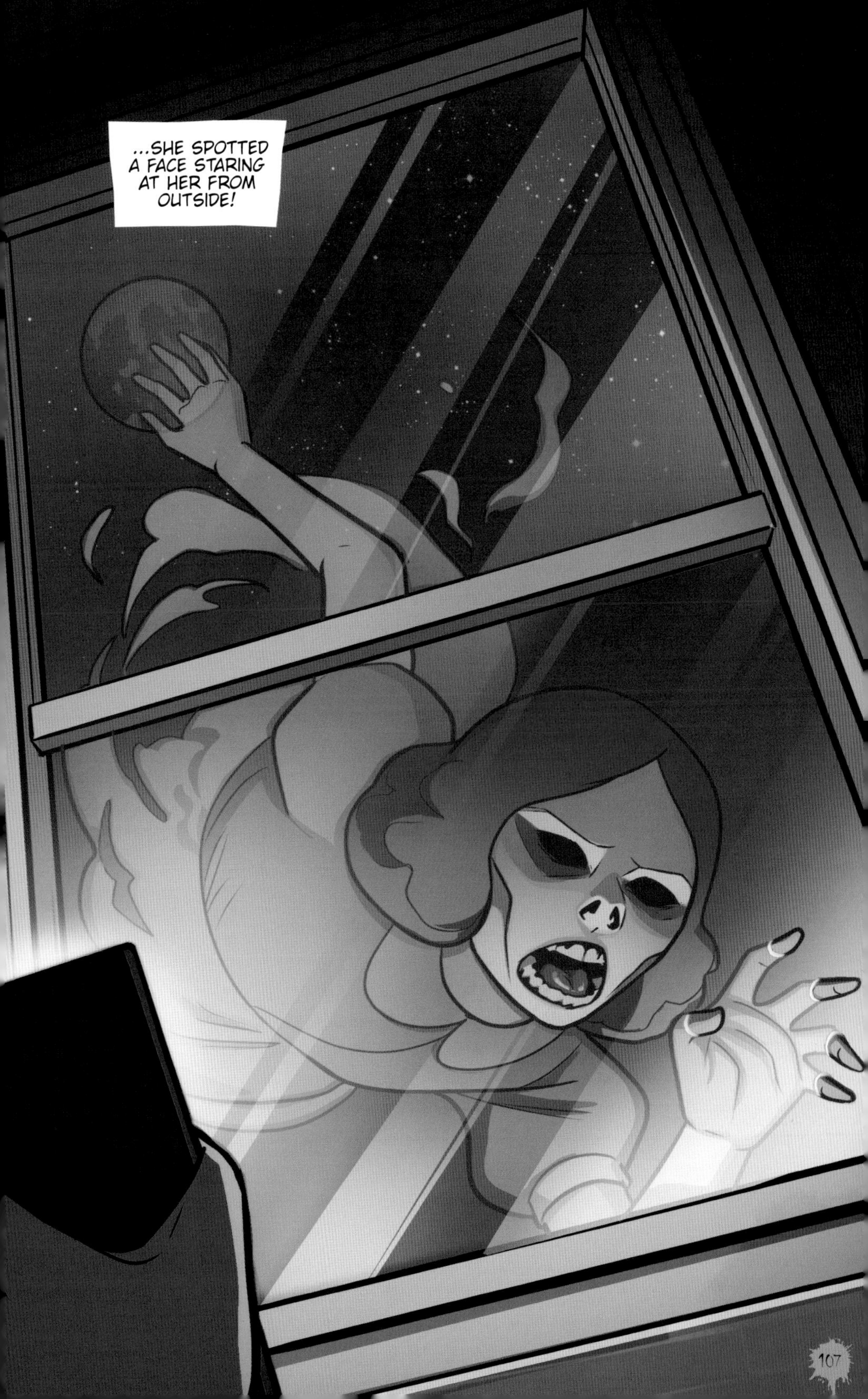
...SHE SPOTTED A FACE STARING AT HER FROM OUTSIDE!

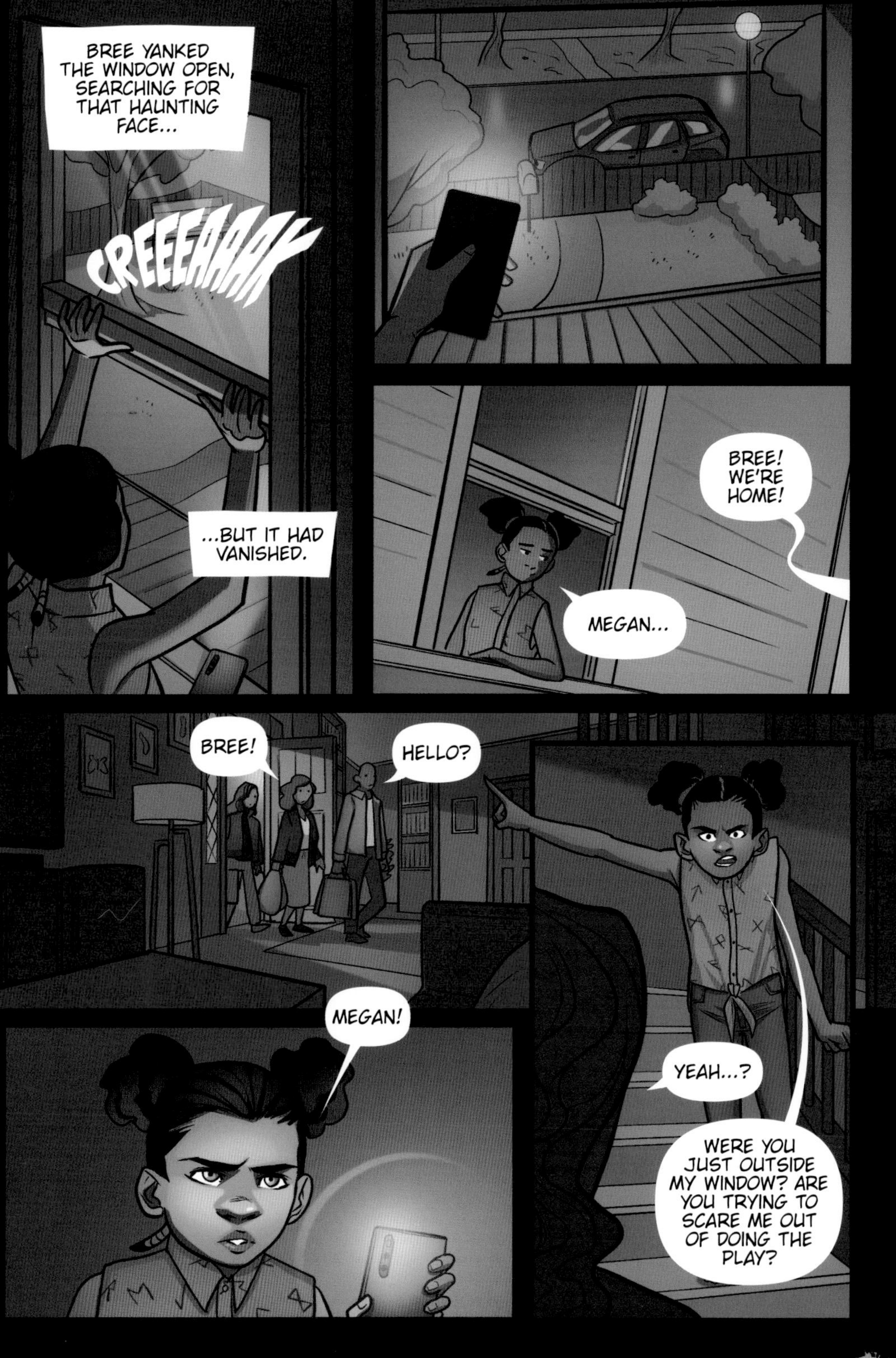
BREE YANKED THE WINDOW OPEN, SEARCHING FOR THAT HAUNTING FACE...
CREEEAAAK
...BUT IT HAD VANISHED.
BREE! WE'RE HOME!
MEGAN...
BREE!
HELLO?
MEGAN!
YEAH...?
WERE YOU JUST OUTSIDE MY WINDOW? ARE YOU TRYING TO SCARE ME OUT OF DOING THE PLAY?

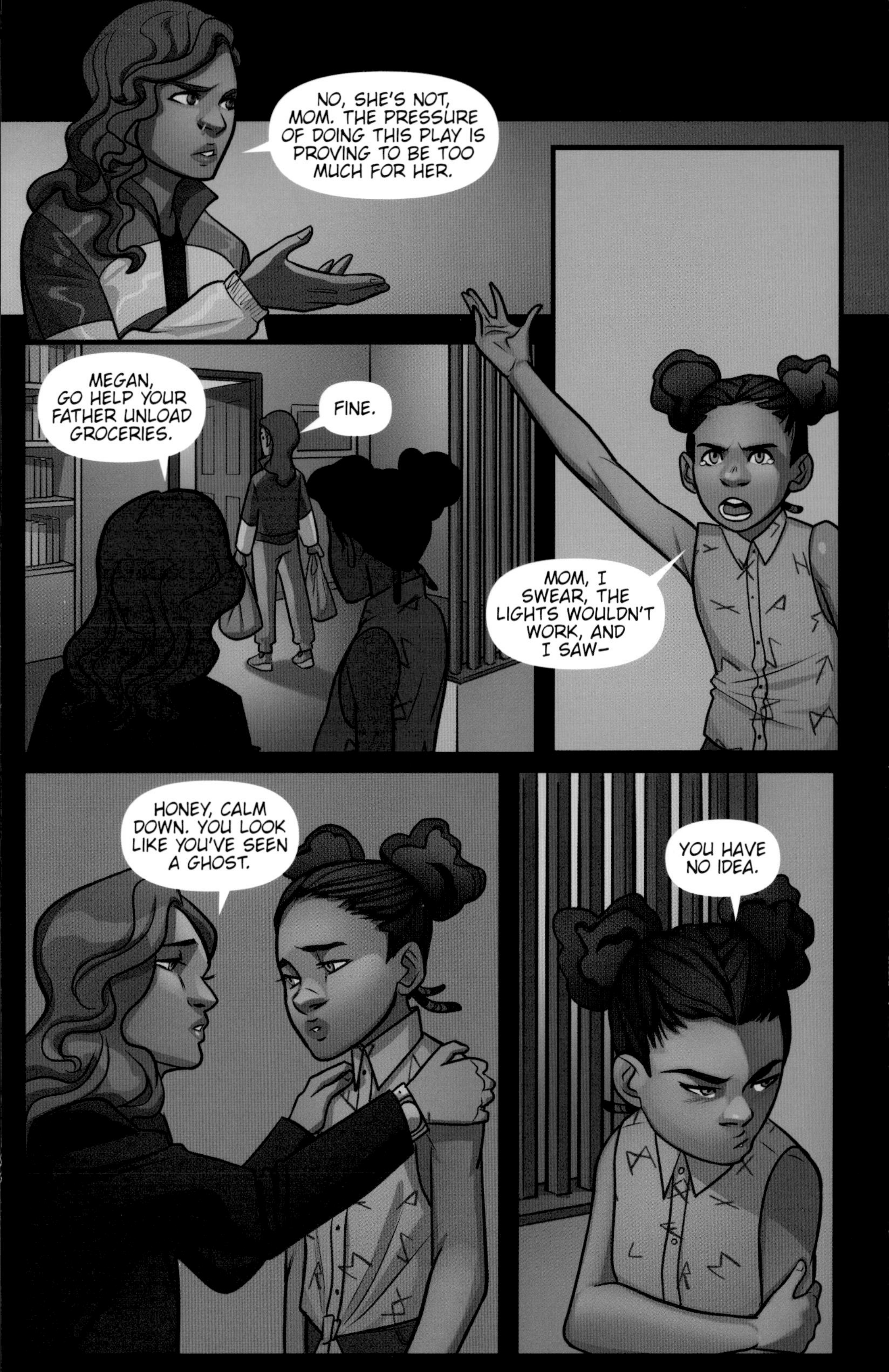
NO, SHE'S NOT, MOM. THE PRESSURE OF DOING THIS PLAY IS PROVING TO BE TOO MUCH FOR HER.
MEGAN, GO HELP YOUR FATHER UNLOAD GROCERIES.
FINE.
MOM, I SWEAR, THE LIGHTS WOULDN'T WORK, AND I SAW—
HONEY, CALM DOWN. YOU LOOK LIKE YOU'VE SEEN A GHOST.
YOU HAVE NO IDEA.

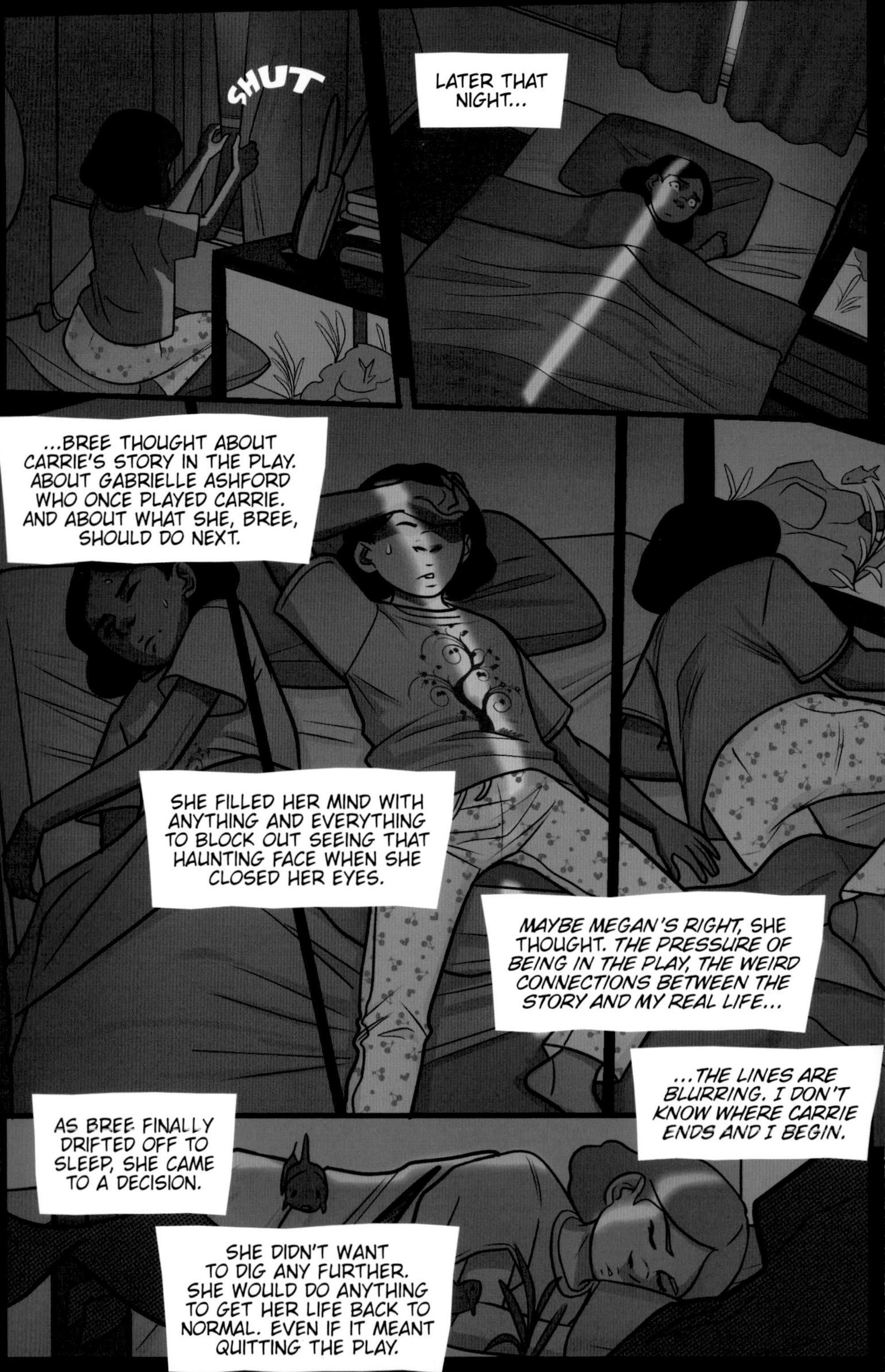
SHUT
LATER THAT NIGHT...
...BREE THOUGHT ABOUT CARRIE'S STORY IN THE PLAY. ABOUT GABRIELLE ASHFORD WHO ONCE PLAYED CARRIE. AND ABOUT WHAT SHE, BREE, SHOULD DO NEXT.
SHE FILLED HER MIND WITH ANYTHING AND EVERYTHING TO BLOCK OUT SEEING THAT HAUNTING FACE WHEN SHE CLOSED HER EYES.
MAYBE MEGAN'S RIGHT, SHE THOUGHT. *THE PRESSURE OF BEING IN THE PLAY, THE WEIRD CONNECTIONS BETWEEN THE STORY AND MY REAL LIFE...*
...THE LINES ARE BLURRING. I DON'T KNOW WHERE CARRIE ENDS AND I BEGIN.
AS BREE FINALLY DRIFTED OFF TO SLEEP, SHE CAME TO A DECISION.
SHE DIDN'T WANT TO DIG ANY FURTHER. SHE WOULD DO ANYTHING TO GET HER LIFE BACK TO NORMAL. EVEN IF IT MEANT QUITTING THE PLAY.

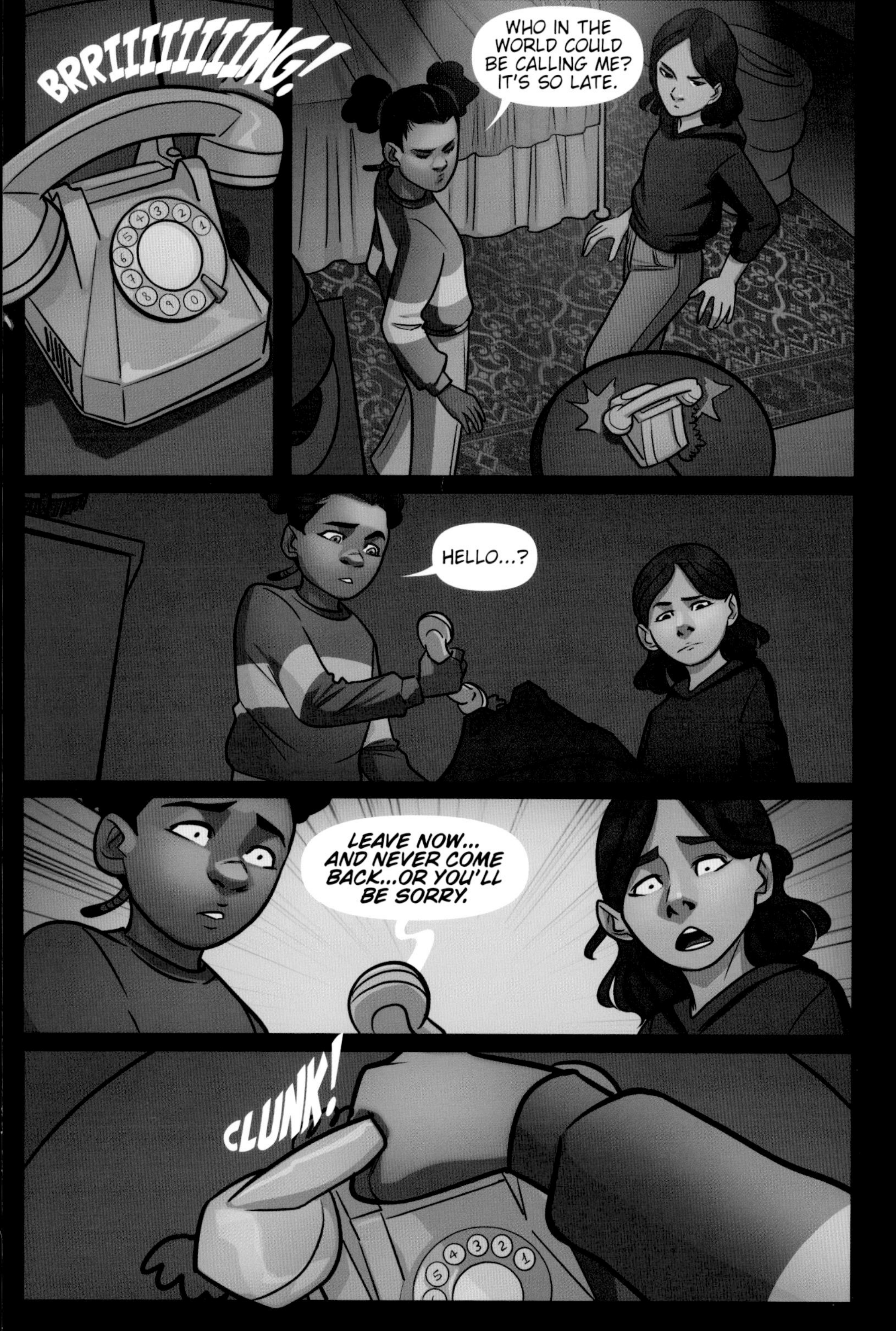
BRRIIIIIIIING!
WHO IN THE WORLD COULD BE CALLING ME? IT'S SO LATE.
HELLO...?
LEAVE NOW... AND NEVER COME BACK...OR YOU'LL BE SORRY.
CLUNK!

A FEW HOURS LATER...

I CAN'T BELIEVE WE RAN THAT SAME SCENE FOUR TIMES IN A ROW. WAS IT ME?

NO! YOU'RE AMAZING! IT WAS A TECH THING WITH THE PHONE NOT BEING LOUD ENOUGH—

GASP!

BRRIIIIIIING!

THAT SCARED ME! I THOUGHT YOU KEPT YOUR PHONE ON VIBRATE.

BRRIIIIIIING!

I THOUGHT I DID TOO.

BRRRIIIIIIING!

Incoming call

UNKNOWN CALLER

BRRIIIIIIING!

DECLINE

ANSWE

117

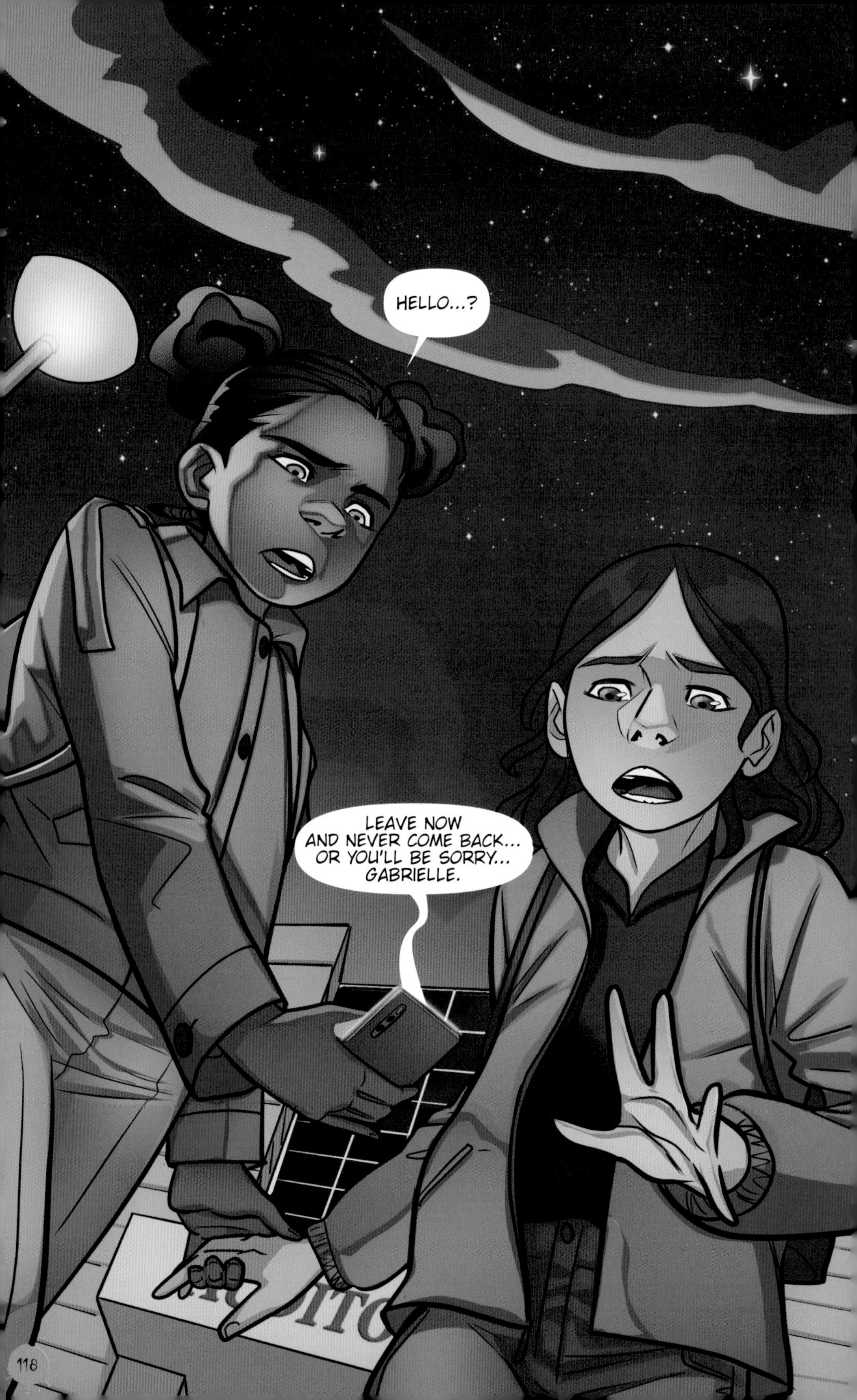
HELLO...?
LEAVE NOW AND NEVER COME BACK... OR YOU'LL BE SORRY... GABRIELLE.

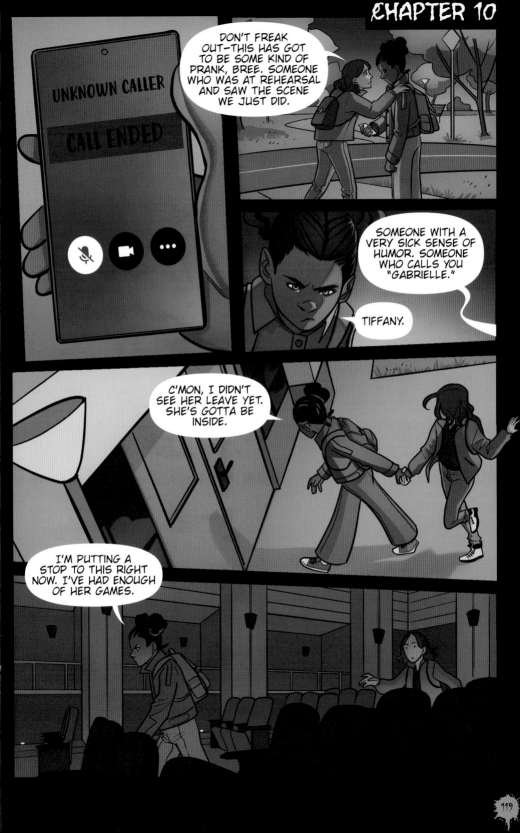

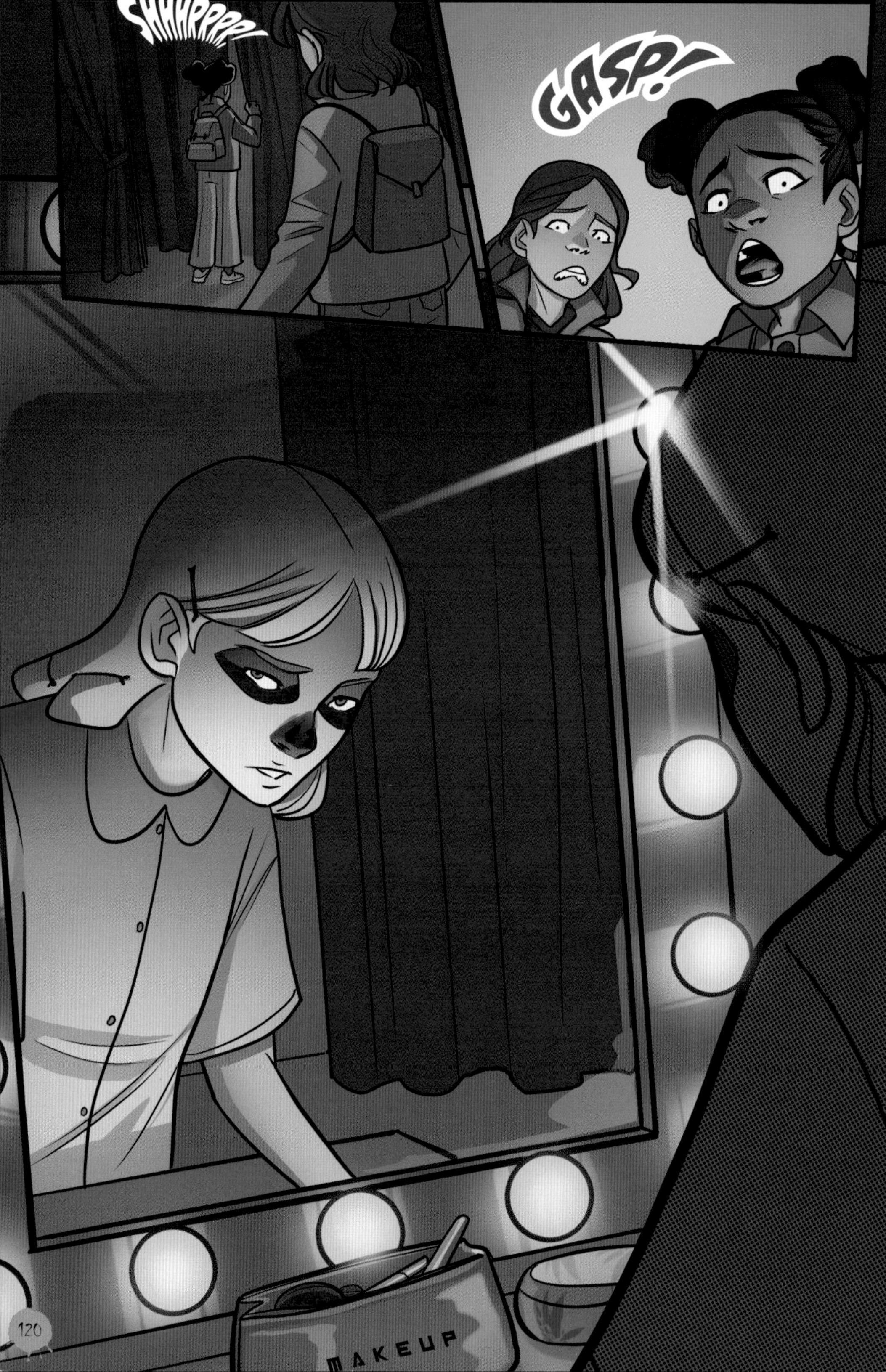
SHHHRRRP!
GASP!
MAKEUP

YOU'VE BEEN MESSING WITH ME SINCE AUDITIONS!

YOU DON'T DESERVE THIS PART!

WHOA, CALM DOWN, TIME OUT! HOLD THE PHONE!

OH NO... IT'S HER AGAIN.

BRRIIIIIIING!

BRRIIIIIIING!

BRRIIIIING!

DON'T LOOK AT ME. MY PHONE IS IN MY LOCKER.

BRRIIIIIING!

Incoming call

UNKNOWN CALLER

DECLINE

ANS

ER

TAP

ANSW

HELLO...?

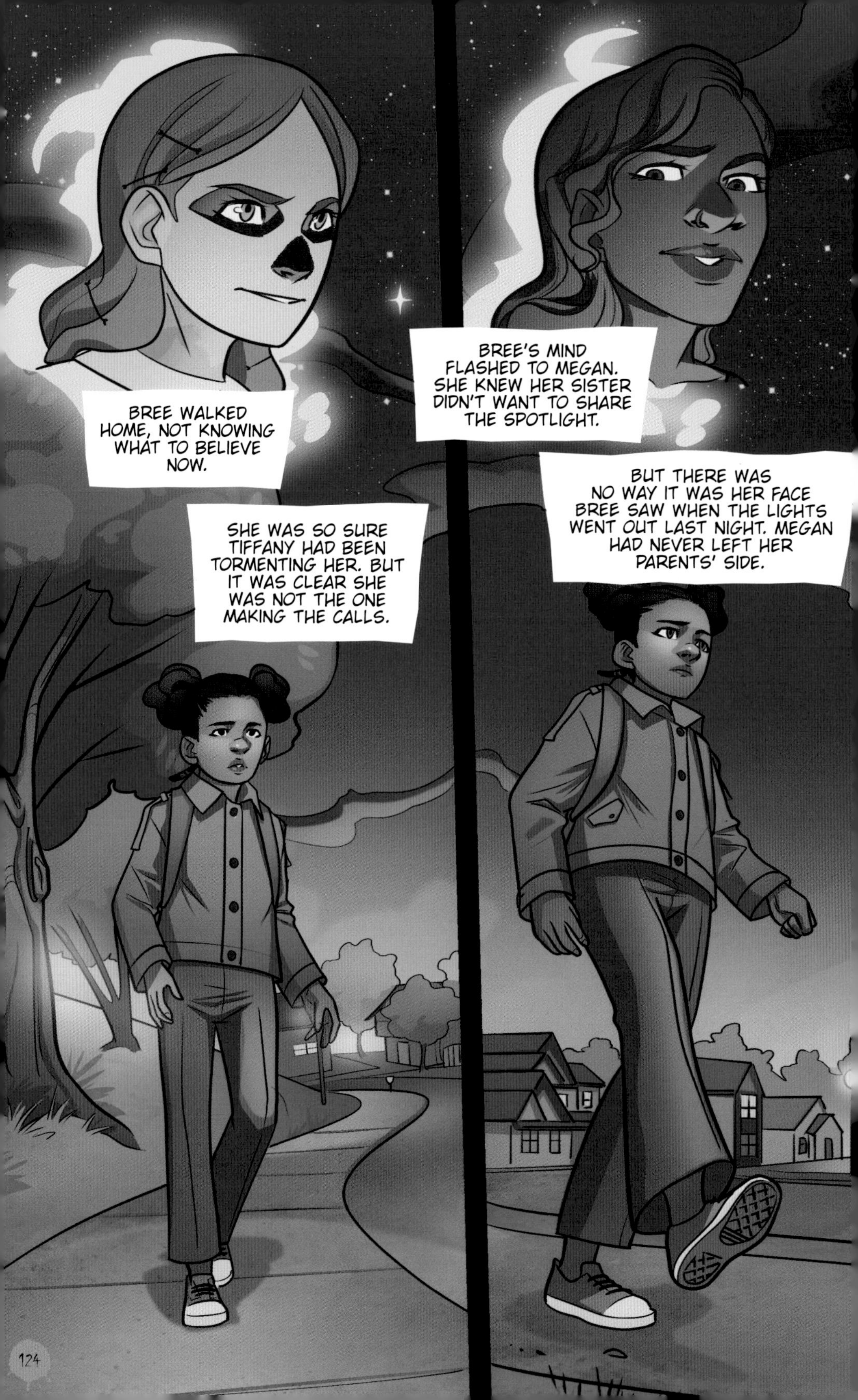
BREE WALKED HOME, NOT KNOWING WHAT TO BELIEVE NOW.
SHE WAS SO SURE TIFFANY HAD BEEN TORMENTING HER. BUT IT WAS CLEAR SHE WAS NOT THE ONE MAKING THE CALLS.
BREE'S MIND FLASHED TO MEGAN. SHE KNEW HER SISTER DIDN'T WANT TO SHARE THE SPOTLIGHT.
BUT THERE WAS NO WAY IT WAS HER FACE BREE SAW WHEN THE LIGHTS WENT OUT LAST NIGHT. MEGAN HAD NEVER LEFT HER PARENTS' SIDE.

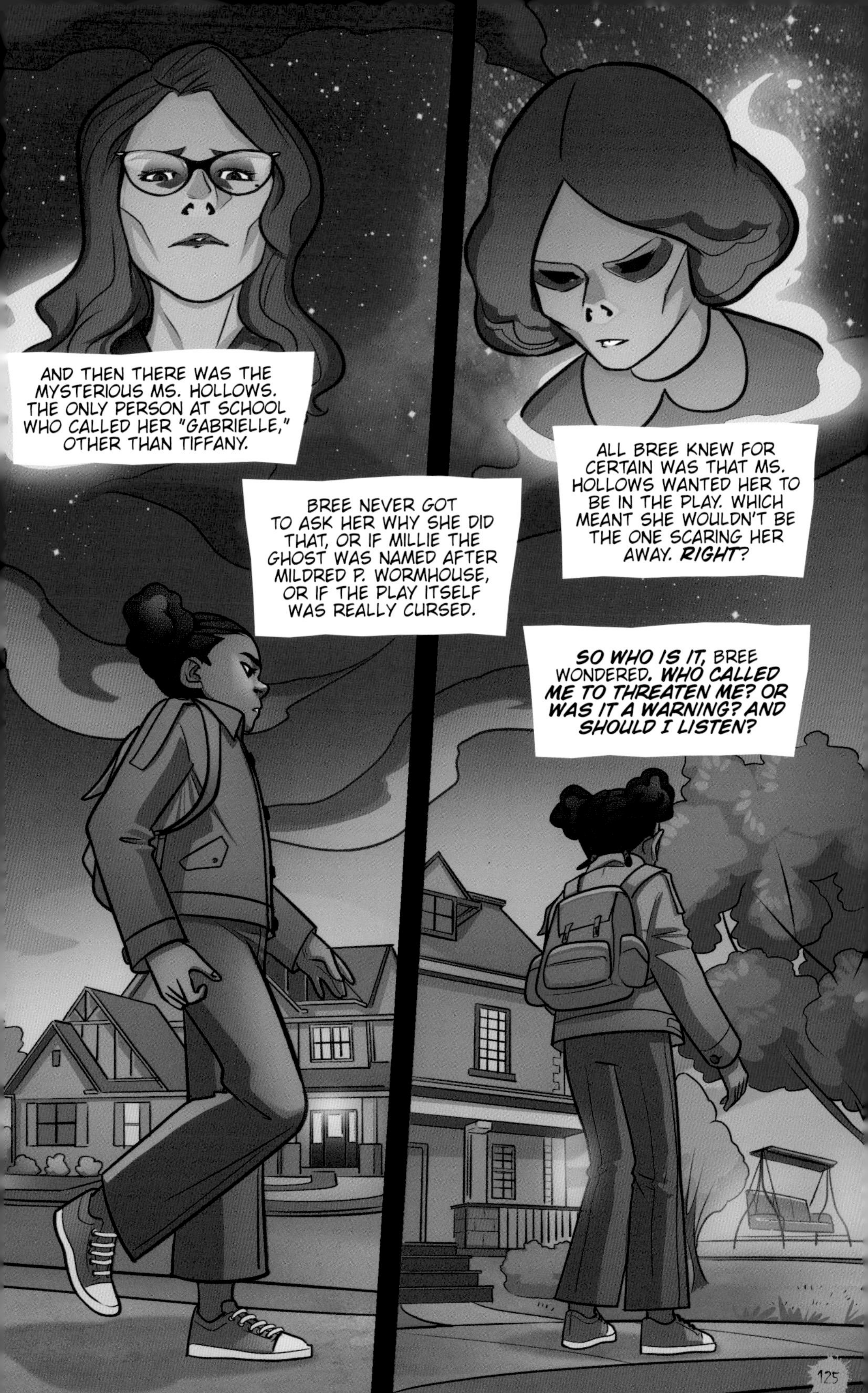
AND THEN THERE WAS THE MYSTERIOUS MS. HOLLOWS. THE ONLY PERSON AT SCHOOL WHO CALLED HER "GABRIELLE," OTHER THAN TIFFANY.
BREE NEVER GOT TO ASK HER WHY SHE DID THAT, OR IF MILLIE THE GHOST WAS NAMED AFTER MILDRED P. WORMHOUSE, OR IF THE PLAY ITSELF WAS REALLY CURSED.
ALL BREE KNEW FOR CERTAIN WAS THAT MS. HOLLOWS WANTED HER TO BE IN THE PLAY. WHICH MEANT SHE WOULDN'T BE THE ONE SCARING HER AWAY. *RIGHT*?
SO WHO IS IT, BREE WONDERED. *WHO CALLED ME TO THREATEN ME? OR WAS IT A WARNING? AND SHOULD I LISTEN?*

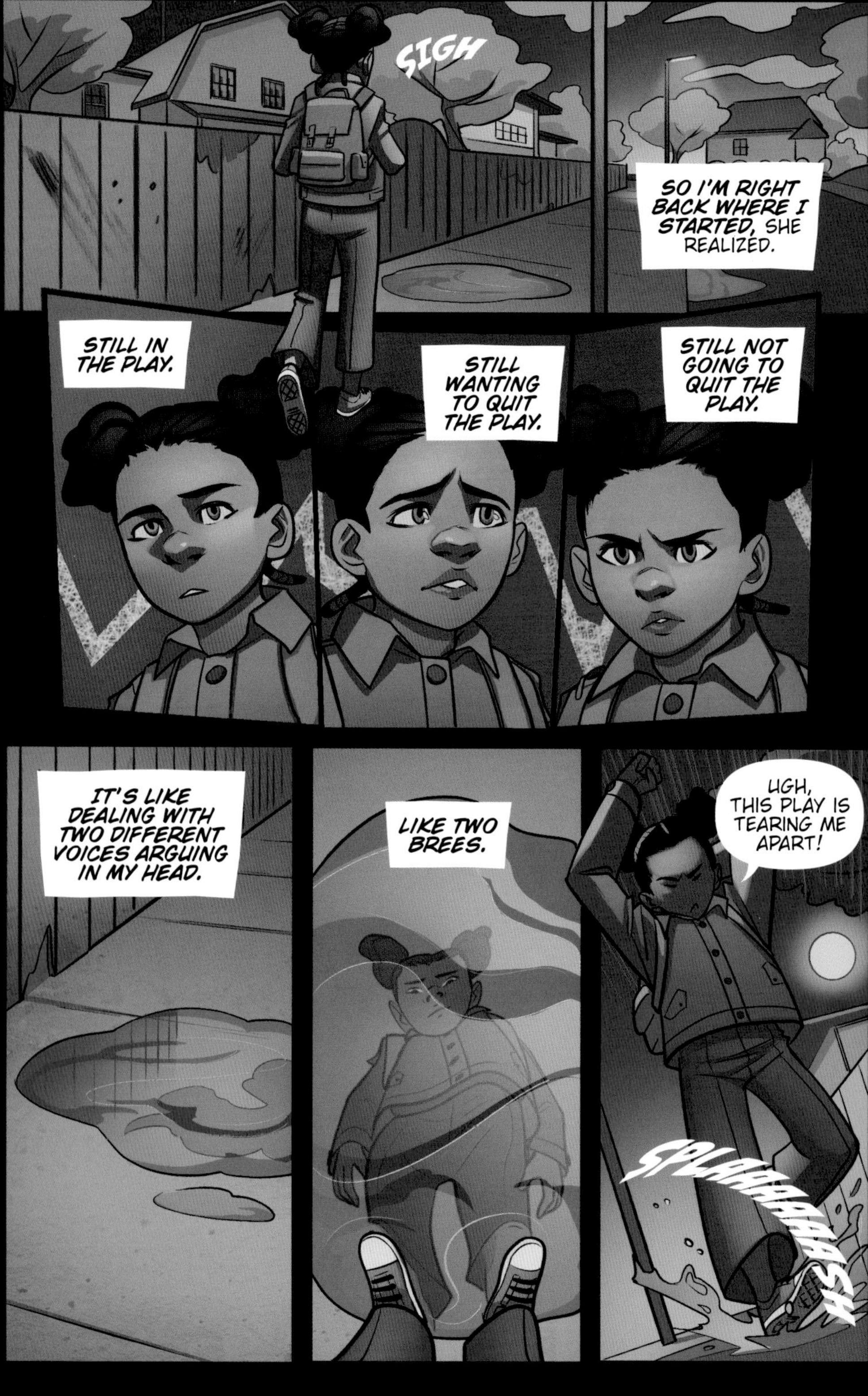
SIGH
SO I'M RIGHT BACK WHERE I STARTED, SHE REALIZED.
STILL IN THE PLAY.
STILL WANTING TO QUIT THE PLAY.
STILL NOT GOING TO QUIT THE PLAY.
IT'S LIKE DEALING WITH TWO DIFFERENT VOICES ARGUING IN MY HEAD.
LIKE TWO BREES.
UGH, THIS PLAY IS TEARING ME APART!
SPLAAAAAASH

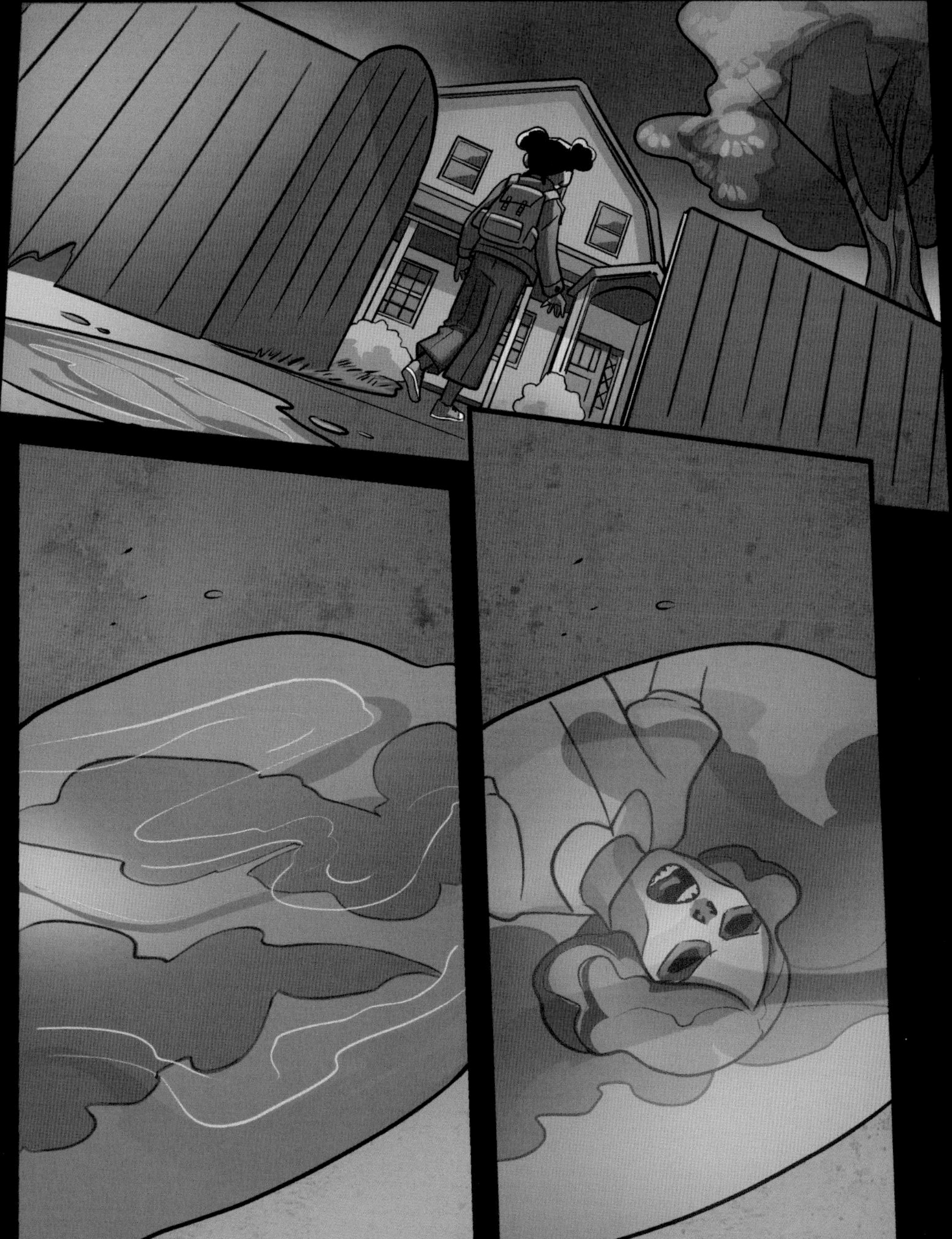

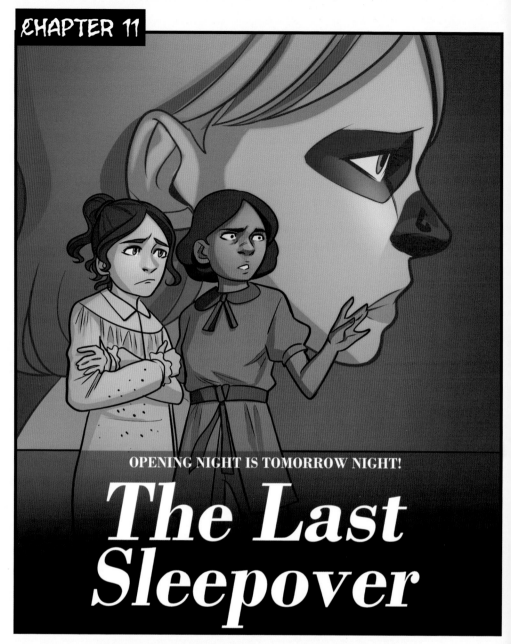

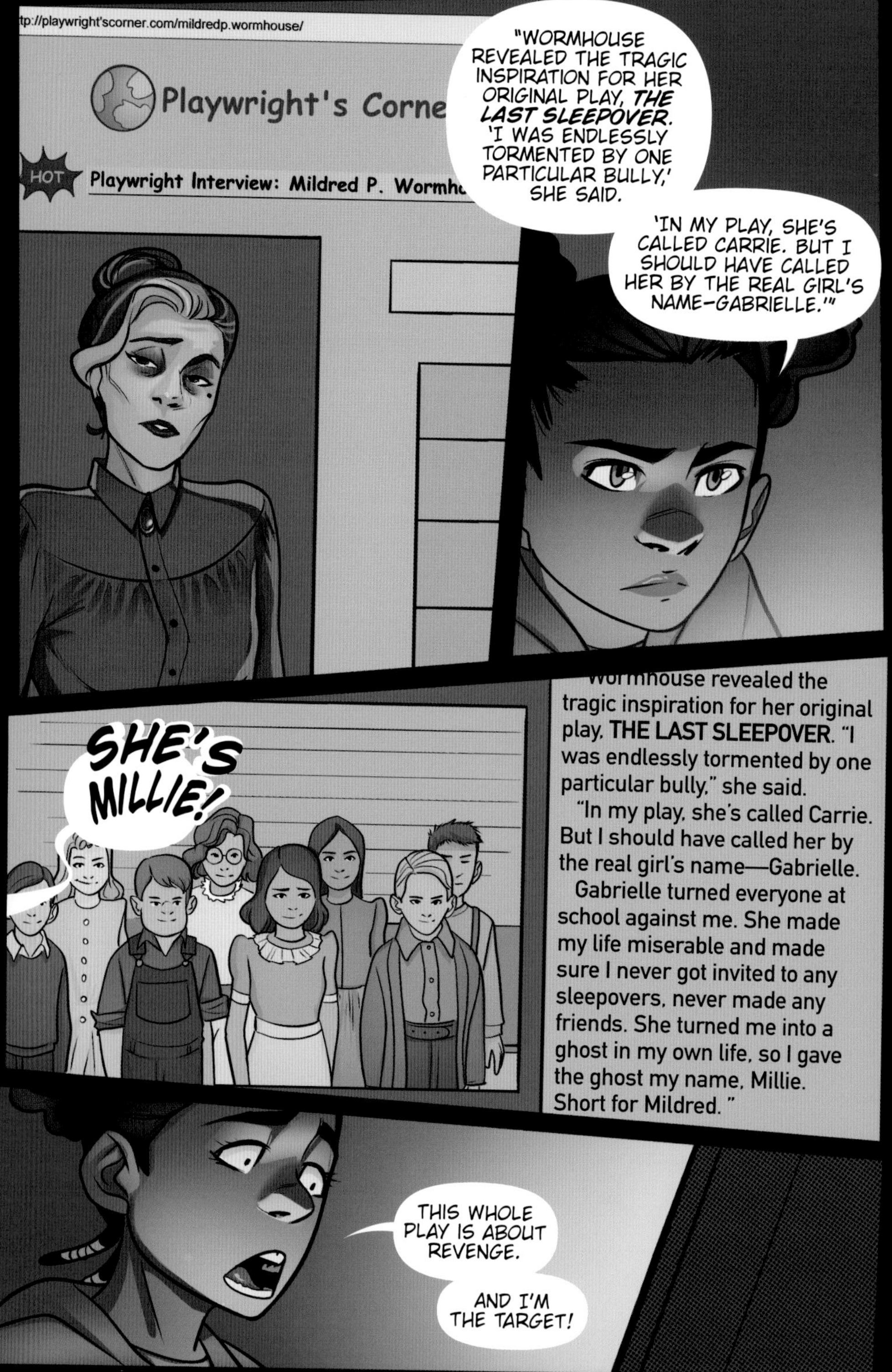

tp://playwright'scorner.com/mildredp.wormhouse/
Playwright's Corne
HOT
Playwright Interview: Mildred P. Wormh
"WORMHOUSE REVEALED THE TRAGIC INSPIRATION FOR HER ORIGINAL PLAY, THE LAST SLEEPOVER. 'I WAS ENDLESSLY TORMENTED BY ONE PARTICULAR BULLY,' SHE SAID.
'IN MY PLAY, SHE'S CALLED CARRIE. BUT I SHOULD HAVE CALLED HER BY THE REAL GIRL'S NAME—GABRIELLE.'"
SHE'S MILLIE!
wormhouse revealed the tragic inspiration for her original play, THE LAST SLEEPOVER. "I was endlessly tormented by one particular bully," she said.
"In my play, she's called Carrie. But I should have called her by the real girl's name—Gabrielle.
Gabrielle turned everyone at school against me. She made my life miserable and made sure I never got invited to any sleepovers, never made any friends. She turned me into a ghost in my own life, so I gave the ghost my name, Millie. Short for Mildred. "
THIS WHOLE PLAY IS ABOUT REVENGE.
AND I'M THE TARGET!

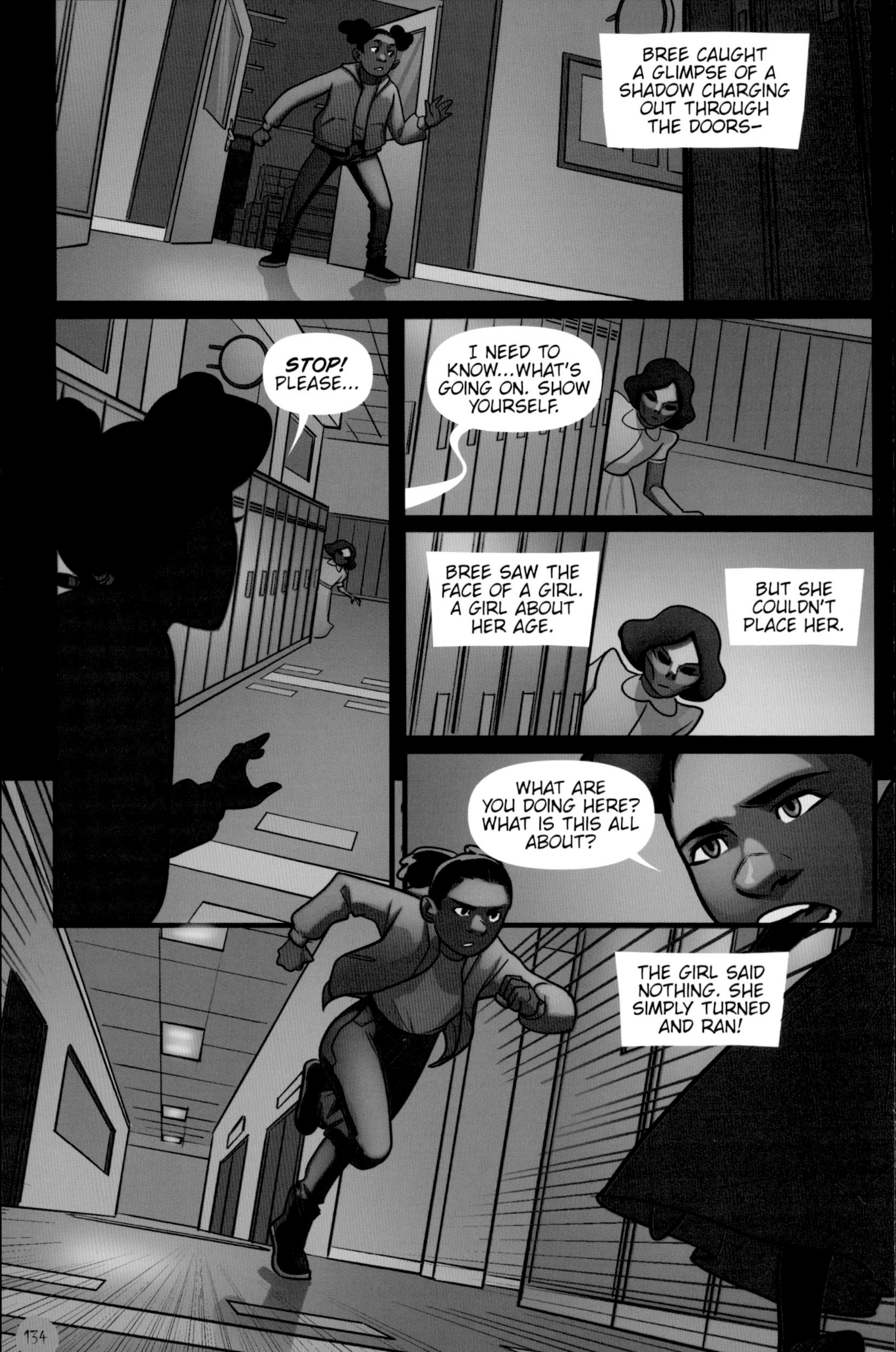
BREE CAUGHT A GLIMPSE OF A SHADOW CHARGING OUT THROUGH THE DOORS–
STOP! PLEASE...
I NEED TO KNOW...WHAT'S GOING ON. SHOW YOURSELF.
BREE SAW THE FACE OF A GIRL. A GIRL ABOUT HER AGE.
BUT SHE COULDN'T PLACE HER.
WHAT ARE YOU DOING HERE? WHAT IS THIS ALL ABOUT?
THE GIRL SAID NOTHING. SHE SIMPLY TURNED AND RAN!

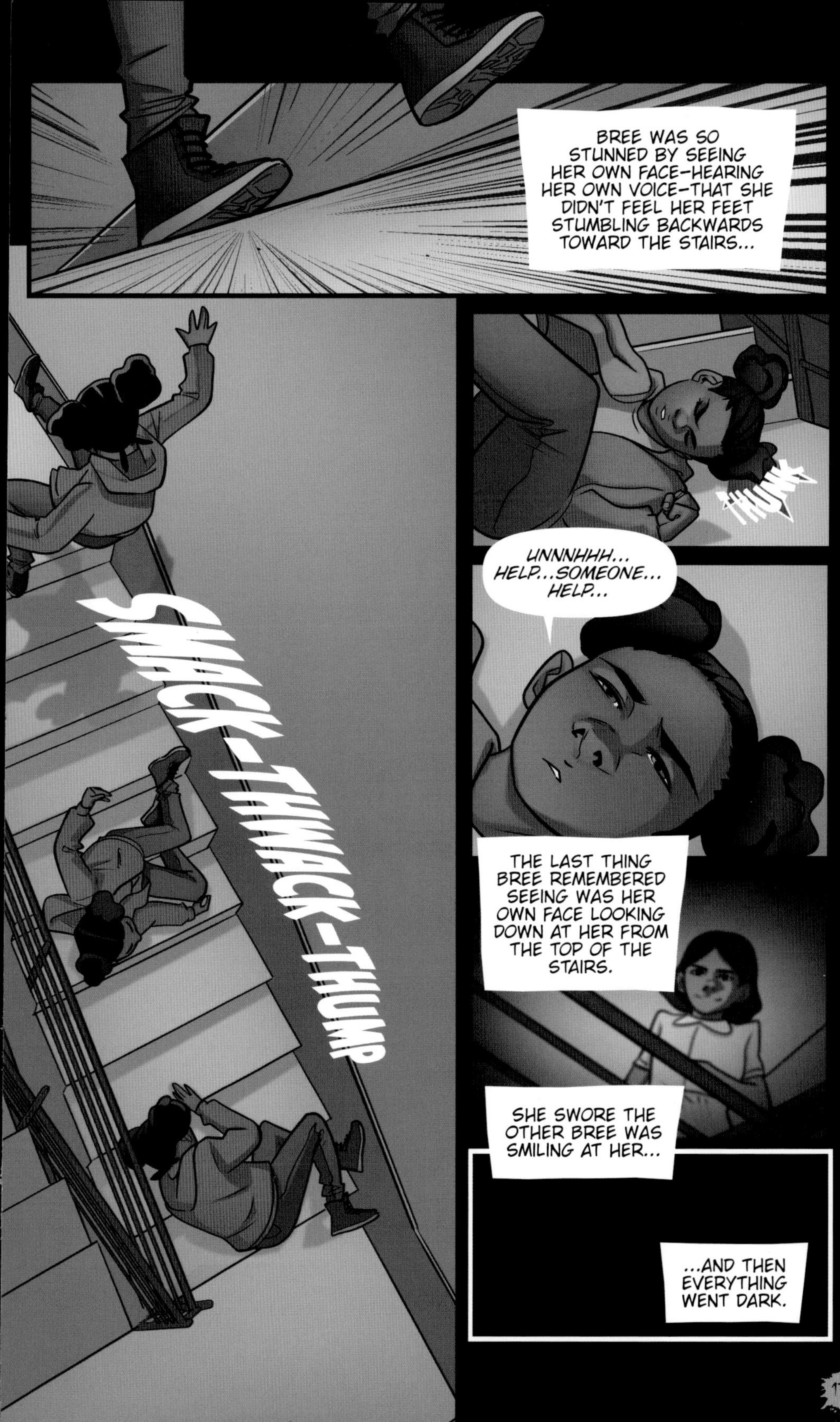
BREE WAS SO STUNNED BY SEEING HER OWN FACE—HEARING HER OWN VOICE—THAT SHE DIDN'T FEEL HER FEET STUMBLING BACKWARDS TOWARD THE STAIRS...
SMACK-THWACK-THUMP
THUNK
UNNNHHH... HELP...SOMEONE... HELP...
THE LAST THING BREE REMEMBERED SEEING WAS HER OWN FACE LOOKING DOWN AT HER FROM THE TOP OF THE STAIRS.
SHE SWORE THE OTHER BREE WAS SMILING AT HER...
...AND THEN EVERYTHING WENT DARK.

CHAPTER 12

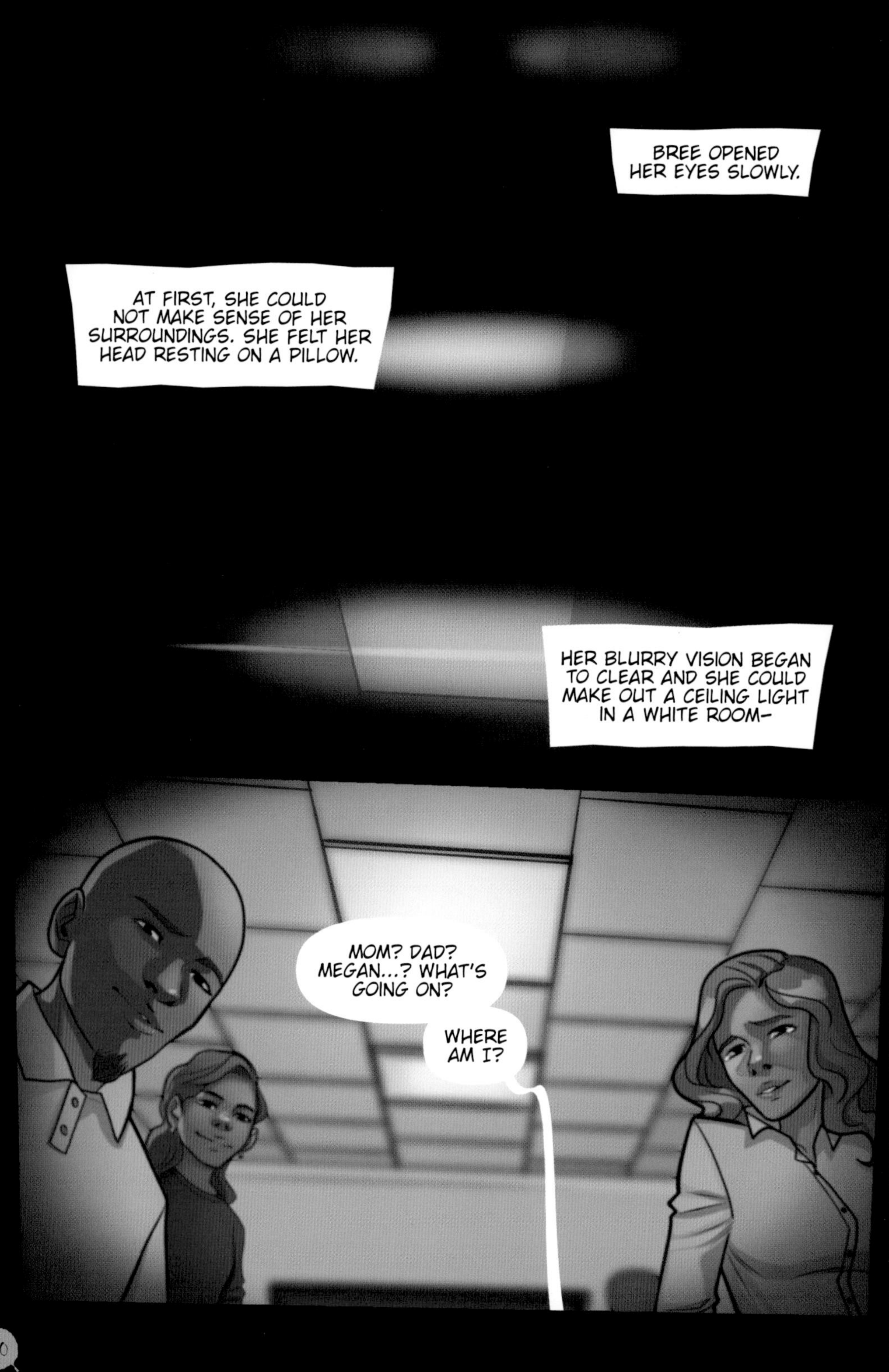
BREE OPENED HER EYES SLOWLY.
AT FIRST, SHE COULD NOT MAKE SENSE OF HER SURROUNDINGS. SHE FELT HER HEAD RESTING ON A PILLOW.
HER BLURRY VISION BEGAN TO CLEAR AND SHE COULD MAKE OUT A CEILING LIGHT IN A WHITE ROOM–
MOM? DAD? MEGAN...? WHAT'S GOING ON?
WHERE AM I?

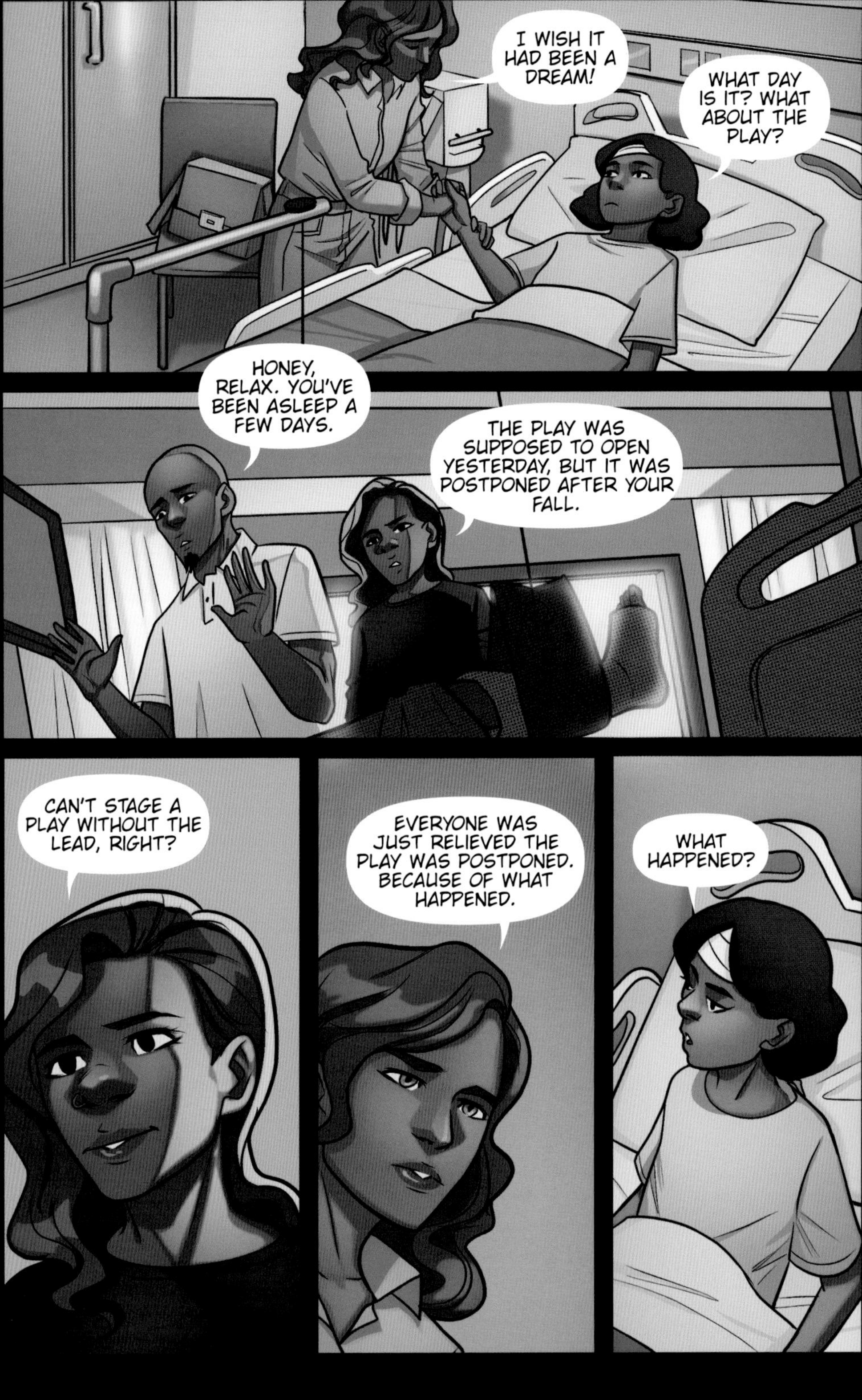
I WISH IT HAD BEEN A DREAM!
WHAT DAY IS IT? WHAT ABOUT THE PLAY?
HONEY, RELAX. YOU'VE BEEN ASLEEP A FEW DAYS.
THE PLAY WAS SUPPOSED TO OPEN YESTERDAY, BUT IT WAS POSTPONED AFTER YOUR FALL.
CAN'T STAGE A PLAY WITHOUT THE LEAD, RIGHT?
EVERYONE WAS JUST RELIEVED THE PLAY WAS POSTPONED. BECAUSE OF WHAT HAPPENED.
WHAT HAPPENED?

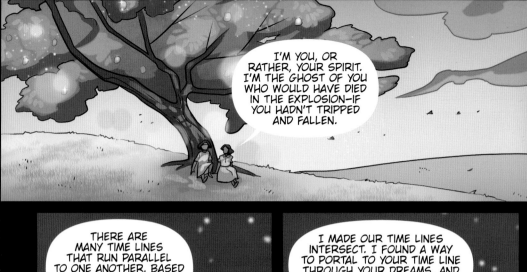

I'M YOU, OR RATHER, YOUR SPIRIT. I'M THE GHOST OF YOU WHO WOULD HAVE DIED IN THE EXPLOSION—IF YOU HADN'T TRIPPED AND FALLEN.

THERE ARE MANY TIME LINES THAT RUN PARALLEL TO ONE ANOTHER, BASED ON THE CHOICES WE MAKE A HUNDRED TIMES A DAY.

I MADE OUR TIME LINES INTERSECT. I FOUND A WAY TO PORTAL TO YOUR TIME LINE THROUGH YOUR DREAMS. AND I USED IT TO COMMUNICATE WITH YOU.

THAT'S WHY ALL THAT WEIRD STUFF KEPT HAPPENING.

YES. SIMPLY TALKING WAS IMPOSSIBLE. I HAD TO USE WHATEVER I COULD TO WARN YOU.

BECAUSE OF HOW TIME LINES WORK, I COULD ONLY DO THINGS THAT WERE PART OF THE PLAY, SINCE THAT'S WHERE OUR LIVES CROSSED OVER.

THAT'S WHY IT SEEMED LIKE THINGS IN THE PLAY WERE HAPPENING IN YOUR REAL LIFE.

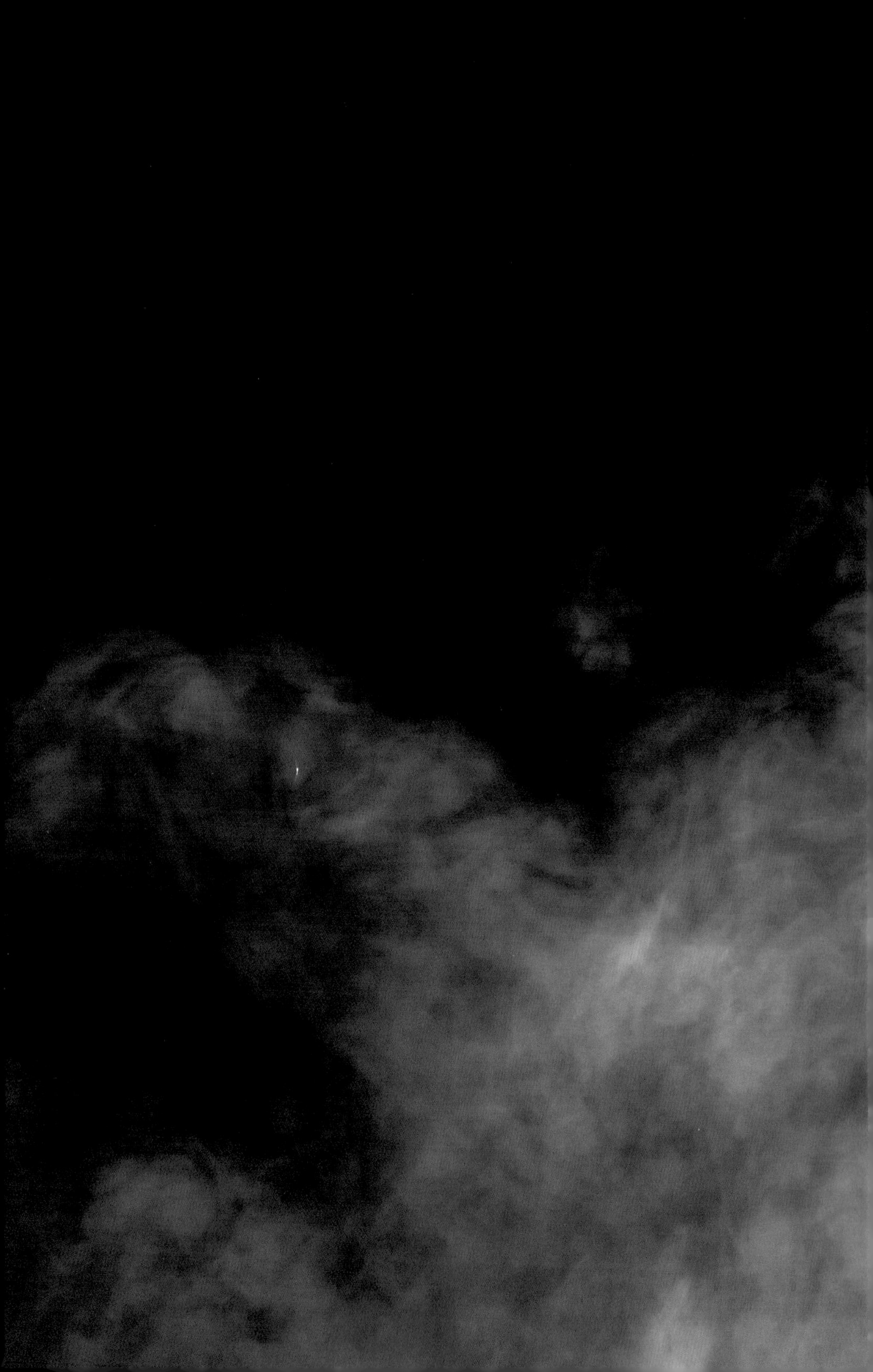

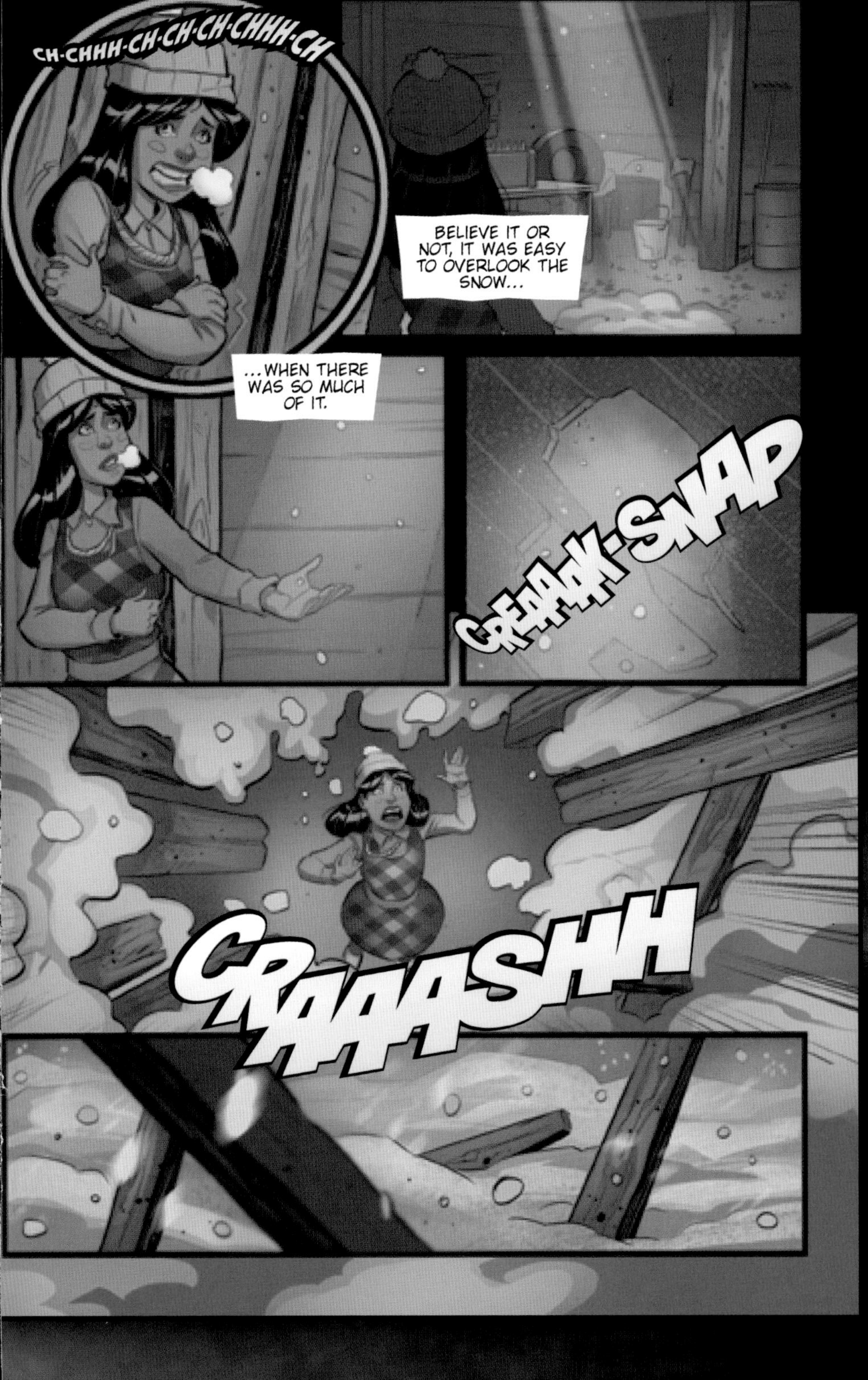
CH-CHHH-CH-CH-CH-CHHH-CH
BELIEVE IT OR NOT, IT WAS EASY TO OVERLOOK THE SNOW...
...WHEN THERE WAS SO MUCH OF IT.
CREAAK-SNAP
CRAAASHH

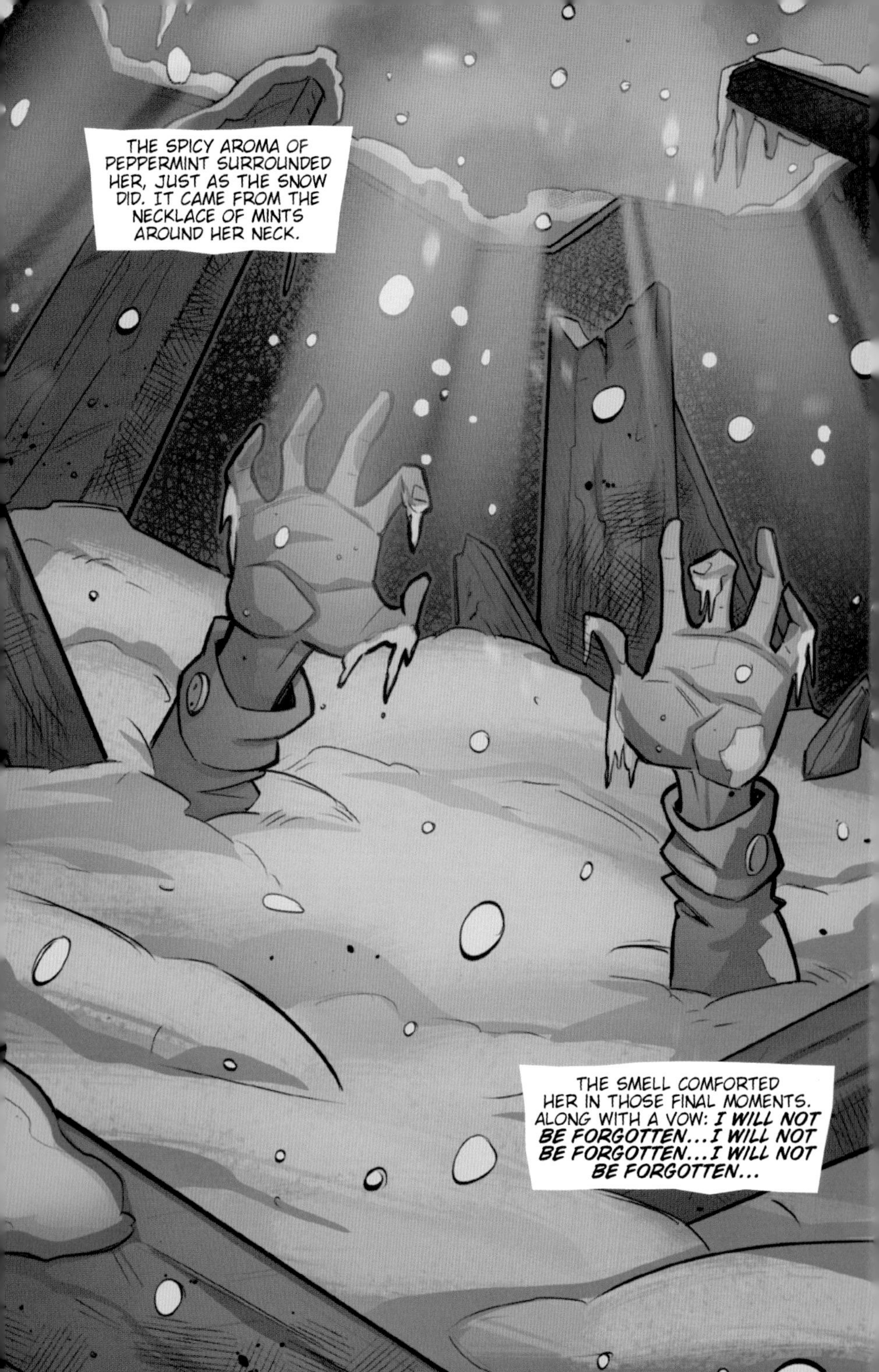
THE SPICY AROMA OF PEPPERMINT SURROUNDED HER, JUST AS THE SNOW DID. IT CAME FROM THE NECKLACE OF MINTS AROUND HER NECK.
THE SMELL COMFORTED HER IN THOSE FINAL MOMENTS. ALONG WITH A VOW: *I WILL NOT BE FORGOTTEN...I WILL NOT BE FORGOTTEN...I WILL NOT BE FORGOTTEN...*

CHAPTER 1

AND DON'T MISS

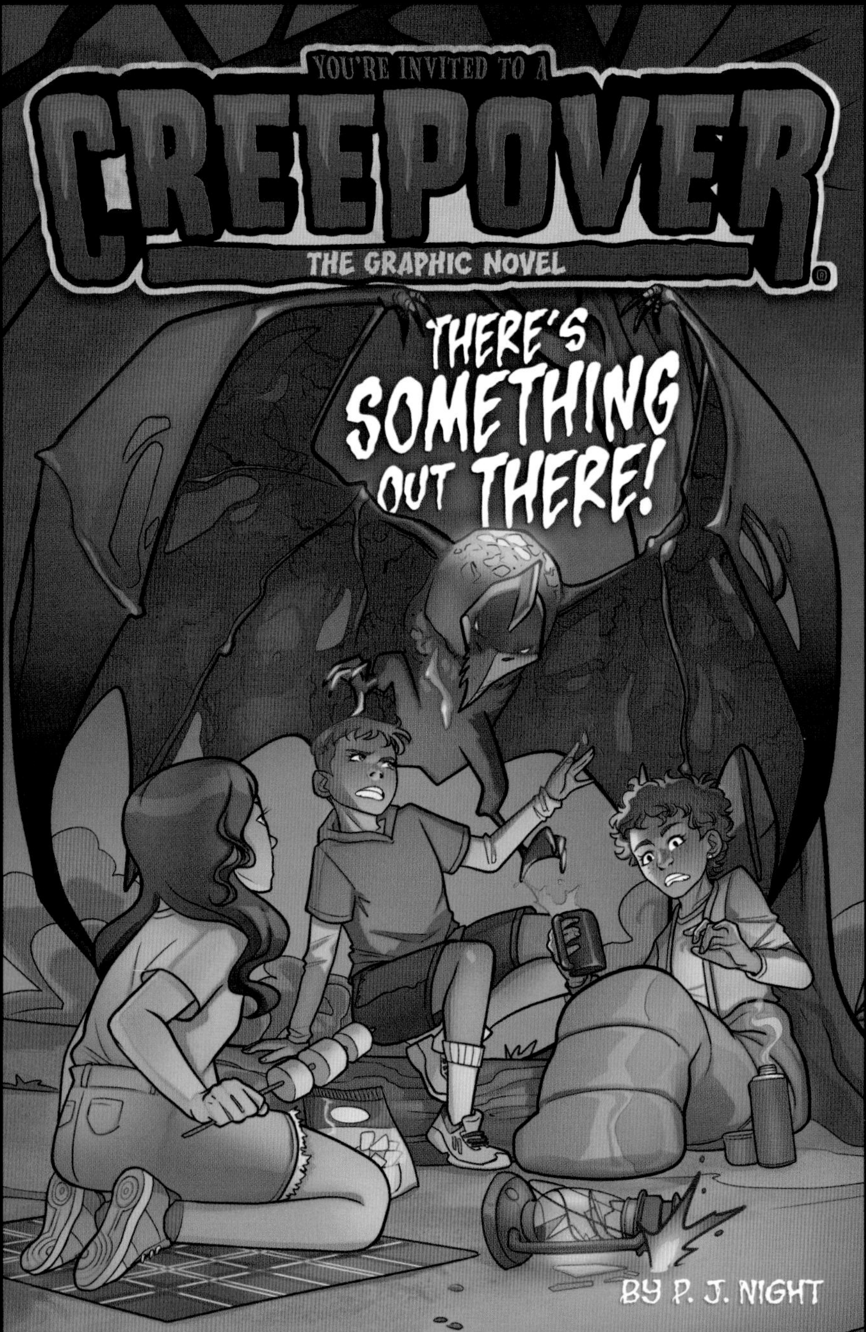
YOU'RE INVITED TO A
CREEPOVER
THE GRAPHIC NOVEL
THERE'S SOMETHING OUT THERE!
BY P. J. NIGHT